Hey! You're Reading in the Wrong Direction!

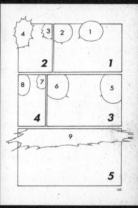

This is the **end** of this graphic novel!

To properly enjoy this VIZ graphic novel, please turn it around and begin reading from **right to left.** Unlike English, Japanese is read right to left, so Japanese comics are read in reverse order from the way English comics are typically read.

Follow the action this way

This book has been printed in the original Japanese format in order to preserve the orientation of the original artw

The Diary of A.O.
BARNABOOTH

CONTENTS

BOOK I
Florence

BOOK I

Florence

I HAVE been nearly four hours in this curious American town built in the style of the Italian Renaissance, where there are too many Germans. Yesterday morning I was in Berlin ; and Stéphane stood on the platform of the Anhalt station and waved his big handkerchief.

I crossed, in the Harmonika-Zug, a Germany still hesitating between winter and spring,—with her dear little nose chilled and cold under her veil. I bowed to her tenderly : au revoir, my beloved Germania. . . . When I return the chestnut trees by the restaurants will be casting a strong shadow over the tables. But I prefer the autumn in the beer-gardens of the suburbs. Then one can be almost alone among the big fallen leaves with a great mug of light beer, very bitter, in front of him. About four o'clock in the afternoon one quietly goes away. Above the exit is a transparency which reads thus : " Auf Wiedersehen ! "

But then comes the winter of Central Europe ! the

9

tremendous cold so full of dignity. Then do I rediscover my Germany, like a pleasant wife, like a warm fireside. Life becomes decent and nice and is filled with serious occupation : it is a time of philological studies, mixed with cigarettes and kisses. And in the evening, on the blue ice of the ponds, one skates until nightfall in the royal gardens ; while far away the lights of the city make the sky seem to glisten with moisture between the snow-covered branches.

Through the tall windows of my wagon-salon I have seen all the little towns come and go and disappear. And I would gladly have spent my life humbly in any one of them : going to chapel on Sundays ; taking part in the local festivals ; consorting with the landed gentry. And, far off, the destinies of the great world would make their useless clamour.

During the stop on the Austrian frontier the waiter attached to the wagon-salon brought me several armfuls of papers. I had a shock : a great Viennese illustrated paper had published my photograph (not much like me, much younger—I looked sixteen !) with only this commentary :

MR. A. OLSON BARNABOOTH
£10,450,000 a year !

A few pages farther on, a note informed the reader that I am "probably one of the richest men on this planet," and that I am at all events "certainly the youngest of the great millionaires." The paragraphist, who made me out a year older than I am, congratulated me on having founded hospitals and asylums in South

America ; but he added : " The young multi-million-aire's manner of living is not different to that of most of the idle men and women of his world."

At first I cursed the impertinent fellow. I was even, for a moment, really distressed as I sat alone there in my wagon-salon ; was there ever a man more unjustly treated than I ? or a character more misunderstood than mine ? The young multi-millionaire founding hospitals was so little like me, my dreams, my aspirations, my physiology, and my enthusiastic impulses, and so like " the others."

And I, " idle " ? I who spend my life in the search of the absolute ! It is you who are an idle fellow, my little journalist, you who spend your whole night stooping over a desk.

But then I soon recognized in the paragraph the ceremonious irony which I find in all the men of modest means with whom (fortunately, more and more rarely) I have any dealings. I meet them without any ulterior thought, as man to man, familiarly, American fashion. And they bow and scrape before me and hang their heads and are ill at ease. In the obsequious fashion with which they shake hands with me I feel their contempt for me. They make no attempt to conceal it when they cut their capers before me : they think a millionaire is too stupid to notice sycophancy. They are so subtle.

At first I thought their irony was only a grin of envy ! Ah ! but that misunderstanding would vanish on the first words. And I used to stoop to any kind of baseness to induce a poor man to admit me to an equality. Well, well. No. It is not envy : it is their incapacity to see and go beyond certain conceptions, certain facts. It is simply stupidity—" But, see here, in spite of my 10,450,000 pounds sterling, I am as good as you !" They do not understand, and go on laughing at the bloated dull rich man. Everything I do, every idea I express, seems to them enormously comic. Think of it : a millionaire taking upon himself to have ideas !

If I were to engage in great undertakings, float huge financial affairs as my father did—my father whom Wall Street, dazzled, dubbed the " Inca "—if I were to disturb the whole economic system of a world, there might be some chance of such people understanding that they are just about fit to be my instruments. And I could do all that. But what's the good ? They will never feel the tenderness of my lonely heart, and the rest is nothing. . . . Once again my experience gives the lie to all that my instructors told me : and I have only found fine minds and delicate souls among the rich and the great.

For a moment I thought of writing to the Viennese paragraphist : " Sir, I am only twenty-three : but do not correct your mistake : it is no use. For the rest, I humbly beg your pardon for having been the cause of your showing your lack of intelligence." But he would have taken it as a joke. And yet . . .

And, as usual, I was able to turn my resentment against myself. At the frontier station of Ulm I left my wagon-salon for a second-class compartment, almost full. A collection of honest Munich worthies. I put on a most genial expression and for an hour I did nothing but talk of my country seats, my villas, my yacht, my automobiles, my "immense properties" (still falling short of the reality, for they would not have believed me ; and taking care not to mention the fact that I had sold the whole lot—for they would never have understood me). "Ah ! You can see in me nothing but a rich man, you poor devils satisfied with your twenty thousand marks a year. Well ! All right ! Laugh, go on, laugh at the absurd upstart boasting of his wealth ! " During all that time I felt a rush of secret burning tears. I was certainly feverish : I was overwhelmed with shame. And they smiled : they were meeting in real life their favourite type, a " bragging upstart of the stock exchange " : that was it. Not one of them understood.

I was very near ending it all with a roar of laughter : " Gentlemen, I have been pulling your legs, hard ! " or I might have said, " Contempt of the poor is the beginning of wisdom," or some such pitiful buffoonery. Not at all. At Verona I got out quietly, bowed to my honest worthies and returned to my wagon-salon.

I was like a child after a burst of weeping. My mortification had left me : I was soothed and calm and felt very happy. I had expiated the hurt done me and harmony was re-established between the world and myself.

I made the last part of the journey, from Bologna here, in a third-class carriage full of young Prussian *Pfarren*. I shall never forget them, hanging like gargoyles out of the windows spewing out all the stupidity of a great people over the Italian scenes that were too clever for them and too simple. The most distant villages were bespattered with it. Art and religion, naturally . . . " Sensuality run riot . . . superstitious practices. . . ." The whole phonograph record.

And over all the Italian light : the sweet, indulgent, intelligent light of Tuscany, blithe, and now a little mournful.

FLORENCE,

12 *April.*

Drove, part of the day : Via Tornabuoni : Via de Vecchetti, Via Strozzi, Piazza Victor-Emmanuel. Met several people (young Count Bettino, etc.), old frequenters of the Casino Barnabooth. Telegrams to Poole, Charvet, Briggs, Thomas and Lock, to tell them to send my summer wardrobe on here. As they have everything ready beforehand I shall have my things in three days.

However, I made several purchases in the Florentine shops : shirts, canes, travelling things, leather things, stationery. They are all laid out on the tables and chairs of my two sitting-rooms. (I have a suite of rooms at the Carlton with ten windows looking out on the Arno, a dining-room, a lounge, a bathroom as big as the bedroom ; and the staff on my floor has been doubled.)

Spent the afternoon and evening in untying all these parcels, hurling myself, scissors in hand, on the strings, sending the papers flying down on the floor, getting drunk on the smell of newness exhaled by all these well-made things, sometimes hugging them and dancing for joy in the littered room. I think I shall never tire of buying luxurious things,—it is as strong in me as a vocation. I remember how I used to welcome my toys, the big boxes painted blue, full of the latest novelties from Paris and Nuremberg, which used to come about the middle of summer, in December, at home. My father used to have the toys sent over for me from another hemisphere where Christmas was celebrated in the snow. I have not changed.

In a few days I shall distribute all these things among the hotel staff, since I no longer have houses in which to store my purchases, and have made it a rule to carry with me on my travels nothing but the little wooden trunk covered with linoleum and red copper in which, arranged according to countries and values, are the little packets of paper money which my bank in London sends me every month.

Will the distinguished men-servants and the pretty Swiss maids of the Carlton be able to appreciate my presents? I wonder what they will say of a man who travels unattended and without luggage and engages the whole first floor of an hotel? . . .

Now the evening is falling. I have seen that evening somewhere before, or an evening very like it : was it at Prague or Eupatoria?

A bath is made ready for me. The noise of the hot water running into the bath and the wreathing steam always fill me with voluptuous thoughts.

I have had my bath and am finishing my dinner. The dishes were fine to see with their tall silver cases. I am pleased with the *maître d'hôtel.*

I shall not go out to-night. Outside the street lamps are already lit. I know the brilliance of the Italian gas in the limpidity of the Italian night. Nothing changes and the age of the world creeps over me.

15

Walked through the deep, fresh streets. In the morning little carts laden with sweet-smelling things fill the dark thoroughfares with noise. Hanging on a cord a pretty basket is dropped from the third floor on to the wall a man's height from the ground. A market-gardener places green-stuffs and fruit in it, and the postman goes by and drops a letter into it. On the window-sill one can see a bare arm, white in the sun, holding the cord. The basket goes up again, jerking merrily. The passing popolane jeer at me. Farther on a little girl crosses the street and cries " Signorino ! " in a shrill voice . . . I stretch out my hands to the warm moist air. I smile at the streaming sun, the bands of grey and green of the perspectives of the winding pavementless streets. And on the edge of the sky, the flat roofs, like great sun-hats, project a little and cast a short shadow down the fronts of the houses : roofs with stays : true and beautiful as an Homeric expression. During the afternoon, a slight north wind drummed on the stones.

My first journey as a free man : since I have freed myself of my social duties ; broken away from the caste in which destiny sought to imprison me ; since I am no longer the slave of my racing stable and my hunters : since I no longer find myself at every turn hemmed in by the demon of real property.

Drove to the Cascine and back along the Arno. The stone quays, the parapet with its double band of faded rose and pale yellow, brick and stone, the narrow hard road : how one clings to Italy ! What beauty and charm are in the provincial scene I see from my windows : the golden reaches of the Arno between the bridges, and, oltr'Arno, the dull mass and the tiresome dome of San Frediano surrounded with houses old and new ; and the little glimpse of the country with one or two yellow villas among the cypresses and the little clipped cedars ? In all this I can feel no trace of the old Republic. Rather a vague distress at no longer being the Salon of Europe and at having seen the end of the Grand Dukes of Tuscany. A provincial Florence, living on memories of the Leopoldine period, and the bustling five years when she was a capital. Old carnivals, masquerades at the Pergola and the Uffizi, chariot races by Santa-Maria-Novella, must not the spring in the old days have been gayer than nowadays ; different from this Denmark of a summer ?

This evening's papers publish Stéphane's portrait, and are filled with extracts from the speech he delivered at the celebration of the royal jubilee in Saxony. We composed that famous speech together, and I made a parody of it which made us ill with laughing. My poor Stéphane. When will you too be free ?

CARLTON HOTEL, FLORENCE,
14 April.

A desire to go to Val d'Ema to see the old Casino Barnabooth. But the stronger desire to lounge in the motley of the centre of the town kept me. Now in the evening I think of it with some regret. I imagine the Casino Barnabooth, a poor house with shutters closed, standing alone in the night on the scented hills. It was perched on the side of a hill between roads full of useless windings. The square garden was terraced, on four grey walls. Everything had been done so that there should be neither shade nor verdure in the garden. Oh, my boxes clipped in the shape of lions, tortoises, guinea-fowls (or were they peacocks?) Oh, black cantaros bending to the thirst of noon! And my lilac bushes that never flowered, and my labyrinth wherein it was impossible, with the best will in the world, to get lost.

Cartuyvels sold it to a syndicate of speculators, and it is now empty.

Cartuyvels, faithful C.—I am glad at length to have escaped from his supervision by selling all my possessions. Under pretext of administering my fortune he tried to be my mentor. There is a misunderstanding between us which only time can dissipate. He thinks he is the only one of the two who takes life seriously. He thinks that I am now doing nothing but amuse myself, scattering my wild oats to all the winds of Europe. He also pretends that it will not be for long and that in the end I shall settle down.

All the fervour of my youth, my burning quest of God, is to Cartuyvels only the "splurge" necessary for every young man "in my position." His experienced eye (his own experience) watches me and waits, waits for the wandering chick to return to the hencoop.

And I think: "Poor man, is your small happiness enough for you? You drink and eat and sleep, and you have never dreamed of solving the riddle of life. You have abruptly rejected the world as in exasperation one throws down a difficult puzzle, and you have chosen routine, animal life, for your portion ! . . ." But I feel that I am unjust towards him.

The sale of my possessions, my escape from the social round, at first dumbfoundered him. He had thought that I was settling down, that I was cooping myself up in habits, and that soon my soul would be crushed beneath the enormous burden of my wealth. His expectations were set at naught. But he quickly recovered. My action, which I held to be of almost symbolic importance, was to him a freak, a little more violent than the rest ; that is all. His eyes said clearly : " Sooner or later it will come."

And at times I am afraid. Will it *really come* ? The day when I enter the service of my money, when I turn my back on the absolute, when I am like Cartuyvels, like almost everybody, satisfied—that day I shall be surrendering ALL ! Ah ! no ! Better to die, Faithful One !

Should I have an explanation with him ? . . . Show him that he is wrong, make him feel what he is, shake him to the very foundations of his being so that he must see—and finally cry out to him : " Nevertheless I do not misregard you, my Faithful One, I hold you rather terribly in esteem, my dear old fellow ! "

FLORENCE,
Thursday, 15 April.

The *Florence Herald* and the *Nazione* announce my arrival here, and call to mind the festa given at the Casino Barnabooth last summer in honour of the American colony in Florence. Certainly the reporters insist that

I am a United States American. The date of the festa ought to make them pause for reflection : the 28th May, the Anniversary of the Independency of the——

In the Boboli Gardens met Maxime Claremoris, the only poor man who has ever dared to borrow money of me. (The rest always seem to say : " But I owe you nothing." That is why I like Maxime Claremoris.) His waistcoat was frayed at the neck. He came up to me and said :

" You see, Archie, my waistcoat is worn out."

He is coming to see me at the Carlton. God knows in what evil hostel of the *chiassi* dwells this worshipper of pure beauty. I shall try to keep him in one of my rooms.

As I went to the post by the Loggia I saw some of the Prussian *Pfarren* in whose company I made the last part of the journey from Berlin to Florence the other day. Smiling like peasants gaping at a great jeweller's shop window, they were commenting on the group of the Sabines, and I saw that they thought it—— He ! he ! dirty rascals ! And to think that the Medusa head held up to them by Perseus did not turn them to stone !

Altogether unmoved they turned towards the Offices, where a group of English parsons joined them. I felt sick at heart to think that my favourite pictures were to be reflected in those hard, stupid eyes wherein the idea does not even stir to pierce through matter, but remains engulfed—in what kind of digestion ? Ah, the Angelico, the Filippino Lippis, the Saint Sebastian of Sodoma, the Annunciation of Leonardo, the dear little virgin of Bugiardini, the drawings of Mantegna, seen by such eyes ! It is as though my tenderest thoughts, my most secret aspirations were to be suddenly exposed to the laughter of the vulgar.

Most of these young priests are barbarians, barbarians possessed of a demon of respectability. To them art is at bottom only a remnant of primitive savagery, and genius is a permanent danger to society.

One wonders what Italy can do for them. They will go away, having blasphemed everything, but sure of having added to what they call their culture, and more convinced than ever of the excellence of mediocre minds, which alone are well ordered and respectable, in fine, the overwhelming majority, the Voice of the People, the Normal Man of the mental specialists, subject only to those passions which it is proper to have, each in its own time : Christianity in the fourth century, patriotism the day before yesterday, Socialism yesterday morning, and love with neither phrase nor Art, and even a moderate taste for moderation.

16 April.

Poole has sent me my summer clothes. Spent the morning in trying them on. No useless trimmings in the work of the royal tailor, a simple cut, very simple and rather heavy, which would seem provincial here and in France. How far removed from the smartness which shop-girls think distinguished !

Linen, walking-sticks, boots, ties and hats having arrived this afternoon, I distributed all the things I bought here among the staff of the Carlton.

I wonder what they think of me. Above all, I

should like to have the opinion of the waiter who so soberly looks after the serving of my meals. Does he suspect that he is serving a vagabond, an expatriated wanderer of a dangerous kind?

For, since I dematerialized my wealth, it has appeared to me more than ever before as, above all, a maleficent power. Sometimes, when I think of the good and evil that I could do with my money I turn giddy, and the good—a few stupid acts of charity bestowed lovelessly upon loveless people—the good seems to me so stale, so remote, so impossible that I cannot even stop to think of it. And, on the other hand, all the faults, all the vices, all the cruelties, all the evil examples, every kind of baseness seem naturally and in spite of myself to emanate from my enormous wealth.

For example, I have occasionally spent a long time in looking at a twenty-pound note. I could then see clearly only the evil I could extract from the slip of paper. The vision of it was so delicious and so sad that I was at once filled with a kind of fever. On the other hand, I did not even begin to see the good that I might have done; and no sooner was I a little tempted by it than some element of cruelty, or at least of curiosity, would mingle with it. Clearly, then, I am naturally vile.

But perhaps I am boasting even in saying that,—perhaps I am simply *nil* : rather bad than good, but too weak to do harm, and am only made harmful by my wealth.[1]

---

[1] Without apparently suspecting it the writer is applying to himself the definition of a slave : *Non tam viles quam nulli sunt.*— V. L.

But perhaps, again, I am entirely wrong about myself. . . . When my faithful Cartuyvels respectfully makes me feel, in such and such circumstances, that I have behaved liked a greenhorn, I accept his remonstrance in all humility: I despair of my intelligence: I feel that all my life long I shall be nothing but a greenhorn. It is only afterwards, when I recollect the circumstances, that I perceive the injustice of Cartuyvels' reproaches.

" I have been a dupe. Yes, but a *dupe of my own free will.* That makes all the difference. Once again you are wrong, Old Faithful! Your explanation of my conduct explains nothing at all. On the contrary, you should follow my example, and let yourself be duped, and go so far in it as delicately to pretend that it was against your will. Every generous nature would have done as I did. It is you who are a simpleton to think that the dupe does not always and everywhere come off best, etc." But how do I know that my first impression is not the only true one?

The danger for us men is that when we think we are analysing our character, we are in reality piecing together a character of romance whom we do not even endow with our real inclinations. We select as his name the pronoun of the first person singular and we believe in his existence as firmly as in our own. So it is that the so-called novels of Richardson are in reality confessions in disguise, while the Confessions of Rousseau are a novel disguised. Women, I fancy, do not deceive themselves in this way.

How easily and instantly at the first glance one sees

the image that every one projects of himself—that is, in mature men ! In myself it is not yet formed : that is all,—and that is what makes me believe in the sincerity of my personal analysis. But with the years no doubt my projected character will be fixed : then I shall write " I " without hesitation, fully believing that I know what it means. It is fatal, like death. . . .

Wrote to Socorro and Concepcion to let them know that I am here. Just before I left Berlin, I wired that I was going to Lussin-Piccolo. It was only at the last moment that I had my salon-wagon shunted on to the Sud-Brenner.

At five o'clock Maxime Claremoris came in. Just the same. Careless of many things because he gives himself wholly to one, which he calls the Worship of Beauty. (The capitals are his.) Always full of vehemence he declaims against the restoration of pictures and monuments ; against gimcrackery ; against the official critics. His constant travelling, and his art review, *Le pèlerin Passionné* consume his small resources. And yet I could not induce him to accept one of my rooms at the Carlton.

" Archie, I could never sleep in a room furnished with so little taste. I much prefer the furniture of wood that once was white in my *trattoria*."

" Yes. You will never rise to an understanding of the New Rich style. By the way, what is your address ? "

" Palazzo Cimiciajo."

I was glad to meet the old " Passionate Pilgrim " again.

Got up too late for the service at Saint Mark's. Spent
the day in the hotel—I should have liked Max to come.
No one came.

Watched the Florentines go by in their Sunday best
on the pavement opposite, along the parapet of the Arno.
Yellow and muddy the Arno went, now and then rolling
down an empty *fiaschetto*, and exuding boredom. With
the first glimmer of the street lamps the black Sunday
Florentines came back from the Cascine. Slow dragging
footsteps. The crowd had an air of intolerable false
elegance. Never had the Florentine Sunday so reminded
me of the Sundays in the great cities of the North, where,
the whole afternoon, one finds a disgusting smell of
congealing excrement. I had to look closely to make
sure that it was an Italian crowd. From it emanated
what is perhaps the true wisdom of life, a resigned mediocrity.

Leaning out over the crowd I sometimes felt that I
bore within myself all the sadness and at the same time
all the joy in the world. I was filled with remorse,
desire of destruction, pity and tenderness. I felt both
very young and very old.

19 *April*.

This morning, took the Galluzzo tramway to the
Porta Romana. From Galluzzo on foot to the Chartreuse at Ema.

The view over the valley of the Greve is, for the
peace and the silent jubilation that rise from it, com-
parable to the view from the hills surrounding the town

of Monmouth. But the Tuscan hills are sweeter and more scented than those of the Wye. Here the luminous silence is full of the scintillating leafy litter of the olive trees, the sun from a greater height sheds a more living clearness, and the great shadows are like limpid waters.

Left with the benediction of the monk who was my guide through the passages of the Chartreuse, at Galluzzo I expected to be seized with a desire to go the few miles which lay between me and the Casino Barnabooth. But no : I did not even feel that a portion of my life was for ever shut in among the olive-trees of the valley. At midday I crossed the Ponte Alla Carraia.

There were letters. The indiscretion of the Florentine papers occasioned them. Requests for money coming from people I had never seen. " You are so good to the poor." That recurs like a refrain.

One of these days I shall reply. I shall say, to begin with, that I am not good : that I have a base soul (I am only too sure of that) ; and that when a man has a base soul he can never be good.

And especially " good to the poor " ! Oh ! I shall certainly end by shouting out the truth : " I hate the poor ! The ignoble Poor ! The infamous Poor ! The penniless, stinking Herd ! I hate them, I hate them with all the hatred fed in the *base soul* of a pariah for the upper classes. Have they not trampled me underfoot, have they not spat in my face, the filthy poor ! How their smiles have pierced my heart, and how well they know how to send me packing off to my millions without giving me time to speak, or making some excuse for myself, or letting me show that in spite of all I am a man even as they. They deny me everything : the power of loving, of understanding things, of thinking for myself, of having sincere friends. And how their gestures say : " Bah ! He will console himself with his bank-notes : let him be ! " Though I had the genius of Dante and the knowledge of Pico della Mirandola, I should still be to them " the American millionaire, the young loafer," a fool, a mindless, talentless grotesque, buying and publishing under his name the books and inventions of others—of Messieurs the Poor, forsooth ! And though I were to devote nine-tenths of my income to the foundation of hospitals and charitable institutions, yet they would accuse me of trying to court popularity, or merely to make myself and my money talked about, or they might say that I had " secret ambitions."

Yes. I may as well write all that and say it all while I am in for it. Tell of the cries of joy I gave when I read in a paper of a whole family dying of hunger. Ah ! That avenged me, me, a man humiliated a thousand times by the " hunger " which the poor are always parading before me. And how I used to rub my hands when one of my automobiles splashed some miserable-looking passer-by, or ran over a blind beggar's dog ! Good, good ! So much the better for me. Ah ! my masters ! You men of purity, you who would do so many fine things and good things if you but had the leisure that I have, and are therefore all superior to me in mind and heart, superior to the " stupid millionaire." You shall be splashed with mud, my lords, over the threadbare clothes of which you are so proud and which you so arrogantly compare with my new Poole suits !

You shall be splashed with mud. Now say that I have not a base soul.

But at once the question arises : Have I a right to say these things ?—" The Colonials, we Colonials." (For we may as well admit that the formula " We Americans " does not mean anything else.) *I am a Colonial.* Europe has no use for me : I shall never be anything but a tourist in Europe. And that is the secret of my anger. For there are still countries in Europe where wealth, which is a force worthy of respect, is respected, where clerks and counterjumpers upset by literature and Ruskinism do not scoff at the rich. There is our Old Home, with its plain white front broken up into squares by the old blackened beams—England. And there is the blessed country of Spain with its great gilded churches. And we come to them, *we colonials*, as if the Discovery were only the other day, full of memories of the Indian wars, the arrival of the Pilgrim Fathers, the landing of Villegagnon in the bay of Rio and the Old Thirteen. It all seems only yesterday.

" Ah ! to sit at the table of the great civilization : to see the Pope, the Kings, the Bishops, to be present at the ceremony of the creation of new knights, at the pontifical masses, at the entry of the Lord Mayor into London ! And to touch the columns of the Parthenon, the Roman ruins of Nîmes and Pola, the pillars of the Gothic cathedrals, the leaded panes of the windows in the Tudor houses ! "

And when he has visited all the museums and battle-fields, the colonial, who is richer than any of the Kings of Europe, expects to take his place in the social order of the old country ; he demands his rank as a rich

28

man at the Emperor's court. But he gets a horrid shock : the social order no longer exists ! The old home is being *Americanized* : the *gachupin* triumphs in the drawing-rooms of Madrid : the new knights wear no swords : Christianity has abandoned the Crusade, and no one believes in the Revolution. Poor Colonial whose mind is away back with Washington and the Libertador. . . .

There is plenty of food for anger ! For it is we who are the ancient people. Sooner or later each of us sees it as he rushes through Europe and the capitals. We think of the serious faces of our children, the direct confident eyes of our girls ; and we see that our faces are strangely like those of the eighteenth century portraits. The pre-'89 heads which are so common in Lima and among the Porteños and in Massachusetts. The ancient people, truly, and there is no room, no future for us in Europe—in the hardly formed democracies which have still far to seek their way.

I wrote that on my return from a café-concert (the Savonarola) where I took Maxime Claremoris. I thought it would infuriate him, for he detests that kind of show, which he calls " low " (his puritanical weakness disguised as a " love of Pure Beauty "). But in the stalls he found a " creature of Beauty " and gazed at him throughout the performance. He took me back to the hotel. It is late.

20 April.

This morning, before I went out, I re-read yesterday's diary. Miserable schoolboy paradoxes (one can even mark the place where I give the necessary twist to the argument). But I was sincere. My great anger was striving with its muttering to smother the cry of my wounded vanity. For it is true that the poor have the right to think that they have more wit than we rich men : necessity makes them subtle, envy sharpens their senses ; let them but get an inheritance and they will let their intellect lie fallow. But for me, it is a long time since I won through to the region of impersonal reasoning and pure thought, and casting off my possessions as a garment too heavy for me, hurled myself into the assault on the absolute. And now that I have got rid of the burden of my real property I can fight on equal terms with the poor in the world of abstract ideas ; I have now as much leisure as they. But suppose I were wrong ? Suppose I were still only at the beginning of the intellectual life where a man begins to weigh the pro and contra without throwing his ego into the balance.

Always the same thing ; I rage against myself for being still so young ; the thought that I am rich tortures me, and I am jealous of my millions because they seem to lower my merits in the eyes of others ; and finally, the idea that I am a Colonial strips me of courage ! And yet . . . Cartuyvels would say : " No one is ever satisfied with his lot."

Kept Max Claremoris with me almost the whole day. His conversation amuses me,—more than that : he distracts me from myself so much that I become almost a part of him ; my personality is enlarged by his. At the beginning of our relations, which were never of any long duration, I used to avoid him, thinking that he obscured my ego, and simply worked off some of his personality upon me ; I even went so far as, when I talked to him, to imitate the intonations of his voice and his charming Irish brogue. And I hated that, for I was so proud and jealous of what I took to be my "characteristics." I have progressed since then ; I have become aware that this faculty of imitation is one of my good qualities. Is it not necessary, in order to understand a character, to recreate it, reconstruct it, and, to this end, to assume the character and become it ? Do the young men who have a fully formed personality in early years ever go very far ? Or am I now only seeking excuses for my sempiternal nullity.

Yesterday evening, at the Savonarola, while I was getting intoxicated with the cymbals and drunk with the drums, Max was sketching in his pocket-book the profile of a young man he had seen sitting in the stalls. It was his way of showing that he refused to take part in a "low amusement." I was thoroughly ashamed of taking part in it, and tried to mock the very sincere emotions called up in me by the patriotic couplets (I was ready to shed my blood for Italy), and I tried to silence the great and noble voices which from the bottom of my heart responded to the jerky and well-modulated music of the smutty couplets of the Neapolitan *diseuse*.

This morning again, as we walked along the myrtle groves of the Cascine, the Pilgrim alluded to "low pleasures." I bent my head and felt guilty, but guilty only from Max's point of view, for a thousand arguments arose in me to supply a justification. What was the good ? And I felt that I should never have anything but a "low mind"—to minds built like the Pilgrim's.

Lunched together at the Cencio, M. talking all the time :

"You can't imagine, my dear Archie, how a man like me suffers through advertising agents. Certain posters make my visual existence a horrible purgatory. It is exactly as if someone were saying over and over again, every ten seconds, one or other of these formulæ : 'Bovril, they want more !'—'Try it in your bath !'—'Little liver pills !'—'Lung tonic !'— 'B.D.V. !' etc. Here again, the lion putting out a tongue on which is written : 'Volete la Salute ?' Positively it will end by reducing me to idiocy ! And the place such insanities fill in our lives. Suppose we have an interview on which our whole future depends : we remember it as having taken place by a wall on which was pasted one of those yellow posters extolling an insect powder !"

I laughed at first. Then I thought of answering :

"Why not ? Would not the poster telling of an insect powder stand for the indifference of nature ? Would it not tell us clearly that there are other occupations than ours, and other interests, and other fashions, and other sorrows ? And that everything is relative ? And what matters it if we perish so the insect powder of Moth et Cie sells well ?" But the necessary words, which I now find so easily, were not then forthcoming. Besides, the Pilgrim was already talking about something else. He told me how he had succeeded in suppressing a little ugliness. He buys all the "gim-crackery" his means will permit of his buying, "the biscuit china St. Johns and St. Josephs; you know, the St. Josephs who look as though they had come out of a country barber's shop"; and he smashes them with a hammer and reduces them to little pieces, which he then throws into the gutter. (I could find a good deal to say to him about that, too.)

Spent most of the afternoon at Gambrinus and Piazza Victor-Emmanuel. A series of invectives from M. against modern architects, the Risorgimento, and what he calls the "national idols." His hatred of Garibaldi exceeds anything one can imagine.

"I have smudged, destroyed and spoiled more than two hundred monuments, prints or portraits of the Knight of Humanity. Of course it is not the man himself, the Husbandman, who disgusts me. No. He has done nothing to me personally. What I loathe is the shameful worship of the hero which finds expression in an intolerably base iconography. It is all the deification that infuriates me. All the filthy literature, and the huxtering enthusiasm! . . . And the Galant-uomo of a King! They've made me love him too with the monument they are putting up to him on the Capitol—a kind of fireman's apotheosis, *the* Fireman par excellence,—a fireman who will be seen everywhere in Rome. Even palaces are being pulled down so that he may be more clearly seen! The dreary symbol of a dreary period. When will they put up statues to the incendiaries? Ah, no. The whole history of the nineteenth century would have to be remodelled, turned inside out."

During dinner (at Max's expense at Lapi's) he broached the chapter of Italian anti-clericalism.

" It is the prime motive force of the illustrious idiots. Oh for a law which would force all those fools to grovel —on pain of death—at the feet of all the monks and priests they meet in the streets ! "

And he drank to the temporal power of the Popes.

Home : rather tired with having heard so many words.

Wednesday.

I was still in bed when Max came in to tell me he was going to Rome.

" I am going to see if there is not some way of ridding the Capitol of the monument to the Fireman. I belong to a ' Pro Roma ' society. . . . Besides, one can always count on the intervention of Providence : the monument is a gratuitous insult to the Pope, and one may hope to see him reduce it to powder, on the day of its completion, with the thunder of God !

" ' Avenge, O Lord, Thy slaughtered saints, whose bones . . .' Ha ! That sonnet of Milton, the loosing of the flight of eagles ! Can you feel that, you rich man ? Ah ! The folly of the age is intolerable ! Down with the Freemason Pope ! Long live Gregory XVI and the Jesuits ! I absolutely refuse to admit Italian unity. By the way, can you lend me two hundred lire to go from here to the Pontifical State ? And a suit you have cast off ? And a few ties which are out of the Piccadilly fashion and therefore out of favour with you ? "

I pointed to my Dalmatian trunk and the wardrobes, bidding him look for himself.

"Don't be shy, Pilgrim. Take as many hundred lire notes as you like. You are the only poor man of my acquaintance who is intelligent enough to dare borrow money from me."

"Poor! Oh, as for that, I am no more proud of my poverty than you are of your wealth."

"Then, why, O poor man, did you call me Rich Man?"

"Hurt, eh? I beg your pardon, your High-and-mightiness."

Lunched at Doney's with Max and little Count Bettino whom I met yesterday at Gambrinus. As Max spoke in English, Bettino was constantly leaning over to me and saying:

"Come dice?"

That was unpleasant, as Bettino never found any opportunity for saying those charming, graceful things which only the Italians know how to say.

Tea (alone with Max) at the Albion: dinner in the Carlton: and as the train M. was to take does not go until half-past twelve I offered the Pilgrim a place in my box at the Savonarola.

"What is this beauty that you find in Beauty, Pilgrim? You see I am quite content with ugliness, stupidity and filth, and I am quite as good as you. I assure you that from certain angles Garibaldi and his cult are quite pleasant to me. And just look at those three beautiful fair girls, yes, the English dancers mouthing their rhythmic ribaldries! Doesn't their healthy plump flesh rising out of the crimson froth of lace tell you something of the people; and the smell of Cavours and Virginias, and the big blithely hum-

ming drum, and the clang of the crashing cymbals?
I mean, the combination of all these things?"

He has a way of replying, "Oh, yes," which flings
me back on my millions, my twenty-three years, and
the presumption that my mind is just that of a weak
stripling who is too rich.

I have been with him to the station, and now for
sleep.

22 April.

M.'s departure has comforted me. I do not yet
know how to maintain my isolation. I ought not to
allow the first-comer to crush me as he did. I don't
mind my rooms being occupied and my time taken up,
but why should my opinions, feelings, etc., be suppressed by the opinions and feelings of others? To-day
all that has stopped, and my inclinations, which for the
last few days have been checked, chided and closured,
are once more expanding and stretching.

But the reaction began last night: I had assimilated
the Pilgrim's state of mind enough to be able to surmount it. But it was not until to-day—pacing about
my rooms and looking out at the yellow, dreary Arno
flowing between the two walls of the quays—that I
found the things I might have said to Maxime Claremoris.

A man who sees nothing in life but lines! How
could he understand the passions which stir and guide
me? All his conversation is outside life, deals with
historical events, with the things that depend on nobody and are arranged by God to His own liking. In
the libraries of the little towns where I have lived I

have found obscure books, generally written by reverend gentlemen in the country, in which the whole history of humanity is ingeniously explained and the finger of God traced therein. The endless meditations of bachelors who never bathed and stank of closed rooms. Claremoris's views remind me of them. How far he is from me ! He knows nothing of love, or pity, or that kind of fury which drives me to desire to do good, or to desire to do evil—I never quite know—though it is a frantic desire, to certain persons. Take the young man of whose profile he made a note the other night at Savonarola's. I should have sought his acquaintance and had glimpses of an heroic friendship, with adventures shared by the two of us : my whole life might have been changed by the encounter.

Yes. Max is ten years older than I am ; which, apparently, explains many things. He has more wis-- dom than I. But what is this wisdom, if not the wear and tear of our feelings, the cooling of our fervour ? The presence in us of a greater quantity of the stupidity of the world (no doubt we absorb a little of it every year) and the acquisition of that *fund of indifference* which is nothing but a fund of imbecility !

But am I not, rather, suffering from being misunderstood by Max ? By misunderstood, I mean, insufficiently appreciated after my own fashion. He too had in his mind the finished type of the rich man who is incapable of understanding and sincerely loving works of art, and he fits the mask on me at once, without thinking, without seeing me. No doubt he thinks he is doing me a great honour by borrowing money of me, and that millionaires like me are only fit to feed æsthetes like him.

Æsthete : yes, that is the word. At heart he is very 1880, the old Pilgrim, hand-in-glove with Oscar Wilde, a Cathedral man, a decadent ; a Leicester Square Montmartrois. In fine, very limited, and incapable of realizing that of us two it is I who am the artist and he the amateur. . . . All that came from spite, and I am unjust to a man of worth who has proved himself. Vanity, always vanity ! But where shall I find coals of fire to put on the enemy's head ?

I have shaken off my ill-humour. Outside the spring evening had been impatiently waiting for me for the last hour—and I went and joined it. Followed the Lung'Arno from the Piazza Manin to the Ponte Vecchio. The evening and the joy of living went with me. I had no desire for anything. We were just like peaceable animals able to be happy everywhere since a little light and air are enough for them. The cherubim placed by God on the angles of the flat roofs showed us mortals patches of their celestial garments. I felt very small, very poor and very pure : and the number of pleasant things was so great that I took heart.

FLORENCE,
Friday, 23 *April,* 19 . . .

A fresh attack of " *boutiquisme,*" if I may call it so. (But it is at such moments that the French language hampers me a little and I find it too much in the " Louis XIV style of dress," jerkin stiff with gold braid, hose and breeches too big, etc.—all that because I can find no equivalent for the word *shopping*.) Among my purchases : measuring instruments (a barometer, a compass, an odometer, etc.) and women's underclothing, which I distributed among the maids at the Carlton. There were chemises and culottes with Venetian lace insertion, very fine. It gave me an extraordinary pleasure to touch them and to give them to *the right persons*. Only one of them said : " Oh, sir, they are too beautiful for me ! " I snatched them out of her hands angrily ; I was very near insulting her. The pride of the woman ! Hulda (that is the young woman's name) believes in her social position and sticks to it ; a row of lace in a chemise is above, and stuff of a certain coarseness of web would be below that position. I felt that I was very humble because I find nothing in the world too beautiful, and therefore too modest for me. (My mania for self-justification !)

Bought also a collection of flat pig-skin handbags (I particularly like the smell of the leather). I have too many travelling things. I shall amuse myself by throwing them, after midnight, from my balcony into the Arno. Really there is nothing more hampering when one is travelling.

24 *April.*

At tea-time, at Giacosa's, met Bettino by chance, and he held forth subtly, with two other men whom I did not know, about the Italian translators of Shakespeare. We were left alone for a moment and he asked me this embarrassing question : " But what have you come to Florence for ? " I replied : " To see the galleries again, of course."

I lied : I came here with the fixed intention of not seeing the galleries again. I have seen too much of them already and absorbed too much. When I made my first tour round Europe with John Martin and Stephane I saw nothing of them : people's faces, the sights of the streets, life in fine, spoke to me too loudly and attracted me too much to allow me to look at anything else. Then, on the second trip, I had to get acclimatized at first, and then reject all the instruction I had painfully acquired, and find my way to works of art through all the horrid pile of literature which for the last hundred and fifty years the critics have been heaping up at their feet. At last I reached a direct contact : I met the reward of my trouble and patience. But must it be that even this pleasure so pure, so gratuitous, so innocent, wears away like the rest ? A little less quickly perhaps, but it also wears away. And it leaves a certain distress, a horrible temptation to analyse the elements which composed it—the temptation to add one more to the heaped-up pile of literature. The other day when I strolled into Santa Maria Novella I felt this temptation : to ponder Ruskin's appreciation of the Ghirlandajo frescoes. I felt that little by little, with enthusiasm, I could become entirely absorbed in it and lose myself far removed from my real life : I saw myself leaving to the world an enormous work, useless even to myself, full of oracles and moral discourse, and remote even from the honours it would procure me ! A work which would win me Cartuyvel's respect, and the regard of all those people who, despising the books which interest them, honour the books which bore them. If ever I wish to win

Cartuyvel's respect I have only to write a " History of Rain through the Ages."

I said : ·" To see the galleries again, of course." In spite of all the novelists and all the æsthetes, Florence would be nothing without the galleries. Apart from the Piazza della Signoria the town contains nothing which is at all times pleasing. The little scraps of the country peeping above the dreary and inhospitable districts oltr'Arno, perhaps. . . . That means you must either leave the town or enter the museums to find the gentleness and beauty of Tuscany. And there is that unpleasant wind from Siena, and the wind and the rude climate : cold or like a furnace, with the sky so often grey, almost always lumbered up or grimy, bruised, heavy with sulphur and rust. There are dark evenings when the North wind cuffs you at every street corner, when the Dome is discoloured like a bad tooth, and everything is dripping and hidden away in the mist rising from the Arno. And empty days when Provincialism reigns with Boredom.

In fine there is only one town in Italy where a townsman can live happily : Milan. No, two : I have just received from Naples a postcard from the Marquis de Putouarey, a good liver who knows not culture. Let us say therefore : Naples and Milan. The rest are archæology.

Bettino is right. What have I come here for ? Ah ! I know : more closely to watch myself living. I mean, without being disturbed by the constant friction of a great city while still having a little movement round me : to watch myself living, to spend these long hours in writing, with a feeling of such futility and isolation.

And yet I have come here with my curiosity still fresh, just the same as it was on my first trip, when I was a boy of fifteen full of obscure sensations and with no power of personal analysis, accompanied by my tutor whose supervision embarrassed and distressed me. A shy, impulsive, timid boy whose ill-instructed eyes stared too much, a little exotic, a young barbarian who left the museums choking and fuming with impatience. But how right I was ! Right against all the art critics in the world ; they could never have led me to direct contact with the pictures if I had not first had my hunger for life sated. Besides, even here, I remain in relation with a little life. With the intoxication of my freedom dying away tired of buying useless things, after the first few days, I go and sit on the stone seats against the Uffizi, in the shade of the arcades. There I sit elbowing a world of beggar men and women stupefied with idleness and deformed by the regular and simple satisfaction of their poor vices. A nose reddens, a leg drags, an eye opens only partially. Sometimes on the other side, under the Uffizi Corti, there will come a number of German vagabonds to rest, with their chops burned to a red-brown and set in a bright down of red hair. About half-past twelve, lovely children come and play ball on the central pavement near the quay. Students pass in front of me. I hear one say :

" Ma è lo stesso anche in Francese : ci sono dei verbi irregolari . . ."

And children crying :

"Prepotente ! lo dico, prepotente ! Perchè io sono piccolo . . ."

And sometimes I lean over the parapet of the Arno, and raise my eyes towards that portion of the sky enchannelled by the two parallel roofs of the Uffizi, at the end of which the Palazzo Vecchio rears to the full blue sky its stone tower and the steel spire where the Marzocco climbs.

Besides, are there not also for me the beautiful streets and the brightness of the shops on the pavements, the smell of the trattorie and their vaulted roofs of hams, the trams to dodge in the narrow streets, a litter of the Misericordia pushed along at a run, shady corners where flowers are sold, the end of a street with a man standing and clinging to the wall, a little lingering piece of history, a murmur that I must catch, the Tuscan C pronounced h aspirate, the words *dice*, *insomma*, which are a kind of spoken punctuation, the severe sad intonations of the Italian language, the *Eh, gia, Eh, si*, so full of resignation, the adorable face of a child, and the songs at the Savonarola where I wind up the evening ?

25.

At St. Mark's. Bettino came up to me as I left. I used to know him eighteen months ago at Basilicate as a much *smaller* man, young and naïf. I wonder if I have changed as much as he : I wonder what I have learned and what I have forgotten since that time. We used to get on very well. We used to go for walks together every evening in the Via Pretoria, munching *pignoli* bought from the pretty seller of *generi diversi*,

43

talking about politics and art and paying the contadine impudent compliments. Bettino used then to write in a local journal *Lucania* verses "à la Banville," with which he was very pleased and signed Willy, because Piccadilly and Regent Street, which he had never seen, were to him the country of all things marvellous.

Two hours spent with him in his victoria (on the road to Settignano) showed him from every point of view exaggerated : he poses as a cosmopolitan and his Anglomania makes me blush for him. It was in order to show himself off before the foreign colony that he came and waited for me outside the English chapel. Everything Italian seems to him dull and low : everything from abroad surprises and delights him. He will end by admiring the middle-classes of Berlin ! The other day he gazed respectfully at Maxime Claremoris, taking his Irish accent for an aristocratic London pronunciation. The fact that the English nobility is entirely provincial has not yet come to his knowledge : and besides, like all Anglomaniacs, he does not know a word of English.

" Oh, Villi, Villi," I say to him, " I despair of you ! When shall I ever be like you ? When shall I have your lively gentle manners, your graceful attitudes, your subtle way of saying things and of making them understood ? In a word, when shall I possess the secret of Italian elegance, the only real elegance ? Though I light my cigarettes without putting my lips to them, though I can without awkwardness wear a heavy cloak thrown over my shoulders, yet I feel at heart that I shall never succeed in being taken for an Italian."

Bettino, for whom elegance has no home save Piccadilly, says nothing, and I continue :

" I am not speaking for you : you have been to
London since we last met and you are St. James' Street
from head to foot. I am thinking of the young fellows whom we meet in the great tea-shops. Those
who mistrust themselves, put up with being taken for
Frenchmen ; but the big guns, the great romantics, are
sublimely anglicized and it is fine ! But let them
only get a little animated and they break out in frantic
gesticulations, and I am always on the look out for it.
I have seen one of them in a café talking of his ' Brit-
ish phlegm ' and with one sweep of the arm upset three
mugs of beer. Happy Athenians : only you can so
disguise yourselves : it is impossible for you to be ridiculous."

Received a long letter from the Yarza girls. My
poor Socorro is dying of boredom at Leamington. I
note the annoyance I felt as I observed that they had
put a sixpenny stamp on the envelope when a twopence-
halfpenny one would have been enough. A faint
stirring which was quickly suppressed. But disap-
proval of prodigality is set in a formula in my mind.
Bourgeois !

26 April.

Received this morning a large basket with green and
pink ribbons, filled with flowers. It came from the
three pretty dancers at the Savonarola (the girls I pointed
out to Max Claremoris one night). The day before
yesterday I sent them a little present, and they have
sent me in return three little paper hens on a bed of

violets and white carnations. I hastened to unfold
the notes. The delightful creatures have insisted on
introducing themselves to me under poetic names:
" Cinderella " (Cheek !), " The Snow Queen " and
" Heart's Desire " (which smacks a little of the demi-
monde and light literature). I have guessed which
" Heart's Desire " is : the one I like best, the plump
fair girl who reminded me of D. G. Rossetti's Lady
Lilith. I was absurdly moved. I wandered aimlessly
through the streets, on the sunny side, and suddenly
found myself in the Viale dei Colli, smiling vaguely
at the great gusts of warm air. " Heart's Desire " ;
but that is everything ! Ah ! I would give all I
have, I would give myself, to the first comer provided
only she were beautiful to me ! Longing for woman ;
a fresh crisis. I have been thinking all day long of the
time when I was in love with Anastasie Retzuch. I
lived again through my flight from the Embassy, one
September morning, when I went to find Tassoula at
the Phanar, to take her away. I followed that horrible road which goes from Therapia to the town ;
the wide sad ends of streets opened up from time to
time on my left, and, beyond the houses with their pink
fronts and heaps of sweepings, showed the Bosphorus
bristling with light. Beyond again stretched the empire
of all things blue : Asia and the sky. How high the
sun was, and brilliant and fierce in the shimmering air !
At Ortakoei I passed a group of eunuchs on horseback.
They were clad in blue frock coats and wore shiny tall
hats. I saw their flat and glabrous faces : I heard their
voices, and when I turned I saw their great shining
horses pass into the shadow of a grove of cedars. Far-

ther on, up a steep road I walked behind a military cart, low and heavy, painted grey. It was drawn by two little humped oxen with horns like trumpets, and it was escorted by soldiers of the Army Service Corps. I can see now the blue-and-grey uniforms, the brown gaiters, the brass buttons shining in the sun, the red fezes. . . . The prince, being away, would not hear of my flight for a few days on his return to the Embassy. We should be far away then ! I was calm and towered over life. I was going to run away with the daughter of one of the richest nobles of the East. (I had been reading at the time that ponderous pedantic invention, *Romola*, the action of which takes place in Florence.) I was in fact the dupe of Tassoula's parents : the Kyrios Retzuch was really dragging me along that road. But at that time (I was seventeen) I thought myself a cunning fellow with whom the world had to reckon. . . . And I was not wrong : since, involuntarily, without intent, it was I who tricked Tassoula's parents.

Our actions are like the rough sketches of deeds, a holding of the arms out to the void. One is on the point of a decisive step, a plunge which will alter the whole of life. The crisis comes : and, some years later, as we look back, we are astonished that we were so much moved and so little changed. We can do nothing to events, *and events can do nothing to us*, whatever we may think.

27 April.

To-day, walked on foot all round the town through the Viali : home by the Zecca Vecchia and the Lung'-

Arno.   The streets in the centre of the town have the depressing aspect of an official festival, and the north wind blows.   A flag here and there marks out a public building, a college, or a museum.   The street lives in jerks, at regular intervals : a cornet à piston drags a few notes along the pavement in an empty street ; isolated sounds rush up, then die away.   On the hills, where the corn and the olive trees spread out their gentle green, where San Miniato shows in the dark verdure a many-coloured face, a deep rich azure, the Italian sky dark ultramarine, a sunset for rich amateurs. And yet in these scenes there is a welcome everywhere. But I could never become a real Florentine.   I know that now.

People may have come to live here from every point of Europe, when it was the capital of a little state, a Switzerland for spring and autumn.   In spite of all, the Salon of Europe has remained a town of passage, one of the old capitals of the argumentative and liberal middle-classes of the nineteenth century.   No room for us late-comers.   Besides, the Salon is no longer as crowded as the grand-ducal period.   For long now, the celebrities have left it : in their stead young midde-class couples from France and Germany come and find boredom for a few weeks and go away with memories of their hotel.   The Germans say " colossal ! " and " pyramidal ! " and the incorrigible French call the Ponte-Vecchio " le Pontet-Vexiau." And the shops with leather goods and the villini outside the gates and the red-and-yellow trams : another Passy !

Another thing : in the great towns which have an important cosmopolitan population, the local life seems to me very remote from myself, almost inaccessible, with depths from which I am separated as by stratas of earth, by the high foreign society to which, in spite of myself, I belong : the native nobility who copy us though they stay in their dark corner : the upper middle-classes who ape our ways, and finally the artistic, financial and industrial worlds which are the same in all countries.

And yet we live in the same places where all this Italian life is stirring. I am fed with the Italian air ; I drink the Italian water . . . (minerals from Nocera !), and in every street I rub shoulders with the Italian life : at every moment it comes and tantalizes me : the charming red of the Casentine cloaks worn by the men who every Friday throng the Piazza della Signoria : the pink carts drawn by a horse and a donkey harnessed together and covered with a beautiful red cloth fringed with a thin gimp of bright green ; the country visiting us, which we feel all around us. . . . And the little cake-seller on the Ponte-Vecchio, the ailing child with the lovely eyes. . . .

I like to remember the little towns where one finds that life in its purity : where one is among Italians with just a few cherished ideas : with the main street tiled from end to end and flanked with high dark *palazzi*, with grandiose *portoni*, and the café-confectioner's where officers drink tall glasses of water and smoke long cigars with a bitter flavour ; and the beggars sitting in the winter sun in front of the white prefecture. A sad smile. Virgil everywhere. And everywhere an air of great architecture. The vivacity of the people : one would say the very animals shared it : the trot of the little horses, the capers of the dogs in the lovely light, and the vigorous vermin !

I can clearly remember in every detail a winter's day at Palmeti, on the Ligurian coast : the wide stretch of grey sea : the wider stretch of sky, soft and warmly grey : the dry palm trees casting no shadow on the pebbles of the garden in front of the Municipal Casino : the enormous snorting trains stopping in the middle of the fields of the flower-growers near the station and along the shore : the scent of the rock-rose and the rosemary coming from the craggy country ; and the little square tower of the beacon, black with age, on the end of the short empty jetty.

And I can catch a momentary glimpse of a summer afternoon at Bari ; a long clamant rain in the wide bright streets ; making freshly green the shutters of the tall new houses and the palm trees in the square : steps of wood have been placed at the end of the pavements ; the water runs and roars beneath them : in Laterza's shop I read " The Raven " translated into the Græco-Salentine dialect with the title *O kraulo*.

But Taranto most nearly stands in my memory for the Italy for which I am trying to find the definite formula (instead of these tentative notes). The little hunchback who frequents the cafés of the new town, with the papers, about six in the evening after the arrival of the last express from Naples ; these cafés (those in the Piazza Archytas and those which look out on the Mare Piccolo and the Turning Bridge) with their inscriptions in Greek lettering on high mirrors swept by the wind from a semi-African sea ; the officers of the Royal Marine, who call to mind the neighbouring nations : Greece, Turkish Tripoli ; the posters of the Politeama Paësiello : the pyramids of oranges and melons on the pavement of a little square, very hot : the great harsh, incessant wind bending the olive trees on the dunes and forcing them to droop their twisted branches down towards the ground in a frenzy : the quays of the old town above the Ionian Sea—the flamboyant gulf all blue, *bleu de France*, on the other side of the ancient burning rampart of stone. . . .

Is that the essential ? Are the dominant notes there ? And is there any necessary relation between the whole of these recollections and the movement of the Neapolitan beggar-woman kissing the penny piece someone has thrown her : or the colour of the Strega liqueur : and the taste of the *Mostarda di Cremona* ; and the *format* of the great dailies of Milan, Rome, Naples, Genoa, and this city ; and the smell of the Virginias and the *spagnoletti* ? Or must I add to my list the sun in the streets of Rome, and the flower-sellers in the Piazza d'Espagna, and the outline of the great flat roofs projecting like long eyelashes over the white faces of the villas of the North, with their façades painted in vivid colours (sometimes at a sham window half open there peeps out the hideous face of a painted woman) : and the Tuscan country : the squares of shining corn-green and blue between the little elms which uphold the hard ropes of the vines. An olive-tree like a group of three girls spinning round with their hair flying out upon the wind. On the slopes thousands of pine trees all together preen out their tufts of green. And companies of cypresses guard the heights.

And, once more, what has all that to do with public opinion, and the ideas of the electors of M. Zanardelli, and the mutterings of the little politicians in the great newspapers and the singing of the great poets in their little reviews, and the directory principles of the Risorgimento, and the anarchy of the dirty trattorie? (But that is much less important than the dreary pink with which the docks at Naples are painted.)

No. I have heaped up words without being able to render the Italian *air* which I can feel so well. It seems to me that I can find something of it in Claude Lorrain, in the verses of Maynard, and especially in Malherbe. I cannot say why. There was also a good deal of it at the Savonarola, yesterday and to-day (I spend my life there). It is time for bed : it is near day and they are already shouting : " Fieramosca ! "

FLORENCE,
Sunday, 30 *April* 19 . . .

For some days now I have been getting up at five in the afternoon. I have my bath and dress about six and then go and have something to eat at the Albion. At eight I have a light supper and about nine I am in my box at the Savonarola. There I have my fill of noise and return to the Carlton about one in the morning full of the sublimest dreams. And until morning I write scraps of French poetry (in *vers libres* which I shall call *Dejections*—so that Cartuyvels may not take them seriously. I am firmly resolved not to be taken seriously by the reasonable and intelligent people of whom Cartuyvels is the type).

52

I can hear exactly what the Faithful would say to me if he knew my new way of living :

" You say you are a poet and you disregard God's good day ! "

" No. Far from it. I love the day so much that I spend the whole night in waiting for it."

Indeed I still have the feeling that I used to have as a child : a feeling of being superior to all those who spend the night in sleeping. I used to say to old Lola and the *criadas* at home :

"Oh, yes. You have been resting but I have seen."

" Jesus ! And what did you see in the dark, milordito ? "

I could not reply. I had seen so many things, beautiful things. I had waged so many battles against sleep, against the custom which insists that one should sleep at night, against all the ideas and principles of my parents and the *criadas* and the other *ordinary* people. And I had conquered : I could let my heated head sink into the lap of dawn.

Meanwhile I am neglecting my diary.

Every night as I leave the Savonarola I have an interview with " Heart's Desire," and I often take her back to supper in my rooms at the Carlton. I know that I could without difficulty win her favours. But . . . She does at best give me a certain pleasure : that of watching her eat. I find that there are not many things more agreeable to watch than a pretty woman in a low cut gown eating nicely cooked meat with a good appetite.

All these days, nights rather, will no doubt be linked

in my memory with the crisis of Malherbian enthusiasm through which I am passing. The stanzas of the great odes go so well with the Tuscan landscapes, which are of the same order as the landscapes of Provence where Malherbe lived for a long time. And the author gives me so much pleasure with his nickname *Père Luxure* ; the pox of which he was so proud ; the knock-down jests with which he used to crush the little enthusiastic affectations of his disciples : the haughty patronage he extended to commonsense, he who had seen the vanity of everything : and the scorn he had for his art, he who was the Father of modern Poetry ! A fine man ! A good workman, building his poetical Louvre on the banks of the Seine ! The great decorator of France ! I can never pronounce his name without being filled with respect, I a foreigner dabbling in the writing of French—after him, after all that he has done for me. And what a slap in the face would the least of his jests at his own expense be for the little prophets and redeemers of the present day !

Once again I have triumphed over darkness and passed through the pit of night, and already (as Malherbe would say) :

> Et déjà devant moi les campagnes se peignent
> Du safran que le jour apporte de la mer.

3 *May*, 19 . . .

I have neglected my diary for some days now. Wrongly : I am now going through a sentimental crisis of which, one of these days, I shall be glad to have documentary evidence.

54

Probably I shall then have a different opinion of my present feelings, just as I already regard my affair with Anastasie Retzuch quite differently from what I thought of it when Tassoula was still alive. But at that time I was eighteen and liked living on illusions, or rather I had not yet learned the difficult art of being frank with myself. I was trying to see Tassoula, who had been flung dowerless into my arms and to whom I was making a considerable allowance, as a lovelorn maiden who had sacrificed everything, fortune, honour, etc., in order to live with me. When the Duke of Waydberg began to court her I closed my eyes and did all I could to make him marry her (though he knew nothing of it) merely to give myself, nay, to buy myself, the pleasure of living intimately with such an exalted personage.

How childish ! I had then the same idea of the world as humble folk and the readers of polite romances : I had a superstitious reverence for what I called " breeding," I believed in " old families " and I had a certain pleasure every time I shook hands with a European whose name was preceded by a great title of nobility. Then came our intrigue, our *ménage à trois :* the Duke and Duchess of Waydberg and Señor A. O. Barnabooth ; it seemed to me very important, very worldly, and devilish European ! No doubt I was paying Waydberg's gambling debts : but was I not his wife's lover ? The pride that filled me when people spoke in my presence of the Duke of Waydberg, and when I read the Duke of Waydberg's name in the papers. There were lordlings simply bursting with envy at the thought that they would never be presented to the Duke of Waydberg; and there was I, a very plebeian young man, at the age when one still regards the seduction of an ordinary middle-class woman as a success, there was I having married my mistress to the Duke of Waydberg and keeping him. Those were the days when my only pride was to be in society and my only desire to stay in society.

I have become harder to please. The only thing that can satisfy me now is to see all things plain both within and outside myself; my youthful simplicities, for instance, as clearly as I can now see through the pure Tuscan light with the sharp haze of the diaphanous olive trees spangled with silver.

So that I have progressed although sometimes I wonder if I was ever deceived by my visions, and whether, as I followed them, I was not just as clear-sighted with regard to everything else as I am now? Ah! At least I have rid myself of such visions. That is undoubted.

I set myself then before all to know myself; and henceforth that shall be my only occupation.

But there is in me, as no doubt in every one of us, a spirit of darkness, a force which makes me dread the boldness of my thoughts and makes me adopt, tricked out as truth, the first lie which emerges from the current stream of lies which surrounds us. And one day I saw that Spirit of Darkness, and—it was my vanity.

Before I set out for good and all to see clearly into myself, my Vanity lived the life of a man of large means, every now and then getting a little pricked, being exposed thereto by my dealings with my fellows; but when happy and peacefully master of myself, it guided me fairly well, and I had no great complaint to make of its domination, since it is apparent that it has led me to my present situation and has made me turn furiously against it. For it is certain that there was a moment when I argued with myself thus : "So the world gossips about me : it finds me ridiculous and full of faults : Cartuyvels says I have no feelings for Propriety, and Guido de S. and Valery L., those inseparables, have marked me out for their jests (envious men of small means) and at every turn life gives a thousand disappointments ; well ! I will examine and criticize myself a thousand times more severely than the World can do." And from that moment, when I began to give effect to that resolution, I saw that the vanity which inspired me was also the great obstacle to my project.

And vanity was the enemy on whose head I was to heap coals of fire ! I have struggled heroically : I have been pitiless : and unceasingly I apply to that open wound the red-hot iron of my self-contempt and the caustic of my inflexible introspection. A duel to the death between myself and the enemy, in the closed house of my soul where no one can come and separate the combatants. I pursue the enemy from room to room even down to the cellar, the last refuge : then at last I close with him and fasten on his throat : " I will strangle my pride," I say, " and from that only will I take . . ."

" My pride ! " jeers the enemy, suddenly springing up behind me while I strive to choke the shadow of a throat with a shadow.

Sometimes I have wondered if I should not do better

57

to make an end by flight. I might quit the house and leave the enemy to stumble over and bespatter the walls and floor : perhaps his own stench would kill him in the end. Yes. Quit myself, and shut the door and throw the key over the roof. Leave myself : but whither should I go ? To whom could I give myself ?

And incessantly I hurl myself at the filthy warrior and shake him and he overthrows me. I have done everything. I have deliberately sought out the company of men who laughed at me, and said just the very things which would ensure their going on laughing at me. I have courted contempt. Whenever I have been misunderstood I have rejoiced. " All the ill they can say and think of me still falls short of the truth : people are too gentle in regarding me only as a vile and infamous creature." And at once I would congratulate myself on having found that formula : and the whole thing would begin over again.

But my disgust with myself is none the less sincere and I feel that it is justified. When I examine myself closely I find myself really vile and stupid, and base, and mean through and through, to the very marrow of my bones, and exactly what I had called myself,—half a line of Corneille, my old device :

A man without honour.

It was at the time when I had begun to discover my faults, though, being dominated by my vanity, I was fain to turn them into qualities and gloried in my baseness (in the moment of absolute despair when I composed a poem entitled *L'Eterna Voluttà*). But now

I confine myself to stating the baseness of my character without the embellishment of note or comment : for my whole care henceforth is to *see clearly*.

And it is precisely my excess of vanity which has brought me to that and still goes with me. Even as I write the Enemy bends over my arm and murmurs :

" What courage, eh ? It's wonderful : you are publicly inflicting on yourself the most cruel humiliation. You may talk of the baseness of your character, but that ennobles you : and it's all very well for you to talk of your cowardice : only the brave dare talk of their cowardice, etc."

" But, you see, I write down at once what you whisper to me."

" Ah ! So you carry your courage so far as to spy on me, O great of soul ! You see, you are beginning all over again."

" Oh ! After all . . ."

Yes. He is always there. So much the worse : we must put up with his presence and try to make him more and more tenuous. (He has already lost half his weight since I began to plague him.) The education of pride : what a programme ! It would consist in giving it free rein, satisfying it, urging it on and on to the point where it would become humility and full intelligence. I shall try it when I have time.

I set out on this long divagation only to come to my project of mercilessly analysing my feelings during the crisis through which I am passing. The devil ! There is none of the sentimental old woman in me, I want to look reality in the face without holding my nose if it stinks. Besides, this desire goes back a long way with me ; I remember disliking my childish books because they lacked realism. They did not give the whole thing. For example, one was never told when Alice left the room and as for the Hatter, if he was constipated, as I feel sure he was, why not say so straight out ?

I turned these thoughts over a few moments ago as I supped in my rooms at the Carlton with the lady who signs herself " Heart's Desire " on little paper notes and is in reality called Florrie Bailey. (And I fancy I even began to compose them and pondered the turning of the phrases and the arrangement of the paragraphs.) Florrie, who had come from the stage of the Savonarola full of gossip and tunes, was surprised to find me lost in thought, and reproached me sharply with being bored with her. That displeased me : I hate women who can never understand a man's being serious in their presence. They do not listen to what one says to them, their thoughts are far away, but if only the man's face smiles and he seems content, that is enough for them. There are other things in her which displease me. I have so far behaved as a respectful friend (that seems to surprise her) and yet she already calls me " my boy " and " silly man." And yet she is not lacking in respectability in the street. Quite the lady (I have been out with her three times). But, *tête-à-tête* with me, she makes her dignity so cheap that I suffer for her, and every time she lowers herself in my presence to please me, I want to throw myself at her feet and beg her to respect herself more, to respect herself as I respect her.

" Oh yes. The life of the poor has deformed you in accordance with its laws : it has not injured your body, but your sweet, pure soul which I can see in your still childish eyes. And from your childhood in white pinafore and red tam-o'-shanter down to this evening when you are sitting here with your smiling lips and beautiful neck and shoulders I wish to know nothing of the ways by which you have passed. Or if you tell me something of them I will listen (that I may love you more) : or of your faults that I may weep over them with you : or of your misfortunes, that I may share them. The contemptuous compliments, the insulting caresses, the kisses of rich men, officers, gentlemen ! everything you have endured, ah ! how I will honour and adore you for all that, *my* dear ! How can I make good to you the horrible years which I see in your past : how can I restore to you the purity and joy that the men of my class have taken from you, the horrible rich men who have dared to use you as a machine for pleasure ? All the inexpiable past . . ."

" My poor boy. Why are you so glum ? If I bore you, tell me so frankly. No, don't be angry ! Smile, naughty boy ! Ah ! That's it ! "

And I smiled at her, but without conviction, as in writing one uses a ready-made expression, saying that one cannot find a better and that one will never have any talent. It satisfies her. These women get worried like nurses when they do not see their babies laughing. I even speak a few words, some silly compliment, but rather too sincerely, and then I withdraw into myself : " A great injustice to be repaired : a human being to be saved. Only a whole life of tender protection, of

61

loving devotion, could repair the wrong life has done you, dear Heart's Desire."

I gaze at her across the flowers and glasses and over the little dishes set in their silver-gilt cases. The plebeian woman tamed : I ponder her big strong limbs soft under the silk of her gown which is put to shame and gives way before her fair childish pink skin, gleaming and full of dimples. The two long blue rays of light move towards her temples, play over her cheeks, and are raised towards me and seem to seek. "Shrimp sauce ? " I anticipate the movement and pass it to her.

"Yes. Go on eating ! I am not hungry : your presence is enough for me. But it is so splendid for me to think that I am giving you to eat. My money is suddenly ennobled by being put to so fine a use : I, poor I, am feeding that wonderful body ! All the girls of Warwickshire are in that body, and this girl, Florrie Bailey (a fine plebeian name) whom I have chosen for my own from among them all, and who is like them as a rose is like other roses. So you have flowered for me, my English rose, so big and fine."

The two blue rays concentrate all their light on me ; her lovely elbows lean on the table-cloth : her round rather high shoulders lean forward and her little face, offering itself with pursed lips, rests on her crossed hands.

"Now, listen. . . ."

I was expecting it : she reproached me with spending so much money in sending flowers. "A whole boxful of flowers for a poor girl like me."

62

" Poor and defenceless and despised ! That is exactly why I love you. Never have I more clearly heard the voice of duty, the still small voice saying, ' You must make her rich, happy and respected '—and I will demand nothing in exchange, oh ! absolutely nothing."

As I was taking her through the sitting-rooms which had not been lit she suddenly drew me to her :

" Let's have a kiss, dear."

I wanted to break away, to protect her modesty against her. I was only kept from it by the fear of being ridiculous, but what a sad kiss it was !

5 May.

Twenty-seven hours without sleep. My only rest has been a cold bath and a friction at dawn this morning. And at eight I was out on the road to Signa, riding along with Bettino.

We exchanged confidences. Of course he disapproves of my amours. In his own he introduces preoccupations with elegance and vanity. I feel that he is wrong. But he judges my position from so lofty an eminence :

The paradoxical fantasy of a blasé mind ! Byron at Venice. A little flower plucked in passing, the caprice of an evening. But it needs a good deal of stooping to pluck, etc., and I dare not tell him that I am really in love and that. . . .

And I lie to him at once, out of fear of being ridiculous, and I play the part of a blasé young man :

" Don't you know that a French poet once said that for diversion one must stoop low in love ? "

And that is how I respect and protect the woman I love. Oh! for a public, blatant reparation! . . .

I began to detest Bettino with all my heart. He is just like the bourgeois young men who made my Florrie what she was when I met her. What she is still for a few more days: just like those odious rich men who have given her their contempt in return for the poor little caresses she gave them like a trusting child. Yes. Bettino in evening dress makes me think of the gentleman one sees in the drawings called *The Lounge at the Ball*, or *Behind the Scenes*: with their *foie gras* complexions, their curling white whiskers like those of a banker baron, all the idiots at whom the dancing girls poke fun, though they come out on top all the same, because they despise, because they pay, and because they do not marry; and because they stand for the " great life " in the eyes of the common young men who will never know it. Who knows? Perhaps Bettino is behind the scenes at the Savonarola while I am waiting in a cab near the stage-door? No. For he would never so demean himself as to go with a café-concert girl. Ah! That cries out for vengeance! I need only make a sign and the old Marchese, Bettino's father, would gladly give me one of his daughters. He would never even dream of an alliance so advantageous as mine. Well, on the day when . . . My wealth makes everything possible, and could I hesitate for a second?

As we returned we met a closed carriage in which I thought I saw Cartuyvels, with his dear old parchment face and little gold spectacles. I must have been wrong.

And now for Florrie.

This morning at half-past one, I made my declaration. I flung a challenge in accordance with the rules at the monster guarding my Andromeda, I struck my glove across the jaws of Society which was on the point of destroying a woman. From that moment dates my great reconciliation with the poor : I am to marry one of their women. Besides, having begun to unclass myself by the sale of my possessions, my resignation as a man of the world would have been incomplete without it. Henceforth I shall not be so disgusted with myself.

It was after supper : we were alone in my smoking-room, sitting in rocking-chairs, Florrie nibbling the end of a Muratti which she did not light.

" My dear," I said, " I have a very important communication to make to you. This is it . . . My name is Archibaldo Olson Barnabooth of Campamento ; I am twenty-three ; my annual income is about ten million eight hundred and sixty thousand pounds. My family, originally Swedish, settled at the beginning of the eighteenth century in the valley of the Hudson. My father as a young man emigrated to California, then to Cuba, and finally to South America where he made his fortune. I am an orphan, and have neither brother nor sister, and am absolutely free to live where I like and how I like. So, you see, I am amply provided with means, am absolutely independent and of honourable birth. That is why I make bold to ask you—Will you be my wife ? "

She clapped her hands and burst out laughing. She had never heard anything so funny ! And it was not a bad joke either !

I had great difficulty in making her understand that it was not a joke. Without saying anything to hurt her I told her all the thoughts inspired in me by her poverty, her youth and her beauty. At last she was induced to believe that my proposal was serious. But it was my turn to be surprised when she replied calmly and quite naturally that she felt greatly honoured by my request, that she would think it over and would let me have a reply in twenty-four hours. I saw then that I had secretly been counting on an outburst of joy, a delirious gratitude, and I girded at my own egotism. Upon reflection, her reserve towards me pleases me greatly.

We stayed sitting there for a long time, saying nothing, hardly even daring to look at each other. I told myself the great news over and over again. I had henceforth a burden on my soul; I had ceased to be alone and unburthened: my life had been augmented by another life, and such a life! The fine young woman, so gentle and strong, so trim and supple, who shows her white teeth when she laughs. Another world added to mine, with this creature of another race and another caste giving herself to me to be fed, protected, loved. I welcomed all my new duties one after the other, to restore her to the world's respect (half a dozen duels in view): jewels to choose, dresses, her trousseau—the trousseau of the richest woman in the world: Paris, mind you! Paris, the Rue de la Paix. . . . And the house for our wedded life to be prepared: and, above all, the fight with the girl herself to pluck her out of her surroundings and habits (money and gentleness will provide for that, I think).

So, I was beginning to live ! I was no longer the useless rich man rightly despised. And, compared with these new interests, my dearest occupations of the old days seem frivolous and tiresome to me : receptions, polo, reading, the peace of little towns, shopping, even the composition of *Borborygmes* ! How I shall love her. . . .

She began to talk to me of my past : since I am ashamed of already having a past. She had heard certain tales of my relations with the Duke of Waydberg and Anastasie Retzuch. (So : these stories have spread even outside the World ?) I described for her the last beautiful afternoon of that adventure : a week before poor Tassoula's operation and a fortnight before her death. I lived again through the drive in the Bois de Boulogne, the stop, on the way back, outside Cuvillier's in the Rue de la Paix (to buy a little bottle of salted almonds, the last she was ever to eat). She was pale and she lay back on the cushions of the Victoria, while the footman, standing on the pavement, wrapped her up in a great blue-grey fur rug : and the winter sky fading away in despair towards the Opera sorted well with the agony of such great luxury.

She spoke to me also of the Yarza girls. (She is well-informed, upon my word.) I told her the truth and that, in spite of anything she may have heard, she would not find a rival in those two girls, whom, at a distance, I protect. If she clings to it I shall marry them off by giving them a dowry as soon as the eldest is twenty. I hardly think of them at all except as two dolls whom I love to dress and undress.

"You see, if they were here, I should dress them in

the old Lima fashion : black silk skirt, rather short, pink stockings and black shoes with large black ribbons. And the black mantilla too ; the 'little roof' over their eyes and forehead—you can't imagine how pretty it can be. Oh ! They could live quite quietly with you and me : they respect me as an elder brother. They are resigned little creatures and yet their life is profound. *Ay, nosotas pobdes mujedes. . . ."*

I would have liked in my turn to ask her about her past. I do not know Warwick where she was born. But I imagine it to be like St. Albans, Canterbury, and the little country towns that I have for a few minutes filled with the roar of my automobiles. Empty streets between little houses where people are so virtuous that their virtues are displayed in the triple framed windows in pious inscriptions on shiny cardboard. On Sundays the whole place groans with family hymns sung round the table in a drawing-room loaded with Victorian furniture. The eldest girl sits at the piano, and the rest sing, with their souls lost in the heavy Sunday and eternity. The grey stone church, worn by the ages, sleeps in the midst of its little well-kept cemetery, where from the turf the tombstones raise their flat heads and the great tottering tombs rear their grey horns. In summer the wide pink domes of the hawthorns scatter shade all over God's acre and the laburnum weeps over it with its long clusters of gold. On Sundays for each grave there is a little girl in white frock and black stockings. And there were you, with your heart full and sounding with hymns. Round the church there are the old houses with their small merchandise set out in the long low windows. Did you love the coco-nut cakes, white and red, with a carmine red and vivid as a transparency? The low gables, the little white fronts of the houses cut up with black beams, and the Rose and Crown inn, painted horribly greeny-brown or pinky-brown, with fat gold letters near the roof, and its bar with doors of sham mahogany, its mirrors with great white frames, and its brass just like London. And the streets of new brick houses naked and glaring. Every morning the maids in shiny black straw hats clean the frozen steps. . . . And the poor districts, yours, where at night shines the greasy blotch of the red blind of a pub, where the women, in white aprons and cloth caps, are waiting on the doorstep for their "good man" to come home to tea. . . . You were in the alley to one side of it : two little boys were sadly playing cricket in a neighbour's back garden. A voice cried : "Florrie" and it was you. You ran back, stopped for a moment—perched as it were on your long legs—to tie up your garter, and said to your dawdling little brother : "Come on !" in a shrill voice that rang out along the red walls. . . . And you have known those days when life was so heavy that all the hours were wasted in trying to lift it. . . .

It is queer how awkwardly we sat there opposite each other all that evening. In a fortnight perhaps I shall introduce her to Bettino's sisters. All the illustrated papers in the world will publish our portraits. What a commotion in Leicester Square ! I would prefer to have no talk but it is impossible. And all that is part of the process of rehabilitation, and at the same time what a splendid dramatic touch ! Cartuyvels will go mad and he will go about raving over the ruins of his nonplussed social prejudices. But on the other hand, how fine and glorious to make a woman happy! Even if I were good for nothing else, that would be a fine thing. . . .

FLORENCE,
10 *May.*

Now that the crisis is over I shall become the impartial historian.

The day before yesterday, in the morning, as I was waiting in my rooms at the Carlton for Florrie Bailey's reply, Cartuyvels was announced. He came in, made me his best bow (which he learned in the old days at the Court of—when he was Chief Valet and confidant to the late monarch) and sat down in the arm-chair which I put forward for him.

" Are you quite well, Cartuyvels ? "

I remembered then that I had fallen into the habit of speaking more familiarly in the imaginary conversations I have with him : while in reality feeling that he disapproves of all my ways, I treat him with a certain deference which is full of hypocrisy.

Oh, no ! He had not come to talk business with me ; he was only too well aware that it bored me. But he was going to Naples to await the arrival of the steamer which is bringing his nephew Tournier de Zamble from the United States, and he was reluctant to pass through Florence without meeting me.

But what about the little leather box he has placed on the table ? Private papers, no doubt. . . .

He carefully puts his gold spectacles with square glasses on his long thin nose. I look at his bald head and cleanshaven face, calm, set, like the face of an old goat in whom there is no trace of wickedness : his grey eyes full of softness and his really fine mouth. He begins to speak with his Anglo-Flemish accent, breaking his sentences with "ha" . . . and "hem" . . . not from awkwardness but from habit, just like the flourishes he adds to each word in his slightly trembling hand.

"I was in Dresden the other day : I met His Highness . . ."

"Stéphane ? "

"Yes : he is well and wants to see you. Are you going to Russia this summer ? He asked me. And also, he is astonished, as I am, that you have not been seen at the polo tournaments this year in England. It appears that the Mato-Suarès brought forty-two ponies from their *estançias* at Corrientes to play against the Duke of Christminster, the Prince de Xaintrailles and Lord Mollard. All your compatriots are there just now : the Santa-Paus, Pablo Barnevo, Ladislov Saenz, José Maria O'Rourke. The Peña-Taratts have moored their house-boat by the terrace at Richmond and Lord Worley has taken his (your *Hooligan* which we sold him) to Hampton Court. There are charming people there ! Several house-boats have a garage on board, and the young men motor along the Thames from one house-boat to another : some of them have steam-launches and go by water to pay calls. I was really distressed when I saw your beautiful *Hooligan*, all white, with its two storeys of windows and flower-boxes, the terrace and the girls lying in hammocks slung between the columns of the per-

71

gola, and thought of the time when it belonged to you. But you wanted to sell everything. I'm not going back on that ! You know my opinion about it. Your stable has been a sorry affair from two points of view. First, as you would not have the horses sold in one lot, we were bound to refuse Vanderkilt's very advantageous offer and sell Braila II and Anade at a loss. Yes, I know. It matters very little to you. But another aspect of the affair will, I think, interest you more. The impression produced on the financial market by the sale of the Barnabooth stables has been disastrous. Certain papers did not let slip the opportunity for circulating disturbing rumours : there was proof, they said : the Barnabooth stables were being sold. It produced a terrible rush on Lombard Street. There were people camping in the street outside our three offices. . . ."

" Great excitement in guanos ! "

" You haven't seen anything about it ? The faces of the old maids who had put their all into Andean Funds. Scotland Yard had to send a special force to the place to clear a way for the traffic : the hawkers had great days hiring camp-stools."

" So they did think of sitting down, all these distracted people ? Well, so much the better for the hawkers of London. They owe their great days to me."

" No doubt : but the small investors are indebted to you for some very bad days. All the more as certain unscrupulous papers exploited the panic and we know for whose benefit ! 'After the Barnabooth Stables, the mansion in Mayfair was sold : two days later the yachts, the *Parvenu* and the *Narrenschiff* ; then the large house in the Champs-Elysées, and the Casino in Florence : then the villas at Mustapha and Lussin-Piccolo ; everything down to the motor-cars.' They even mentioned your Majes—— I mean, your jewels. One man who had put his whole fortune (two hundred thousand pounds) into Andean Funds shot himself outside the door of our central office. Rest assured. He missed. For the rest : here are a few illustrated papers which will show you . . ."

And he took a few English papers out of his little leather box.

Ah ! Now I understood. The photographs give a fuller account of it than all Cartuyvels' drawling words. *Scenes outside the offices of the Industrial Company of the Andes and the Pacific Coast on the 7 and 8 April,* 190 . . . What ! While I and Stéphane were speaking a poetic farewell to the beer-gardens of the suburbs of Berlin ! Yes. I saw the small investors in the tail of the queue of people standing on the wet pavement in the moist air hardly warmed by a molten sun. I knew the Small Investor with her decent gown smelling of lavender, her worn gloves, her ribboned bonnet and the faded roses of her soft face, and her wan smiles, and her little round old forehead, full of wisdom. There she was, looking straight in front of her, never moving outside the line marked out by the policeman. She made me think of Battersea and Clapham, of all the decent, commonplace districts far from the centre, of which I know very little having only driven through them. O Small Investor ! And it is I who have brought you out of Battersea and given you that fixed stare and that unhappy expression and perhaps a few white hairs

73

under your neat little bonnet? How can I ever expiate my doing? . . . I will go to London. I will put my name down as a valet in a servants' registry and I will do your housework for nothing and perform the most menial tasks for you. . . . I asked Cartuyvels:

" Did all those people think of me? "

" Most probably they had never heard your name until they heard of the Barnabooth stables."

" How they must curse me! "

" Not at all! They were too busy thinking of their money to think of you, of whom they know nothing except that you must be somewhere, a bankrupt American."

" Then they pitied me? "

" Oh no! They could think of nothing but their money, of their threatened lives. Put yourself in their place."

" I don't want to put myself in their place. I prefer to amuse myself with looking at their photographs. What delicious expressions they have assumed! It's a pity I was not in London at the time. I should have gone and hired out camp-stools to them! Yes. You are right: there is no love lost between them and me, They had no pity for a bankrupt American. Why should I have any pity for them? My only regret is that a man who tried to shoot himself in my honour missed. As for the rest. Ah! what a good thing it was that I had everything sold! And what delightful consequences the sale has had! Look at the head of the old spinster in the first row, Cartuyvels. An allegorical statue of the Small Investor in distress. I was near pitying her. But I am thinking of her moral dirtiness : her pinched lips and her narrow eyes fixed on the bank. I know her, dear creature. Virtue herself, with Backbiting and Hypocrisy walking by her side as usual. She takes all the tittle-tattle of her neighbourhood from house to house, and loudly deplores the slips in conduct of her neighbour, while secretly she rejoices in having a competitor the less on the road of the domestic virtues. She is always trying to put the whole world in the wrong and she tortures the unhappy servant girl who is at her beck and call. I know the wicked old woman ! What she respects above all, is the most contemptible thing of all : the social order. All the members of the Royal Family are saints or men of genius : the nobility have all the virtues and all the talents : and she herself, the Small Investor, is the very model of life as it ought to be lived ; does she not go to church every Sunday and does she not from the bottom of her heart despise all the sinners who do not go, and all irregular people who, like myself, have no saving habits ? Oh ! I am trying to think of all the most dreadful irregularities into which I might fall to her knowledge in order to deserve all her contempt ! Or rather no : Tartuffe ! Better by a false assumption of virtue and piety to gain her esteem, to seem to her as innocent as she thinks she seems, and suddenly to pounce on her, rob her, and laugh aloud in her face. And how did this charming comedy end ? "

"There was a counter-campaign in the press and money was paid out over the counter for a fortnight, at the end of which the public regained confidence and brought back their money. Haven't you been reading the papers these last two months ? "

" What do the papers matter to me ? Besides if I had known the story I should have given orders to suspend payment and to have myself declared bankrupt. To have the pleasure of ruining the Small Investor : to force her to think of me. I should have been sentenced to a few years in prison, purely nominal, as I should have put myself out of reach of Scotland Yard. Why didn't you tell me, Cartuyvels ? For I stand greatly in need of being disparaged now that I am trying to get myself driven out of the exclusive circles to which I still belong. It was a fine opportunity : what a splendid way of getting out of the world of affairs and the world of clubs. ' Latest news ! A hundred million crash ! Mr. Barnabooth in flight, etc.' Business : what a shameful affair ! Prison is less ignoble. It is still one of the maxims of the Small Investor that everything that promotes business is good. But prostitution is excellent for business. Business is prostitution. How can I who am in business be anything but a Man without Honour ? "

" These philosophical reflections, sir, are beside the point. The directors of the Andes and Pacific Company have arranged everything for the best in your interest and the public's ! "

" So much the better then, since I have not had to worry about it. But here you are, Cartuyvels, talking to me about business."

" Our conversation has naturally led us to it. But I should like to point out to you, by the way, how dangerous it often is, how risky always, voluntarily to quit

76

the social position in which destiny has placed us. In order to unclass yourself, as you call it, you have very nearly brought misfortune upon thousands."

" What does it matter, so the brutes have been pacified ? Besides, have I not succeeded in shaking off the demon who was bestriding me : the demon of real property ? Real property ! How degrading ! A houseful of servants, luxury, social importance ! What ridiculous things for a solitary young man ! "

Cartuyvels looked like a sorrowful goat, a goat who has had misfortunes. Not a spark of mockery in his eyes : at least I think not ; I can't see them clearly behind his little square glasses rimmed with gold. What does he think of me ? He knows that I am not mad and that I am less puerile than what I say. Attacks on the social order, virtue, bourgeois respectability never move the cunning fellows who know that there is only one great fact : money. And I end with a last childish sally which I am childish enough to think bold.

" Cartuyvels, must my father have been a great financial brigand to leave me such enormous wealth ? "

Cartuyvels patiently packed up the papers and replied at once :

" I am glad to have found you in such a jesting mood. I have been told something : Are you about to get married ? "

" Cartuyvels, you have been spying on me. I thought so."

" It is not a matter of spying on you, but of looking after your safety. When you set out on your travels alone, with a box full of bank-notes and unarmed, I provided for your safety, that is all. In Bosnia, under the very noses of the German police, travellers are kidnapped and held up for ransom. Last month in a village in the Apennines the peasants nearly killed Vanderkilt under pretext that his motor-car had killed a child. A story invented, of course, to squeeze a big cheque out of him. Besides, your bodyguards are discreet : you do not even see them."

" But they send you reports on my private life."

" A man like you, young, fearlessly going everywhere, upon whose life great interests depend, is continually exposed even when he keeps the strictest incognito. It is my duty."

I did not even argue. I resigned myself to the mercies of Cartuyvels. A miserable young millionaire must go through the world with a string tied to his leg. And to think that I had thought to break away from Cartuyvels' guardianship by selling my possessions !

" Cartuyvels, you are like Mentor and I am like Telemachus—a very undocile Telemachus. You won't suddenly turn into Minerva ? Let me know. And, tell me, have you been having me 'protected' for a long time ? "

" Since you left Berlin down to the last few days. I can assure you that Mr. Maxime Claremoris had nothing to do with it."

" I had not suspected him, Cartuyvels. Who is it that follows me ? "

" Two detectives whom you do not know, trustworthy people."

" I must have seen them ? "

" Possibly. But they assured me that you had never noticed them."

" Have they been following me about every day ? "

" Yes. One one day, the other the next. Only by day."

" And by night ? "

" By night someone else watches you. A woman."

" A woman ! I wish I had known it. Perhaps she was hidden behind the curtains in my bedroom."

" No. She was not hidden. You saw her and talked to her. You even asked her to marry you twenty-four hours ago."

" Florrie Bailey ! "

" Some such name. In any case she was to have introduced herself to you as ' Heart's Joy ' or ' Heart's Desire,' or some absurd sentimental pet name of the kind."

" It is false ! "

(I roared that out and with all my soul I desired it to be false indeed.)

Cartuyvels, impervious to my interruption, went on in his hesitating voice :

" The young woman has been very useful to me. She is a prostitute, but clever enough. Pretty, too. But I need not describe her to you."

" What a yarn ! The Lady-Detective one sees announced on the last page of the newspaper ! As soon as it was known that I was here your private detective agency sent her to Florence : when she got here the Lady-Detective found out that I went to the Savonarola and got an engagement as a dancer, for she knows every trade, like a character in a police novel. But how could she manage to arrange for me to choose her ? You see, the whole thing won't stand for a moment."

"Quite so. But the thing is much more simple really : when my agents saw that you were after the girl they had an interview with her, and she consented, for money, of course, to help them."

"It is false ! She has been making fun of you all. I am sure of it. It is funny too to take your money like that. I will pay you back. And to prove that she was making fun of you, I will marry her."

"No, you will not marry her."

"You will prevent it ? "

"I know my place too well and my duty towards you ever to oppose your will. But the fact is that the girl entrusted me with the reply she thought she ought to make to your proposal of marriage and that reply is in the negative."

"Proof ? "

"This. It is, as you can see, written and signed by her as a receipt for a certain sum accepted on condition that the undersigned shall leave Florence and Italy within twenty-four hours. You understand : I have no further need of her services : I pay her and dismiss her. We can be quite sure that she will not lack discretion."

"Cartuyvels, you are too strong : but what is there to prove that the receipt really was written by the girl in question ? What is to prove to me that you did not procure it by threats ? And what is there to show that the whole thing is not an invention of your own ? "

"Go and see her."

"There is one thing that I can't explain : how

could she consent to serve you at the risk of annoying me when I offered her a thousand times more than you can give, and when I was no doubt the greatest chance of her life? It is monstrous that she should hesitate between us two. You are her lover."

"Oh, Mr. Barnabooth, at my age!"

"I can easily make her see reason. You shall give her to me at the altar. Yes. Even if what you tell me is true, I will marry her."

I feel that I am falling into the snare, that the game is lost, or rather that there never was any match, that I have been tricked from the very beginning in this affair, and that I am wrong, and that every word I utter but makes me more wrong and more ridiculous. Yet a malevolent power drives me on.

"You will marry her? Well. I am the happy possessor of a large number of photographs of Mrs.— what's her name?—Florrie Barnabooth in all sorts of curious attitudes. Would you like . . . ."

"Give them to me."

So that was what the little leather box contained. The house of horrors. I turned over the album with my head in a blaze. My poor beloved, how could you ever sink into such an abyss of infamy and make your shame thus public?

"She gave them to me," said Cartuyvels gently. "She carries them with her wherever she goes. They are souvenirs, you see."

And that was the terrible past of which I so whole-heartedly absolved her. And I still absolve her of it! A cycle of hell and the postures of the damned! Tenderness flung on the dung heap: and the soul slimed

81

with spittle. Oh! how lovely is chastity! And to think that death might clothe you in innocence again and that be left behind: that! . . .

"These photographs are much appreciated by collectors: she has sold a great many of them," said Cartuyvels. "You will observe that the young woman adds to her talents as a choreographic artist and a private detective, certain particular aptitudes on which you will not need my insistence. She is absolutely a suitable wife for an honest man."

So she had to suffer the jests of the first comer! Oh, how greatly I pitied her! I was near dying of pity. My *naïveté* filled me with shame at the thought of such degradation. Oh! If I could share with her the world's contempt! For it is intolerable to me to think that while the world respects me and all the society columns in all the papers in Europe carefully register my movements, and I am A. O. Barnabooth, the son of the Inca, the well-known rich collector, the popular sportsman, etc., etc., this, my sister soul, should be used for the debauchery of every passer-by.

"Cartuyvels, at yours and no other hands I will receive her at the altar. I will marry her. I tell you, I will marry her at once."

"Once more, I will not oppose it, if she consents. But go and speak to her, I beg: we shall the sooner bring this painful discussion to an end."

"I will go."

"Very well. Take the album back to her: I don't know what to do with it, and it is not a thing for a self-respecting man. . . . Wait a moment, please:

82

I arranged with her . . . I mean, without a word from me, she would not receive you. Here is my card."

I went on foot, almost running. I left Cartuyvels at table : I hardly thought of eating. She was at home and received me.

" Forgive me for having amused myself the other day by making you talk about your past and your lady friends. But I was hard put to it to find something to talk about. I could not tell you the truth, the part I was playing with you, could I ? But I hope I helped to amuse you a little, and many thanks for the charming suppers you have given me. After all, my dear, we had a jolly time, you and I, on the first floor of the Carlton."

She took my hat and the album with a very polite smile.

" Rather filthy, isn't it ? " she said, alluding to the contents of the album (and truly I had not the least desire to laugh, so humourless was I). I said that I had come to find out why she had refused me and ex-pected her to give me a full and frank explanation.

" My poor dear boy, are you so simple ? What do you want me to say, except that I don't want to be married ? That I want to keep single, and become a horrid old maid with spectacles and no more fair hair and no more step-dancing ! Oh ! Please don't take on that unhappy expression ! It annoys me. Do you want to know the real truth, my boy ? Do you know, there are two kinds of lovers, my dear : the good kind and the bad kind, of course. I saw at once that you belong to the bad kind because you did not laugh when I was with you. Those who laugh are the good kind : men who come to us as we are, to amuse themselves, to forget their troubles : old business men, young officers on leave, married men who know what life is. And also a very few young men who in their everyday existence are occupied and serious, too ambitious to be so stupid as to fall in love with girls like us. And they are gay and charming and kind and good companions for sure. There are some who are happy to dress us and give us jewels, to show how rich they are and also to give us pleasure. They love showing their money. Who can blame them ? It was in order to be with such young men that I became a Gaiety girl : my temperament is like theirs : a happy laugh, suppers, champagne and kisses, the sunny side of life and all care driven away. We are the people who get the best out of life, and no useless sentiment. The married man comes to forget in my face his wife's peevish expression : as the song says : ' the wife's mournful face.' I console him and in return he gives me his gaiety, his good moments, and I must take care to be worth the trouble. I too have a social mission, and as for the contempt of fools and hypocrites, I don't care that for it ! My poor dear boy, I'll tell you what you lack : you are hardly at all a man, nothing like a gay dog. I was told that you travelled with a harem. That seemed to me all right for a rich man : there are so many who only think of horses and gambling, and the poor girls wither away outside the shop windows. Well, I told myself that I should be quite glad to enter your harem : I could have got on very well with my sultan's other wives. And I saw that the facts were not at all like that. You could not have a harem : you are too mortally serious in your love. You don't come to us for amusement but for boredom and duty. No. Let me go on ! You don't know what you want. But I know : you are only thinking of finding a wife, my dear boy, and you ask the first girl who pleases you, me, of all girls ! But I could not be a good wife to you. Oh, yes. I should have nothing to do but please my lord ? But to please my lord I must have a well-kept house. I should have a housekeeper ? But who would look after the house-keeper ? You see, I am not even capable of keeping my poor little theatrical lodging tidy. No, my dear, it isn't possible. I could love you, my big stupid schoolboy, but marry you ! You might as well ask me to turn nun. Oh dear ! Oh dear ! Isn't it funny ?

"And if I were to say to you : follow me, without any marriage ceremony and come with me. Well, you would come just the same and you would follow me from town to town, and you would be sitting like a solemn child in front of the house while I was laughing with my friends behind the scenes. That would be convenient for me because of the money. But I should feel you near me with your jealousy and distress. You would weep every day over my butterfly life (I have known stronger men than you who have wept all day over their dear girls) : and that would not amuse me at all, you know ! You would come, I know, because you would hope to persuade me little by little to marry you : yes, to leave the theatre, and then one thing and then another until I have become

85

a good wife to you with the wife's sorrowful face. No, I've been bored that way once : I don't want it all over again. And I don't care about money really. So long as I can send a postal order at the end of every month to my old mother in Warwick I'm satisfied. I am an artist in spite of everything and, really, I don't care about money. . . . Would you like me to give you some good advice in return for the presents you gave me ? And I would like to give the same advice to all the unambitious and idle young men like you : don't love a Gaiety girl ! Look round you and marry a girl in your own social rank. Those who work and labour to raise themselves in life seek amusement, and we are there for them. But those who have nothing to do but amuse themselves seek responsibilities, and they therefore take the girls of their own social rank. Now, as for me, if you are still a bachelor, come again in fifteen years and perhaps I will say yes."

" You have thought of . . ."

" The chance you are offering me ? Oh ! I can find another. You are not the only rich man in the world. And must I tell you again that I would rather be poor and free than rich and tied ? And so, my dear, good-bye. I am going to Austria, and perhaps we may meet again, but don't trouble to arrange a meeting. You will hear of me in all sorts of ways. Yes. In the newspapers, all over the world."

" How ? "

" You will see. Something I have had in my mind for years, a long, long time. A great thing which will bring about a change in many little things in the world. I'm becoming interesting again, apparently. I tell you it is a thing of which no one has even thought : very simple, very good, which will do everybody a lot of good. But you don't expect to know it before everybody else ? I shall have to live for some time in Germany . . . Oh ! in four years, or two years and a half perhaps : it is hard to tell : the world is not quite ready for it yet. Well, well, good-bye. Remember my name, Florrie Bailey : everybody will know it one day."

" Something social, I suppose ? "

" Suppose nothing. My dear boy, I must send you off : my box isn't packed and I am off at six this evening."

She held my hand.

" Let's have a kiss, dearie," she murmured, drawing me to her as she had done in the room at the Carlton one night. " And a hundred kisses, two hundred, as many as we can get in in an hour. I'll be a little quicker over my box. You have been so kind . . ."

She smiled, staring fixedly, with her upper lip stiffening : I passed her brusquely, without kissing her : she filled me with disgust. The moment before I had seen her in one of the great variety theatres in a capital, suddenly stopping the orchestra and calling out a few words which left the whole world amazed : the solution of all problems, a delirious happiness. Now I saw in her only the prostitute, the obscene masseuse, the filthy bawd : the reek of her life stank in my nostrils. Her anger rose immediately to meet my contempt : behind me the door was viciously slammed.

Cartuyvels whom I had left at table had waited for me for lunch. I felt at my ease with him and that was a thing for which I had not looked. Is it simply because Cartuyvels is nearer my social rank than Florrie Bailey? Above all, I felt relieved. Cartuyvels did not triumph over me : he kept his respectful attitude : he was as calm as if he were sitting for his portrait.

"Well, my annoying resemblance to Cato the Elder has got me another refusal. I foresee that I am going to be difficult to marry."

Cartuyvels had not expected to see me come back so gay : perhaps he had a moment's uneasiness.

"Yes," I explained. "It is just like my tale of the poor shirt-maker. 'Mr. Barnabooth no longer loved the shirt-maker's daughter.' Oh! the instability of our affections, the mysteries of the human heart, etc. There is perhaps the material for a burlesque history in this intrigue between a dancing girl and a millionaire, with unpublished discourses by the Poor Rich Man, and dedicated to Gætan de Putouarey!"

"I am glad to see that you have been able to rid yourself of your affection for this unworthy person."

"Unworthy? That seems doubtful to me. Perhaps it is I who am unworthy of her : not plebeian enough : too remote through my education and very mixed origin : incapable of understanding her, to put it briefly."

"Of course not!" said Cartuyvels, and for the first time his icy smooth face grew a little animated. "From the moral point of view, the girl is a brute and she realizes that she is unworthy to be your wife. . . There is something, however, which perhaps I should have told you before : the second day after they met she became the mistress of one of the men who is watching your safety."

" She had done worse than that : she offered herself to me just now in return for what she called my kindness."

" Of course. She is like all these women. Their favours are their small change."

(How true that is ! We are so convinced of having discovered life that when a person of an earlier generation proves that he also knows it we marvel.)

" Cartuyvels, I give in ! You are too strong for me and with you I feel just like the little schoolboy I was with John Martin. How well you contrived all that ! and your masterly touch, when instead of pouring out moral formulæ you worked on life. Oh ! It was fine ! My esteem cannot but go out to your virtues. Really, my dear Cartuyvels, I must tell you that I love you. I know that you despise my literary attempts. Don't protest : one day when you were waiting for me in my study in London, I was in the smoking-room just off it and the door was ajar. To make room for the business papers you had brought with you, you cleared the desk with a sweep of your arm and brushed aside the loose sheets of my *Borborygmes* which I was then copying out ; and as you did so, you murmured : 'Poetry, his famous poetry !' I heard it as plainly as if I had been in the study. I said to myself : 'Lord, he doesn't understand.' That is what every author thinks when he is roughly handled by a critic. But, in spite of myself, I was furious with you, and I concluded from that that you could not have the least understanding of anything in life, and that

89

as my whole life was organized in relation to my *Borborygmes* and my *Dejections* (the title of my next collection of poems) you would disapprove of it altogether. And I was not wrong : I write nothing, say nothing, do nothing but in your heart you disapprove of it. And yet I say to you : Cartuyvels, I love you. Everything you wish is for my good. My life is contemptible, grotesque, full of contradictions, shameful things, blunders, hag-ridden by all the demons of sensuality, pride, sentimentality, stupidity. It is so ! And your life is admirable in your eyes : there is in it nothing but devotion and respect and again respect and again devotion. After having lived for an old Emperor, you now live for a young millionaire—without enthusiasm, O excellent servant, with no delirious self-denial, no basic ideal, but in the simplicity of your heart. How you must despise me ! "

" Despise you for what you have just said ? "

" No. For my whole life, for selling my possessions, for the adventure with this woman."

" On the contrary. I have a higher opinion of you : it is well to desire firmly what one desires : and as for the adventure with the woman, it has shown me a chivalrous quality in you of which I knew nothing. You are twenty-three. When you have more experience you will be able to master these altruistic flights . . ."

" It is the same old story (and I hate the word *altruist*). No, let us talk of something else. Are you going on having me followed by your private detectives ? "

" If I told you No, you would not believe me. And

if I told you Yes, you would still have doubts. So what then ? "

" Oh ! Better and better ! And it is true that I lack experience ; and when you credit me with chivalrous feelings you do me too much honour : it is vulgar sensuality, neither more nor less. And Florrie Bailey was right when she said it was chiefly a desire for marriage. When I had my motor-cars and carriages I was constantly turning to my right, to the empty place beside me. And it is funny that this desire should always go out to the daughters of the people. I should prefer even a middle-class woman to the women of our world, because she would be nearer the people. What do you object to ? The very lack of education is an added reason for my choice ? The journalists, who sometimes in their paragraphs express astonishment that I am not yet married, and Florrie Bailey who advised me to marry a girl in my own class, never suspect that the little princesses whom I might marry do not move me, while a look from the humblest popolana, or the dirtiest little slut I meet in the streets of Florence, always sets my heart wildly beating."

" And yet you will admit that there are differences of intelligence, kindness, gentleness, as there are differences of stature and beauty ? "

" Oh, yes. That is truth, a series of complications. I had just discovered the grand principle : that all men are equal, or rather that the irreducible and hidden thing—the soul—is equal in all men. And that everything which can be added to it, genius, knowledge, intelligence, good manners, is no more than a shrub on the slopes of the Himalayas. Good, it was a simple general idea, and I only asked to stick to it. But now life insists on my regarding the whole scale of differences, even down to the smallest subdivision as important. And there are people so subtle that to them the great fundamental equality of men disappears under all the differences, even under the differences of education. And instead of having as much respect for Florrie Bailey as for themselves, they despise her. No, that's beyond me : my head is bursting. Enough ! What I see clearly can be reduced to this : that the women who are my social equals bore me even to look at them, and therefore I feel myself morally compelled to marry a poor woman."

" What fantastic stuff ! "

" No, Cartuyvels : I am king of Vanity Fair : if I wished I could be a king to-morrow (and you know of what country I should be king : every day I am asked to go and place myself at the head of the rebels. And then you would have no more need to take care not to call me Sire). I would like to find the poorest woman in the world and invite her to share my royal splendour. Oh ! If only it might happen once that a king married a shepherdess. The King Cophetua married the beggar girl ! Sometimes I feel inclined to go into the nearest hovel one morning and choose my wife and take her away, still sleeping, dead drunk, and bear her to the altar. To avoid the chance of another refusal, perhaps."

" Possibly. It is a kind of indolence. . . ."

" Slothfulness of the heart ? "

" Yes. Exactly, which makes most people prefer the mediocrity to which they are accustomed, to the wealth which would change their habits. And all purchasable ladies are like that. . . . Would you like to hear a story of my own youth with which I once had the honour to amuse His Majesty ? "

" Yes, yes."

" You must not be shocked at hearing such words on the lips of an old man, but it was at the time when I had a mistress in Paris under the Second Empire. . . . She was a woman of the people : what we used to call a grisette. I used often to dine with her in her room. Simple dinners they were, though they seemed to me the more charming as I had been used to very luxurious food in the servants' quarters of the Duc de Morny, to whom my father was valet. To be brief : one day I took my mistress a pretty little porcelain cruet-stand, her own (ours) having been broken at our last meal. As soon as she saw my present she was annoyed and thanked me curtly. Her temper lasted for a whole day : ' It is too beautiful for me : keep it for the lady you will marry,' she said to me. I insisted on her promising to keep it, but I never saw it on our table. And when the breach came, with a packet of my letters she sent that same cruet-stand. Forgive my telling you such absurdities."

" But it is a charming story."

" It amused His Majesty."

" It is nearer moving me to tears. I can see the porcelain cruet-stand. And the little Frenchwoman pouting, bending her head and watching her shoulders droop in her wide sleeves. You should have married her : she would have had a right to the cruet-stand."

" She was only a caprice to me."

" How odd that is ! I can only conceive of marriage. The idea of a temporary liaison has never crossed my mind, and if the Duchess of Waydberg were not dead . . ."

" I suppose you have heard of His Excellency's death."

" Bodo is dead ? "

" Yesterday's papers were full of obituaries of the Duke of Waydberg, setting out his career, etc. Look. The *Wiener Tageblatt*. They say he died in a cabaret, in the company of . . . At sixty-seven. . . ."

I could find nothing to say. The flavour of the past has returned to me. Poor Bodo ! He was of another school. To him, the realities of life were suppers, parties, horses, all the things that are called pleasure. And yet they talk of his career and he was famous in the *Carrière* : he helped to avoid a war between two nations. He used to work from seven to twelve every morning. He served his country and his sovereign well. What have I done to set against that ? I who count myself morally more pure than he. But what he did with his life excuses his pleasures a thousandfold, while my cherished moral purity is a thousand times condemned by my uselessness. That is the truth of it.

Cartuyvels respected the silence into which these reflections plunged me. However I would have liked to defend Florrie against him and to talk of the famous secret. I did not dare. Cartuyvels finished his little glass of *zabrowka* and got up to say good-bye, and we parted coldly enough. He went the same evening, and no doubt is now sitting on the terrace of the café in the Galleria Umberto I at Naples, telling the story of the dancing girl to Maxence, who will roar with laughter at my simplicity. He is a sly fellow who will only marry for money and a lot of it, just one of those ambitious men who please the Florrie Baileys of this world. Suppose he were right ? Suppose the need of loving were only folly ?

I have written all night without once raising my head. I must conclude. I have concluded : a yawn.

BOOK II
Florence, San Marino, Venice

BOOK II

Florence, San Marino, Venice

NOW that the crisis is over, when feeling was everything, I am beginning once more to see my
surroundings : my walls and furniture once more take
on their reality for me. I had never even seen the room
where Florrie Bailey received me : though I ransack
my memory I can find nothing but a blurred impression
of bluish walls and a painted ceiling cracked and peeling
in places. The room must have had a tiled floor : my
memory has registered a feeling of hardness under my
feet and coolness round my ankles. So I return to

> Objects of all kinds
> Ineffably faithful,

and I rediscover even the streets of Florence, the hard
dry pavement which makes one think of a world brought
altogether into man's domain, and smoothed out and
fashioned in accordance with human will. I rediscover
my favourite shops : the sellers of travelling things in
the Via Calgaioli, the bookshops, the haberdashers and
confectioners of the Via Tornabuoni, and the Cerretani,

99

Mai dei Cavour, streets, and the drapers of Calimara :
(I am beginning again to be interested in shop windows.)

And yesterday, Thursday, to recover from having
written so much, I crossed the Arno and went to Boboli.
It is hard to like the patches of dried greenery divided
by paths and beds of dried sand. A garden where the
seasons cannot make themselves felt. In the midst of
the squares of greenery—hornbeam, olive, and ivy—one
looks in vain for any sign of spring. All these beautiful
trees—even down to the smallest blade of grass—seemed
to have been dead a long time and preserved, naturalized,
by some chemical process, like one of those gardens
glued together round a doll's house. And as I parted
the branches suddenly it seemed to me that the paths
were long cascades of hot sand pouring unbroken down
from a stifling blue sky here and there stuffed with fat
clouds of dirty wool. And as I returned and came to
the end of the Via Maggio, the river and its quays appeared
to me like a great piece of jewellery : an Arno of dark
emerald bordered by quays and palaces of clear amber,
and crossed by bridges of old ivory inlaid with silver,
aquamarines and gold.

While I was playing the fool with Florrie, while I
was wasting my time in arguing with Cartuyvels, all
that had been going on around me and I no longer saw
it. No. No. The crisis has not passed : the cause of
the crisis subsists. As I walk I know that my eyes rest
too intently on every woman, and that I am still just as
uneasily looking for my wife. " Tutte le femmene ! "
as the Neapolitan song says. But especially the popolane. I put the matter to Cartuyvels as an absolute rule
of my disposition, but my desire for the *Popolana* is quite

recent. I began by preferring the mantilla to the hat, and now I prefer a bare head to a mantilla. I close my eyes and I say ecstatically several times over : *le donne*, as if in the very sound of it there were something feminine. And indeed it is " women " who attract me and not " ladies." So in Florrie it was her fine big plebeian limbs that pleased me. Was I lying to myself once more with that idea of a social injustice to be repaired ? . . . So recently ? . . . Come. I have remembered an old story to which I never gave a thought, though my affair with Florrie must have reminded Cartuyvels of it, for he had it from John Martin : the story of Marika, my first essay in gallantry. I will record it here. (Perhaps I shall not think of it again for years.)

When I was sixteen and we lived in the castle of W. near Kharkov, Stéphane and I, we used to go and spend a month's holiday in Constantinople. (It was also during that first visit that I met Anastasie Retzuch.) I was tired of an innocence to which I attached no value, of which I was even ashamed, and was determined not to return to Russia without a mistress. But John Martin, my tutor, who went with us with orders from the prince to keep a sharp eye on us, was an almost insurmountable obstacle to my project. We had to slip out of our rooms in the Pera Palace at night and run through the alleys of Galata at the risk of having our throats cut. And while we were out wandering we used to tell each other that a dog-fight or the cries of the watch might wake my tutor, and we would imagine him going and knocking at our door, receiving no reply, going in and keeping awake to surprise us on our return. And that would be terrible, for the prince's anger knew no bounds. Nights of great adventure they were! Stéphane, who was eight years older than I, would go his own way, but we used to return together. Our meeting-place was opposite the gate of the Petits Jardins at the beginning of the main street of Pera. (I remember one evening when he was late and I stood shivering there in the creeping dawn, stared out of countenance by the infantry patrols coming up from Stamboul.) At last, I don't remember how, I found a Smyrna girl of twenty, with a complexion of gold that looked as if it were lit up from behind by a flame. Her name was Marika, and she agreed to go with me to Russia. The preparations were very exciting. She was to disguise herself as a *baba* and wear a white veil: I bought everything necessary. Marika was charming in her rough costume: she was no longer the girl of the alleys of Galata of my first encounter with her. (Oh, yes. Florrie is right once more: even with that girl, the first, I should not have turned from the idea of marriage one day, when I had rid her of her past. And even while we were in Constantinople I respected her.)

I had bought her a second-class ticket on the boat which took us back to Sebastopol. From the windows of our private state-room I watched her come on board. So it was true: I had a mistress: and my tutor and even Stéphane knew nothing of it! At last I had my own life and a kind of intrigue!

After dinner I hastened to find Marika's cabin and I entered, choking back a cry of joy. She answered my "*kalispéris*" with a groan: I had reckoned without sea-sickness. I spent the whole night in the most repulsive attendance on her, amused all the same and not without thinking that life had a certain wit of its own, rather coarse but full of sound sense.   Marika, abandoning all modesty and coquetry (and that also was interesting), alternated between tenderness for me and cursing me for having dragged her off on the voyage ; then she called on her mother and began to invoke all the saints of the orthodox calendar.   I never knew more than a few words of modern Greek, and our conversation was continually getting tied up in the most ridiculous misunderstandings. At last the blue shield of day appeared on the wall of the cabin : I climbed upon the berth above Marika and looked out at the sea heaving to rest, tired of having laboured all night to turn windlasses, turbines, transmission belts, and mechanical pianos.   Dawn's eyelids were raised a little more.   In a fold of the water bobbed a green pumpkin.   Then the mists melted away and showed the sliced chalk of a coast quite near.   I said to Marika : " We are arriving."   I saw her face and body almost nude, livid, with spots of green shadows : exhausted as I was, in the bitter reek of the cabin, she filled me with a great disgust and no pity, and that also was interesting. The throbbing of the boat ceased and as the sea all around us heaved away, a bell rang.   I had to implore her to get up.   When at last she thrust her legs out of the berth we were moored to the Grafskaïa Pristan under the enormous ladder.   John Martin was already looking for me, and I had to invent an excuse for being late.

I thought she would never be ready to take the train in which my tutor, Stéphane and I were already settled down. However, she had her passport all in order, and I had told her over and over again what she was to do on her arrival. I imagined her already wandering through Sebastopol, falling into the hovels of the military port, for ever lost to me. At last she appeared on the station platform just as the second bell was going : her lateness, her appearance, made her noticeable. A group of officers in helmets and white tunics pointed her out and laughed. They thought : " Look at the little Greek going astray in the north." I saw her climb up into a carriage. And I almost fainted when John Martin's voice behind me murmured :

" Don't be afraid. We shan't go without her."

I turned sharply and muttered : " Who ? She ? " But my tutor only replied by puffing a great cloud of blue smoke towards the big lamp in the ceiling, and just then the provodnik brought us a cup of tea. And the fifteen hours we spent in the train were fifteen hours of hell. I said to myself : " My tutor knows everything from the beginning, from my nocturnal rambles at the Pera Palace : and he hasn't interfered just to give me a severe lesson. To-morrow evening, no doubt, when I come into the drawing-room, or at dinner with His Highness I shall find Marika by my side ! " I imagined the prince's fury and the ineffable absurdity of the scene. I was filled with a desire to plunge into excuses. I renounced Marika : I was terrified. And yet I pretended to read a novel by Emile Zola, which had just appeared : *Rome*, I think it was. I had bought it the night before at Pera. I found in it no terror equal to mine and the meaning of the words hardly reached me. But every now and then I would take heart : after all John Martin probably knew nothing definite : he had simply observed that I was looking closely at the Greek girl, and was making fun of me. The last thought at which I stopped was not funny. " After all, *he* won't kill me."

At least I thought I had better warn Marika that we were discovered, and that it would be as well for her to stay in Kharkov, where she should spend a few days in the hotel until I could come and fetch her. At Simferopol (I have never forgotten that Province scraped with a knife, the great stretches of light earth under smooth turf, the bold rolling of chalk hills trying to look like mountains) I got down to the platform and tried to find my little Smyrna girl. Impossible : the bell had already gone, the horrible funnel had already given its mournful " Hoo ! " and I had to scramble back into our own carriage. Finally in the buffet at Alexandrovsk I was able to take Stéphane into my confidence. He had only just time enough to tell me to keep quiet and to promise that he would help me : my tutor was just behind us. And then again to look unconcerned. I bought some idiotic French book full of indecent passages. Marika did not come to the buffet. We took our places in the train again, and ran straight across the worn billiard cloth of Russia, every second bringing us nearer the prince's wrath.

The day after our return Stéphane came into my room very early and told me that everything had gone off well, and that Marika was concealed for the time being in the cottage of one of the gardeners at the gates of the park.

" With Demetrius' wife, you know. After breakfast we'll saddle our horses and ride round that way."

Demetrius' wife was of all the babas of the country round W. the only one for whom I had a certain fondness. I loved her from afar purely and respectfully. Whenever I read the words :

" In Esther everything breathes innocence and peace," I thought of Demetrius' wife : whenever I read that virtue is a pleasant thing I at once imagined virtue with the features of Demetrius' wife : and virtue was indeed charming with Demetrius' two children playing at her feet. I had seen her one day at a fête, with a brilliant scarf over her head, in a dress stiff with embroidery and gold braid. Her clean-cut sweet face shone more brilliantly than her scarf, and what one could see of her arms in her wide open sleeves was more beautiful than her whole costume. Purity itself ! I was shocked to hear that she was embroiled in the affair.

We set out. I felt like a general going over a battle-field. Perhaps we were being watched !

As we got down from our horses, the young woman curtsied low to us, and Stéphane questioned her. I heard them muttering together, and was irritated not to understand and impatient to see Marika, when Stéphane turned to me and said in French :

"She has gone. Yes. She slept in the room they got ready for her, the day before yesterday, and yesterday morning little Theodore found the door open and the room empty. They have looked for her in vain all round the house."

" Did they hear any noise, that night ? "

Stéphane translated my question. No. They had heard nothing.

Ten minutes later we were rolling towards Kharkov

in Demetrius' cart. Three hours across the billiard-table, at first with no marked road, through the stream of air set up by the two big black horses. The horizon drew nearer and vast green roofs and gilded domes appeared. We stopped at the Hôtel Prosper. The Smyrna girl had not been seen. M. Prosper advised us to go to the French Vice-Consulate : I went there. A secretary, who received me with extraordinary rudeness, became very polite as soon as he heard that I was not French. Yes, he had seen the young woman, the day before, about midday : a monk had acted as interpreter. She had come to have her passport endorsed, because, having been brought up in a Catholic convent, she was a client of the French Consulates in Turkey. Finally, after a lot of useless chatter which served only to display the secretary's wit, I learned that the Smyrna girl must have left Kharkov at once. I ran to the station. Yes, the day before she had taken a ticket to Sebastopol. We had still a chance of making sure : by going to the police. But neither Stéphane nor I dared go there.

We returned to W. next morning. I said that I had been to the town to buy some books, and John Martin tortured me by asking repeatedly to see the books. Not a word did he say of the adventure. Was it he who had discreetly sent Marika back ? Was it not rather she who had fled, terrified by the aspect of the country, or doubting my promises, or fearing the wrath of the people upon whom I was dependent ? She must have found a carriage to take her to the town. On leaving Constantinople I had given her a good sum of money, certainly enough to buy return tickets. I saw that I should never know the truth. It was like a dream. "Don't be afraid. We shan't go without her." At last I came to believe that my tutor had never said those words. Twenty times I was on the point of provoking an explosion by asking him for an explanation. But I hung back. For him and for me it was better so. Cartuyvels must have had the story in mind : the intrigue with Florrie Bailey was no less *young*.

As for Marika, how could I regret her ? I did not know her. I had only a great desire to know her. I had selected her to teach me the psychology of love. She had been exactly, to use the expression of Jules Laforgue (whom I met later in Paris) :

"She who was to put me in the way of knowing Women."

Yes ; instinctively I had entrusted that duty to a mercenary. And yet my curiosity had been mingled with a vague sentimentality. I purchased her, yet I was ready to receive with adoration the gift of Woman.

And in spite of all I felt a certain comfort in being rid of this pitiful intrigue, and I tried to trump up in myself an artificial and poetic despair. I even began an elegy :

"O little Smyrna girl, with thy golden face . . ."

I got no farther.

Some time after that I dragged Stéphane once more to Demetrius' house, and the pretty baba once more sank down at our feet as a mark of respect. She repeated what she had said the first time, word for word. I was convinced that she knew the whole story. She added a few words and bent her head under her white veil and smiled. I thought I understood and Stéphane translated :

" She says it is not worth while bringing women from so far away when there are so many here. You understand. She says that for her own benefit. I will leave you here. Demetrius is at the village."

But I had turned my horse and was galloping towards the castle. Stéphane followed me shouting :

" Stop ! Stop ! You crazy idiot ! "

The baba's words had shaken me to the very depths of my being. I had thought myself very wicked and perverse in bringing Marika to W. And the young mother, whom I had adored from afar as an image of conjugal purity, had showed me, in the most natural way in the world, a heart a hundred times more corrupt, more inclined to evil, and more perverted than mine. I wept over it that night in bed. I was ashamed of being so simple, almost innocent : a little saint believing evil to be so rare and exceptional that one needs to go a long way in search of it. Never again did I go near Demetrius' house. And once when I met the woman in the village I looked at her severely with austere morality in my eyes : she blushed. Ah ! I would gladly have had her whipped there and then. And I should still want her.

Yes, the crisis, though fainter, still persists. As I write down these recollections, I am so clearly reminded of those two women that I am filled with a desire to see them again. Marika must be twenty-seven now and Demetrius' wife thirty-two. I have never seen another face like the Smyrna girl's : even in the full light of the sun it had that inward clearness, that tragic, solemn vehemence of colour.   How they despised the little light of love I bore within myself, those two ! One by allowing herself to be so easily taken from me : and the other by offering herself to me so lightly, as a substitute, a makeshift.

14 May.

A visit from Bettino.   We sat in the smoking-room· and looked at the Arno rippled with blue by the wind, and the sky covered with grey and blue felt, and the mournful cupola of San Frediano with the hills of oltr'-Arno where the olive-trees are as tender as bracken and as green as gaming-tables—and we talked quietly.   A fat lady passed along the pavement opposite.

" Quanta carne ! " cried Bettino.

I had told him of the impressions made on me by my crisis.   It made him coarse, and he is seldom that :

" But, my dear fellow, for such urgent cases we have certain artistes at the Savonarola : and even something better and dearer."

(He knows nothing of the end of my intrigue with Florrie Bailey.)

" Villi, please understand that if I could satisfy myself so cheaply as that I should not even mention it to you, and I should only speak of it as sometimes I say : my bath was delicious this morning.   No.   Please understand that I want something else than such a perpetual seeking, the grotesque and shameful hunt.   Your attitude towards these things is shameful, don't you see ? "

And I became coarse in my turn.   There are people with whom it is impossible to talk about certain very important things.   I knew that.

Villi was not at his best : and he had nothing amusing to say with his delicate precise voice which makes every word precious.   I did not keep him to dinner.   I preferred to mingle for a short while in the bustle of the Central streets, round the Piazza Vittorio Emanuele and under the arcades.   There have been races at the Cascine.   The " newsvendors " were shouting : Al galoppo !   Al galoppo !

It is good to stand for a long time on the edge of the pavement, among the moving shadows of the passers-by, and watch the heavy traffic on the roadway shaking, while at the end of the street stretches a whole expanse of the Duomo in black and white.

15 May.

The crisis is over at last.   This morning I received a bombastic letter full of flattery from a mother asking me as a " magnanimous patron of the arts " if My Lordship would not with his spare coppers assist an extraordinarily gifted girl who was prevented by poverty from continuing her study of singing.   And this same mother, who honoured herself by calling herself My Lordship's servant, gave me her name and address.   I had only to cross the Arno and turn to the right at the end of the Ponte alla Carraia, she lived behind the Piazza di Castello.   The girl was at home, awaiting the turn of her destiny.   Yesterday I should have gone : a girl in distress, an artist . . . I tore up the letter without a regret, thus, perhaps, rejecting the great chance of my life.

Went out into the deep sunk streets, even into the Viali which always drive me back to the heart of the town.   Now I feel nothing but the bitterness of woman.

I like this comparison : just as the King is by nature the source of Honour, so Woman is the source of Virtue. And that is what distresses me : I find virtue inactive, monotonous and stale.

It is no good : woman is not a creature of pleasure. For an hour or so, at dinner, she may seem to love pleasure as much as we do. But as soon as she makes room for a man in her everyday life, it is not long before he discovers the fund of boredom beneath the few happy moments, the black earth between the flowers. Whether he likes it or no, the man who lives with a woman learns wisdom and settles down. Tournier de Zamble, who has already lived pretty fully, said to me one day : Love affairs begin in champagne and end in camomile. And how can this relaxation in the life of a man under the domination of habit not be extended to his spirit ? Just as he puts up with not going out in the evening, and not travelling, etc., so he resigns himself to giving up the search for truth. And he surrounds himself with comfort, with commonplace pleasures and meagre lies. But the woman is always there, seeming to say : " Am I not the truth ? " " Not altogether, my dear," replies the man, with his lips on her soft hair, and he catches himself thinking of Nietzsche and Pragmatism and the New Theology. . . . Woman is a limitation, and sometimes they even go so far as to refuse us the only thing for which we tolerate them.

I am going to begin to read a book the first chapter of which shall contain nothing but new truths, exact images, just thoughts, echoes, music, and then six hundred pages of moralizings, witticisms, cookery receipts, verses composed by a sentimental police official—and I shall swear to read such a book through to the very end.

Strange : the aversion I feel from what is called virtue. I must look into that too. I am so often forced to admit that there is in me a certain emulation of vice. Virtue seems negative and easy to me. Wickedness seems positive and difficult : and how should I not go towards evil ? I constantly hear it speaking to me and crying out in a great voice : " Lazy fellow ! Leave your room and come and find me : you know perfectly well that you must conquer yourself and drive back a thousand fears, a hundred prejudices and a million timidities before you can lift yourself up to me. I am on high and difficult of access : come ! "

And it enrages me, indeed, to think that the dullest of the maids at the Carlton has more wickedness in her than I. Oh ! I long to reach the grand activity of vice.

FLORENCE.

I have tried. It was very simple. I went into a stationer's shop in the Via Ceretani where they sell horrible and expensive souvenirs of Florence. There was a table covered with little bells with handles like red lilies. I had an excuse : I wanted some sheets of blotting-paper of different colours. I took up my position near the table on the left. I spoke to the girl who served me about the weather. I took out my handkerchief.

" No. Not that green : I prefer the pale blue."

I made a sudden movement with my right hand, while with my left I dropped my handkerchief on the table full of bells.   And at first there was the horrid dread lest it should ring !   And then, as the girl went to the till with my five-franc note, with my left hand I lightly picked up my handkerchief and (with my middle finger holding the tongue of the bell) put the whole thing into my pocket without altering a single fold in the handkerchief or moving a single muscle of my clenched fingers.

And when the girl came back her eyes went at once to the place where the bell was missing.   It was a fine moment.   But she did not see what had attracted her eyes.

" Nothing else, sir ? "

I took my time, pondered, seemed to hesitate   Nothing else, thank you.   I went out slowly, and I even stayed for a few seconds outside the shop window.   I was certain I had not been seen.   But the whole evening as I lounged through the shops I almost fainted every time a customer came in.   Even when I returned to the Carlton I asked the porter if anybody had been to see me : No, nobody.

I ought to be pleased : I have got the better of myself and done evil.   I wonder if Florrie Bailey would have dared to steal from a shop.   I ought to be proud.   I tried to persuade myself that I was proud.   But no : it gave me no pleasure at all.   The little bell is beside the note-book in which I am writing, but I never had the least desire for it.   Not that it worries me.   To think that I have not even succeeded in procuring a little remorse !

First of all I exaggerated the risk.   They would have made no pother about it : they would simply have made me pay.   My name, my references, my address at the

Carlton alone, would have proved that I was not a thief but a kleptomaniac. And suppose the girl did see me ? A shop where I have bought three thousand francs' worth of stationery in a month ! I thought I was committing a theft, and I was only playing a silly prank.

And that is how I employ my time as a free man, as a man who can endure no constraint and will have no bounds set to his activity and permit himself to do everything ? No. I have not got the better of myself, and wickedness is too difficult for me : for I spend my time in avoiding not only constraint but effort. I am only the prey of a few base feelings which fight among themselves for the possession of my soul, and of all these feelings fear and indolence are the strongest. Beyond Good and Evil ? I am lower.

I sent to the Assunta an English family who, under the arcades of the Piazza Vittorio-Emanuele, asked me the way to Or San Michele. It might have been a good thing for me to go to the Assuunta myself. It is a positive evil. " You can thrash the beast : it is tied up." But physical disgust is too strong.

I shall write to the governor of the prison at V. for permission to see over it. I want to see how the thieves live there.

Tuesday.

I don't know why, but I have done it again. In other shops. The same procedure (the handkerchief) : same success. With practice I shall soon be able to rifle the big jewellers' shops. I should come to it in time : with each little operation my emotion grows weaker. Not even the tiniest thrill.   Decidedly the game is not worth the candle.   One doesn't know what to do, and then one " lifts " some little thing in a shop : then a drive to the Cascine, then tea at Douey's, then a stroll round the Piazza Vittorio-Emanuele, then dinner at Lapi's.   Gertrude Hansker, who calls that the sport *par excellence*, made me expect an extreme pleasure.   Not at all.   It is an insignificent action (except for the shopkeeper), and it does not even leave the smallest regret.   If I had spoken rudely to a servant at the Carlton I should have some remorse : my thefts leave me very tranquil : but I do try conscientiously to blush when I see the things I have stolen.   Bored, discouraged, disgusted with myself.   Not a single friend, not a single enemy (except a few jealous people who do not know me), I feel like standing in front of one of the mirrors in my rooms and hitting myself hard for a whole hour.   What's the good ?   It would not express a thousandth part of my contempt for myself.   No desire, no passion, no will, my snout in the trough. . . .   What about my life as a free man ?

Thursday.

Went to the prison at V.   The governor came to fetch me in his automobile.   A man with perfect *signorile* manners (I can't find the word : " gentlemanly " ?)   We crossed the Tuscan campagna, where I happed on the elements of a short French poem, which I have placed on a Sunday in March in spite of the overturned baskets of spring flowers everywhere, and the big green butterflies, their wings, poised on the hoops and the twisted grey branches of the shining fig-trees.

Was hard put to it not to tell the governor of the prison of my thefts. I should have liked to have his opinion about it. No doubt he would have talked about kleptomania : to be a real thief a man must be poor. I constructed a whole theory about it and I should have liked to put it to the prisoners I was going to see. But the prison is not at all what I imagined it. As soon as I breathed the air of it I felt that the ideas I had just been promulgating could not live there. The speech I had prepared had no relation to the reality. There was not a single thief, not a single criminal in the prison : there were only prisoners. Almost soldiers, not at all sick men. There was a picture representing remorse in the director's drawing-room. (Remorse is an almost naked gentleman much upset, because his eyes are starting out of his head.) That was the only trace of remorse one could find in the whole establishment. The need of expiation in a few tormented souls ? Well, they were there for that ! As for the rest, they counted the days and the months, but that was only idealism : meanwhile they accepted their days and months and the food and the distractions of the day's walk : a change of living : nothing more.

Through the gratings of the cells I saw a hundred times the same pierrot in green-and-yellow stripes, lying on the same bench under a rectangle of bright blue daylight. The punishment seemed to me useless, and even more useless the act which had led to the punishment. Life had taken that form here and that was all. Life itself was useless.

When I left I was on the point of saying to the charming governor of the prison : " I have a friend who steals from shops " and tell him of my exploits.   But I corrected myself.

" I have a friend who wants to write something about prisons."

" Ah ! I shall be very glad to show him over ours."

30 *May.*

Another day wasted in watching the Sunday Florentines in their black go along the quay beneath my windows along the pink stripe of the parapet.   The parade of the prisoners of daily work.   Resigned ?   No : poor timid souls who ask nothing of life and get angry when other souls do demand something of life : the poor dumb crowd of commonplace people who point the finger of scorn at a man who tries to taste of the world, the man who lives irregularly, the artist.   And I am glad to have been cut off from them, made invisible to them, by my wealth.   They would all be capable of yelping at me.   There is really something to be said in favour of my friends the thieves in the prison at V. No, nothing.   There is nothing to be said in favour of anything.   The rumbling of the footsteps of the crowd yonder affirms that.

Formerly I was annoyed to find a kind of satisfaction in the very excess of my sadness.   And that was at once complicated by a certain satisfaction in admitting that I was annoyed to find a kind of satisfaction at the bottom of my sadness.   But this afternoon, above the green reaches of the Arno, between the bridges, above the diagonal crack of the dam where the hard water slips over in a curve, opposite the cupola of San Frediano with its mournful windows, as on the night when I wrote my *Gift of Self*, I have touched the void within me. Misery ! My whole life is organized for egoism, and I seek only to please myself and I do not love myself and I love nobody.

Want of exercise perhaps ? A game of hockey would put me right. Meanwhile I shall go out and mingle with the crowd in my best clothes, with plenty of jewels, my gold crutch-handled cane, all the things that will make the small shopkeepers stare. I wonder if I am the only one of the great millionaires who knows how our luxury disturbs the souls of the middle-classes (the people, who are accustomed to deny themselves nothing, understand and admire). Sometimes I see an angry contempt in the eyes of the avaricious.

FLORENCE,

2 *June*.

I reproach others with indolence of the heart, and I am still in Florence on the 2nd June.

But at least I am saved : saved for the moment : as I write this entry in my diary the Marquis de Putouarey is snoring in one of the rooms of my suite. I have clung to a human being. It was time.

It was Putouarey who brought me back to the Carlton : I should never have gone back alone. A frenzy of despair made me wander at random for three days, never washing, sleeping for an hour or two in cabs, on the streets of the outskirts, going into a restaurant and leaving it without eating any of the food put before me, and at last walking about all night along, like a sick bat, sucking the dregs of the night in the dark alleys. Often

I must have been seen dragging wearily across the Piazza Cavour, the hideousness of which was so well in accordance with my state of mind.

I remember now that I saw summer enter Florence and penetrate even to the darkest *chiassi*, where the battered houses are in a cold sweat even at full noon, where there are hidden old fountains of leprous stone which make one think of pillories and instruments of torture, and gurglingly vomit forth a stream of greasy water. Particularly the alleys between the Lungarni, the Borgo SS. Apostoli and behind San Firenzi, Via Fillipo Via Borgoguona did I haunt, where the pavement seems to have been heaved up by earthquakes, crushed by cataclysms, and the gaping doors slobber up a sticky cold shade, while high palatial windows, set in black carved stone, in full mourning, look down from their height on all the haggard misery and do not deign to take pity on it.

I remember how all through the city the summer opened out, in spite of the days of despairing skies, when the wind from Siena gustily swept the dry pavements driving the dust in all directions. Then the ice-cream sellers took up their stands near the station behind Santa Maria Novella. Then the passer-by turning away from the cold blast of a dark *portone*, saw beyond barriers of carved wood and glass doors, the sunlit heart of the black palazzo, the enclosed garden, all staring with leaves, light and water. The cabdrivers replaced the red woollen rugs of their horses with holland or pink horsecloths. No more does one hear English or Russian spoken on the terraces of the Galabrinas and the Guibbe Rosse. And one knows which is the shady side of the street, morning and evening, and sticks to it.

And one evening Bettino came to the Carlton and brought me a live cricket in a little wire cage. He explained that it was Ascension Day and that everybody bought a cricket then, and that the little Florentine girls went very early in the morning to the Cascine to catch the *Grillo Canterino*. Then came the Savonarola anniversary : the bronze plate let into the pavement of the Piazza Signoria was surrounded with a garland of flowers that soon faded : and hard by a hawker was selling some medals or other. And there are all kinds of celebrations on the 28 May, the anniversary of certain battles, and yesterday, on the first Sunday in June, the national festival : that is, a long day of sadness and mediocrity, with miserable glass bowls containing three candles hanging outside the gates of a barracks by the Piazza d'Agaglio and discoloured flags marking out the official buildings.

But it was in the Chiassi where I had taken refuge that I saw the Florentine summer appear suddenly with a terrible aspect : like the face of an old prison warder, painted red and blue, behind green shutters, and beneath this face, the body belonging to it, the sweating shoulders and bare arms of a buxom wench. In all the Chiassi was the same face and the same bare arms at every window—the laundress, the bearer of burdens throwing off her bodice to avoid the heat. And a horrible voice as I passed let fall on me the cry : " *Venga !* "

And I went on wandering through such desolation that reminded me sometimes of certain poor quarters in Hamburg and Copenhagen (the savage North), from arch to arch, from urinal to urinal, going, returning, tasting the bad smells, every now and then gulping down a mouthful of hot, thick, greasy air. Only my fear of vermin kept me from answering the call of the red and blue faces behind the shutters : I could not see why I should not settle there in one of those rooms with the old prison warder with bare sweating bosom. Perhaps we should have made a jolly household. After all, no one else said " Venga ! " to me. (And I so sorely needed someone to say it.) The Galleries? Oh ! I thought of them when I got to the dregs of my weariness. But only quickly to fling away the idea. And that is three hours ago. I was dragging along an endless dark street, behind Santa Croce, when suddenly I saw, at a corner, the lights of an enormous automobile which had stopped in the middle of a little street.

" Here's something to take me out of my boredom," thought I. " All the more as if I bungle in getting her away I run the risk of being shot."

I had intended to drive the machine straight to the Carlton to fetch my trunk, a rug and this notebook, and then to make for Genoa or Milan, whence I would send a cheque to the manager of the Carlton. I would make things all right with the owner of the car, if he were to trace it to me. Anyhow, it was something new. And what a trick to play on Cartuyvels' detectives, who would certainly lose my tracks !

I was hot for the adventure, when, as I came up to it, I seemed to recognize the car, a huge limousine, an exhibition model, with a 70 h.p. engine painted yellow with dark blue stripes. And the little flag waving in front of the hood on top of a little semaphore, and the varnished doors showed me a coat of arms which I had seen somewhere. I sat in the driver's seat and at once saw a gold plate riveted to the dashboard with the name of the huge machine. Good Lord! It was my old "Voracious" which I had sold the year before to the Marquis de Putouarey. And why had I not observed before that the house outside which the Voracious stood was Madame Assunta's, where the whole night long, surrounded by her nieces, she receives her friends? A few seconds later I entered the drawing-room.

"So here you are, my little guano-seller, my million-aire with periwinkle eyes?" cried the Assunta.

And Putouarey got up from an arm-chair, of which he was not the sole occupant, and said:

"My dear Count, what a lucky meeting!"

On that I sank down on the cushions of a divan and lost consciousness. A brief stupor: I recovered to find myself surrounded by a bevy of pretty faces and lovely flashing dark eyes. I was surrounded by the nieces of Madame Assunta, and they were slapping my hands and putting handkerchiefs soaked in cold water to my forehead. I got up painfully and slowly and took Putouarey out into the air of the street.

"Come," I said. "It is the result of fatigue and hunger. You have come in the very nick of time: I put myself in your hands. I don't know where to go really. A prostitute of whom I craved hospitality jok-ingly advised me to sell my hat. But the shops were shut. She could not understand that I was really very poor, fallen low in the world: she told me she could not afford to waste a night. And I was in such dire need to hold someone's hand and lay my head on some-one's bosom. Idiot. When I left her, I would have given her a cheque which would have given her an income for life."

Putouarey looked at me in astonishment. I was showing him a part of myself which I should not have liked him to see in other circumstances, but I was dead beat. All the causes of my boredom, all the things that had been secretly devouring me for a week past had turned back on me and submerged me : the repercussion of the sale of my possessions on thousands of people : my lamentable romance with Florrie Bailey, the lessons which, in spite of himself, Cartuyvels had given me, my whole future life stretching on in the likeness of such a beginning, my baseness and my folly, my shame, my disgust with myself, overwhelmed me. And I had not even the strength to cry out : " Forgive me ! Forgive me for everything that I have done, said, written since I have lived in the world. I will not do it again. Tell me what I must do and I will humbly obey. Ah ! I want to be wise, I want to be pure. I want to die ! "

" You are very tired, my poor fellow," said Putouarey. " Haven't you a bed anywhere ? Anyhow, I'll take you to the Carlton. I meant to sleep there to-morrow morning."

He laid me back on the cushions of the Voracious, and that is how I come to be back in my study after a good supper, already feeling better.

CARLTON,

3 *June*.

" Cospetto ! You were in a fine state that night, my dear Count. No ? Did you really ask a fly-by-night for a night's lodging? What a joke! I'll try it."

Putouarey, in China silk pyjamas, with a big gold-backed brush in each hand, is vigorously brushing his hair in front of a mirror. Impossible to explain to him that it was not a joke. And soon I am taken out of myself by his activity; his rich, satisfied vigour and I began to persuade myself that it was indeed a jest that I imagined.

From my bed I watch the Marquis. I like his handsome French face: his bright speaking eyes (rather too loquacious): his little dignified and at the same time impudent features (I suspect Putouarey of getting himself up to look like Henri IV of France): his well-trimmed hair: his shiny black beard turned up in two snail-shaped twists in front of his chin: flowers in all the windows and a charming smile. He is rather short, and it is by way of excusing his height that he is for ever reminding me of his rank as a lieutenant in the cavalry reserve. By his side my long bony face and red hair rather distress me. Fortunately, I am a head taller than he is. And his vivacity! When we walk along the streets together I seem as though I were holding him at arm's length on wires like a jointed doll.

" Please don't call me ' dear count,' Putouarey."

" Why not? Aren't you Count of Aquibajo? "

" I bought the title without knowing why, as I have bought so many things. The degenerate Spaniard of whom I bought it made a better bargain than I did. The arms, the coronet, the name (I had been offered a selection of patents of nobility) determined my choice. At once everything I had, my dumb-bells, my cigarette papers, my horse-cloths, the skin of the fruit served up at meals, bore my arms and coronet. And at the end of a month I could not bear the sight of them. Pure vanity ! Barnabooth, though it shrieks of money, will always sound better than any of your Counts of Aquibajo or Aquirriba."

"As you please, my dear C—my dear fellow," and Putouarey consoles himself with the thought that it is just as flattering to be able to call the Richissimus " my dear fellow."

I like the humble vanity of people who are proud of their relations, their money, their titles, their know-ledge, their talents. It seems very touching to me, who suffer from having reached the centre of indifference, to see that people can let themselves be deceived by the appearances of life. So there are still men simple enough if they are noble to despise those who are not ? And if they are learned, to think themselves superior to the ignorant, or, rich, to set themselves above the poor ? Why have I not the freshness of soul of these children ? Oh, to be the grocer who with all his heart despises the grocer opposite, or the rich retired merchant who is sick with longing to be received by his neighbour the lord of the manor, or the man of letters who thinks himself important because people talk about his books ! But it is not the great vanity and pride I feel in know-ing myself superior to all their little vanities, also very touching !

"I am surprised, my dear fellow, that you didn't turn up at the polo tournaments this autumn in Eng-land and on the Riviera in March ! I was there with the Prince Xaintrailles, the Duke of Christminster, the Prince of Aunis, and Lord Molland.   There were quite a lot of your compatriots too : the Mato-Suarès, Pablo Barnevo, the Santa-Paus, Ladislov Saenz . . . a wild lot ! "

" Yes, I know.   Where have you come from, Putouarey ? "

" From Naples.   You smile ?   You guess the kind of life I lived there, with the Assuntas round the Piazza Plebiscito.   Yes.   I added a few interesting pieces to my collection of memories of women.   A few Neapolitans and Salernians . . ."

" No Capri girls ? "

" Scusi Signore : one, but she was a German.   Enough. Basta.   Now for serious business."

" Certainly.   What exactly ? "

" I want to go to the republic of San Marino, the little circle one sees on the map, you know, the rosette Italy wears in her buttonhole."

" To study the San Marino women ? "

" No.   To see the country and gain instruction.   It is a very serious matter.   I want to visit the country, examine the rock, take a few specimens, and send postcards to my friends : and also add to my collection of new postage stamps, you know, the sheets of four stamps : the finest collection in the world it will be when it's finished.   Tell me, shall I take you with me in the Voracious ?   I have an excellent French chauffeur, capable of taking down the engine and putting it together again in an hour.   It is too hot to *dimorare qui molto di più*."

" Is that the Italian you culled from the lips of the Neapolitan beauties ? "

" Yes, it is," said Putouarey, slightly uneasy.

" My dear fellow, you speak like Dante ! Very well then, I'll go to San Marino with you. At least in that little circle, as you call it, there will be no works of art. Here I feel as if I had the weight of all the museums on my shoulders."

So we arranged to set out to-morrow morning. I am sick of stopping still. " Why not to-night ? " I said to Putouarey. But the roads over the Apennines are awkward, and it is a hundred and forty-eight kilometres to Rimini, our first stop.

And now I am absorbed in Putouarey's personality. Many things shock me in that illiterate bourgeois, who is commonplace even in his pleasures, idiotically pleased with himself, with his Marquis' coronet, his money, so much so that when I think of him it is hardly more than as an amusing fool. No. I feel I prefer him to Maxime Claremoris, the great aristocrat, the son of every kind of culture. With Putouarey I do feel at my ease.

A note to tell the Yarza girls I am leaving—and so to bed.

One last look through the window—the empty quay, the reflections of the street lamps waving their long golden spindles in the black water.

RIMINI. ALBERGO DEL RISORGIMENTO,

4 *June*, 190 . . .

Full of joy. The open air : speed : the Marquis' confidences. Anyhow I feel heroic.

Left Florence this morning at six. I wanted to leave quickly so as to escape the vigilance of Cartuyvels' agents (if he is still having me " protected "). But Putouarey had to go to the Central post office, and I wanted to buy a manuscript book to begin arranging my latest poems. I was driven to the stationer's in the Via Cerretani where I stole the little bell. (*And to think that I shall never dare to speak of it to Putouarey!* So there is one man who does blow his own trumpet.) When I had bought the manuscript book the girl said :

"Nothing else ? You don't want one of these Florentine bells ? "

It was the same girl, and she pointed to the table on which I had operated. At once I lost countenance, muttered a refusal, and hurried out to join Putouarey in the limousine. So I had been seen ? What then ? And then I thought the girl had not asked me intentionally. She had been told to sell the bells as quickly as possible. So. I shall never know the truth.

And I shall never know the truth about Cartuyvels' agents either. We were certainly not followed as we left Florence. Then as we crossed the Apennines, after Rocca San Casciano, where we lunched, we were passed by a torpedo going at full speed. There were two men in it ! "It is they," said I to Putouarey. "Who do you mean ? " Then I told him what Old Faithful means by my "bodyguard." The torpedo was already a long way ahead. Then, near Forli, we met it again, stopped by the side of the road : a tyre had burst. We offered them assistance. They refused, and one of the two men shouted in Italian that they would be in Ravenna in three-quarters of an hour all the same. And, indeed, soon afterwards we saw the torpedo raising a cloud of dust, on the Ravenna road which cuts the road to Rimini, along which we were going, at right angles. It was all quite natural. But they might turn back and follow us to Rimini, or reach Rimini by another road. This evening in the streets I have tried hard to recognize them. But the two men in the torpedo had leather and glass goggles : what then ?

Putouarey also goes through life surrounded by mysteries. It appears that he was on the point of making a fool of himself over a dark-haired popolana in the Via Mezzo Cannone in Naples. He was even going to take her back to France and instal her as housekeeper to his young wife. (He tells all this with violent gestures, which, as he cannot use his arms which are holding the driving wheel, are driven back into his shoulders, his head, eyes, and even the tips of his ears.)

As soon as we left Florence, Putouarey wanted to drive the Voracious himself, and we sat in the front seats, relegating the chauffeur, that useless organism, to the luxurious solitude of the inside. And the Marquis talked, talked, talked, all through the spiral drone of our career, through the grinding of the changing gears, through the eddying backwash of air we made.

At first he tried to give me a favourable opinion of his taste by expressing a few ideas on art and Florence.

" Ah ! Raphael. Titian ! Perugino ! The Tribune ! My dear fellow, and Giotto ! When Ruskin . . ."

(Of course he has not read Ruskin and his absurd pretensions make it impossible for me not to despise him, to feel that as regards culture I am a great European and he only a little bourgeois, and that is precisely what I do not want to feel. Putouarey is worth a hundred times more than I : if only he would show me the side of himself on which he is my superior ! I am sick of admiring myself.)

"The Tribune ! The Tribune ! My dear fellow, don't talk to me of the Tribune ! Why don't you admit that all these things bore you to tears ? I can appreciate them perhaps a little more than you, but I've had enough of them this long time past : they make people talk such rot. No. Don't make me believe that you like the culture of manuals and guide-books. You wear it exactly as it is worn in the circle in which you were born, that is all. In the salons of Paris you gush over Berlioz, Saint-Saëns and Debussy, and when you return to Putouarey you play Théodore Botrel. And you are right, because you like it ! And it is the same with literature and painting. I can see the library at Putouarey. Your great-grandfathers ! Voltaire and Rousseau are packed off to the attics, and instead of those old unfashionable *sans-culottes* there are shelves full of the little fashionable books, indecent and tiresome, which your bookseller makes you buy. No, my friend, it is not for your artistic tastes that I like being in your company, but for your charming humour, your good sense, your coolness in handling life and your handsome French face. What I love is Putouarey the petticoat hunter, Putouarey the true of heart. And don't let us talk of Ruskin, or even of Florence."

"By jove, you are right : and from this out I shall be able to play Botrel without a qualm : you know those little songs of his move me. I'm very much of the people like every real nobleman. So much the worse for great literature, great music and great painting : a little chemistry, a little geology and, mogaril ! the fair sex, that's what I've a head for, and *basta*. My dear fellow, a lovely girl, Angiola ! Via Mezzo Cannone, you know where it is ? "

(I saw the hard new boulevard where the sun scorches you up, with all the vulgarity of Marseilles, and all the most Senegalese quality of Greece, and the little parched streets smelling of slums and dirty linen to the right of the Piazza Municipio, opposite a statue of the monarch whom Max called the Fireman.)

" A tiled room furnished with three iron bedsteads, six cane chairs, and a copper dish full of charcoal which the children swing round to warm the air a little. The North Pole. And the cat on a chair stretching her legs to persuade herself that she is warm, poor beast. Do you know any country where it is as cold in winter as Italy ? "

" Greece, Spain and certain parts of Iceland."

" Angiola was the youngest of an innumerable family. Her mother, oh ! her mother, too fat for the street. I used to think : she is the whole *Cannone*. Angiola was married : yes, she had two charming babies though she was only twenty. But her husband had no time to waste in barracks and cleared out the day after he was declared fit for service, to seek his fortune in Argentina. And she was to go and join him with the brats as soon as he sent them the money to travel second-class."

" That is how the foundations of a new world are laid. How did you meet Angiola ? "

" Through one of those men who accost strangers in the Galleria Umberto I. This fellow was known in the Via Mezzo Cannone as ' Don Pasquale.' I merely asked him to introduce me to a young woman of the people. There is no gallantry in Naples. Before I used to travel, that is, before my marriage, I used to have extraordinary ideas about the immorality of the South. But Naples is a much more moral town than Lyons or Liverpool. Without the foreigners, Naples would never know that love can be put up for sale. I tell you : one evening in one of those salita which go up to the Pausilleppa road I approached a young woman who seemed to be waiting for me : as soon as she understood she spurned me and made the sign of the cross. There are two or three ' Madame Assuntas ' at whose houses one finds respectable mothers and housewives from Torre del Greco and Piedigrotta, poor girls who are trying to give the steamboat English an idea of debauchery by shouting blasphemy and swear-words without any conviction. Don Pasquale was a long time in finding what I had asked him for. It was so abnormal, so monstrous ! At last he told me one day that it was arranged. The meeting took place in another gallery where we could be quieter. . . . When I entered the little café, there was Don Pasquale, the girl herself, and her enormous mamma, all bosom. They had put on their best black silk gowns : they were in black silk from head to foot, with gold jewels, round ear-rings, heavy bracelets and brooches, all rather grubby, but heavy and old, perhaps dating from the Bourbons."

" Or the first French domination."

" Don't laugh : with those two women in their black silk gowns I understood the meaning of History. Yes : the tradition, the continuity of the life of a great capital : it was in their faces, their jewels, their dresses. You don't know how thoroughly of the ' capital ' they were !

A town of which all the inhabitants, down to the very poor, were gentlemen and ladies, and had a right to black silk, as the Roman citizens had a right to wear the toga. And what a capital ! No, the bourgeoises of the faubourgs of Paris and the ladies of the East End with their fur necklets which they wear every Sunday in the year, even in July, would be like peasants compared with the two Neapolitan signores who sat waiting for me in the café. For a moment I felt that I myself was the product and representative of an agrarian civilization in the presence of that antique city civilization. Yes. In that moment, two nations met face to face. Then the social hierarchy came between us, separated us as individuals, and yet reunited us as members of the human community. . . . Don Pasquale did not delay matters. But so much gravity and ceremony was brought into it, the mamma welcomed every look of mine with such kindly smiles, that I was on the point of saying to Don Pasquale : ' I suppose they understand that it is not a question of marriage ? ' But Angiola was married . . . and so was I ! No, the reason why they took the affair so seriously was because it was a question of money. I had promised to make the girl an allowance as long as I stayed in Naples. There was not even an attempt made to colour the matter with some pretext as I had begged Don Pasquale to do : Italian lessons, for instance. The question of the amount per month dominated everything. From the moment when I offered money I had the right at any hour of the day or night to enter the rooms in the Via Mezzo Cannone, as Angiola's protector or vice-husband, if I may call it so. It was, well, a family affair. They must have gathered together the evening before, or that very morning to discuss my proposal and prepare for the interview. I doubt if there was as much discussion when the *ragazza* married! Ah! Denaro, Roba, Risparmio, those are the words I most often heard on Angiola's pretty lips. I told Don Pasquale to begin by offering a hundred and fifty francs and to go up to two hundred and fifty at most. I saw mamma's eyes flicker with delight when two hundred francs were mentioned : but with perfect politeness and a delicious smile she said :

"'E poco, egregio Signore, veramente poco . . .'

"The family were willing to oblige and would feel honoured by my acquaintance, but they were not so poor as all that . . . I might have depreciated the goods of course, but Angiola was really lovely : you know, the white lilac skin with depths of burning sepia about the neck, one of those great creatures of flame and shadow who make one think of the warrior angels. And all that was going on in front of her, and she listened to our words with the lofty disdain of a princess led into slavery. Ten times was I on the point of pulling a few notes out of my pocket and sending them all home. But Angiola's eyes! When she closed them, she had just a little dark face, nervous and thin, but when she opened them life took on a new meaning and they were like two living creatures that one could never tire of watching at play. To cut short the ignoble scene I consented to everything they wished.

"You will feel of course that I should have been the lowest of men had I taken delivery of the goods that very evening. No. I wished to be discreet and to efface from Angiola's mind the memory of the transaction. I wrote her a four-page letter, in fairly accurate Italian,

135

I fancy, in which I expressed (with a little embellishment of the truth) the tenderest affection. I took it to her myself : she read it and gave it back to me saying :

"'Molto bene.'

"To her it was only a duty and she paid scrupulously. But gradually we became more intimate friends : I used even to pay attention to the babies to win my welcome. And then, finally—I triumphed."

"Yes. There was enough between you to make it tolerable."

"Quite so. We became companions : we used to go out together. I used to take her to the little room at Gambrinus. We lunched there once between Mr. Joseph Chamberlain and Coquelin Cadet. Fortunately Angiola was beautiful : it would have been horribly absurd if she had only been pretty. She made me conspicuous, but I did not mind that. Besides I had dressed her well. You can count on that. I think there is nothing more amusing than to go with a woman to the shops where she buys her clothes. And how exciting to go there alone and find oneself in a place full of girls and women and ask for a female article of clothing, reciting the formula given to one with the commission ! The shop girls smile up their sleeves : one feels a little awkward, but one has a certain pride at being initiated into the sweet mysteries."

"My dear fellow, it is a vocation with you ! It's a pity you don't exercise it for the good of Madame de . . ."

"I was wrapped up in her. I even thought of taking her back to France, yes, to Putouarey, as housekeeper at the château. Why not ? Meanwhile I lived in the

Via Mezzo Cannone, and only went to my hotel, Corso Vittorio Emanuele, to fetch my letters. To get a little warmth I bought four or five scaldini and two dozen straw fans, and I paid the children a franc an hour to keep the charcoal glowing all day long. Angiola used to sing from morning to night : *Pè tutta Napole : La Frangesa : Carmé, Carmé : Fior di Zucca*. . . . She used to sing through the howling of the brats. She would even sing in response to what one said to her. The opera ! Even by my side in the street, at the Toledo she would hum : It was embarrassing : it showed too plainly where she came from. So much the worse ! I had many pleasant memories of her ! . . . although it was always distressing for me, a chilly Burgundian, to have to do with the southern girls who will sleep with their arms out of bed. (I beg your pardon. I did not mean to make you blush.)

" And little by little it was all spoiled. I gave up being shocked because every night she used to place under her pillow the pious images she used to wear in her bodice during the day (it seemed sacrilegious to me : I was brought up religiously). We even began to guess each other's thoughts, to be interested together in the same things. But I felt that she would never become attached to me. A German, an Englishwoman, even a Frenchwoman, would have become attached to me in spite of the social differences and in spite of her preoccupation with Denaro and Roba. Angiola submitted to me : even in public she would give me all the marks of respect due from a good wife to her lord and master. But I felt that she did not care in the least for me. Between ourselves and to her I was her Gaetanino, but with her family I was *il Forestiere*, the Foreigner. Gradually the whole tribe began to regard me as a member of the family, as the richest member, whose duty it was to help the others. I was never alone for an hour in my hotel in the Corso Vittorio Emanuele but some blackguard calling himself a relation of her Mamma's would come and ask me for help. At first I used to give in weakly, and then because I feared a scene in the hotel. The whole tribe of the Cacace—*Cacachè*, you know : her name was Angiola Cacace. And every day I met a new member of the Cacace family. All the types of the people of Naples filed before my eyes : and they were all Cacaces. All. A bogus relation in a bowler hat much too high : a black velvet tie instead of a collar, a very short coat : very worn and very dirty, though it looked all right at a distance, and a pair of wonderful new brown boots, one with a square hole cut to accommodate an enormous corn wrapped up in white lint. He would call himself a painter. But, diamoni ! between ourselves . . . And a little shopkeeper with enormous dirty jewels, a waistcoat of the same red as his fat round unshaven cheeks. And an old man all gestures, groaning between every word while his bleary blue eyes did nothing but laugh. And even Albinos ! *Ma chè !* The funicular up the Vomero only worked for the Cacaces who came to pluck me at the Hotel Bristol. I lost my patience and told Don Pasquale and Angiola that I was going to Paris whence I would prepare Madame de Putouarey for the advent of the Italian housekeeper. Angiola should come. She seemed pleased. Paris was to her what Naples is to the women of the faubourgs in Paris : Paris attracted her : see Paris and die !

" But from that time her conduct towards me changed. The Denare played an increasingly large part in her preoccupations. And when we were out together she would constantly stop outside the shops and say :

" ' You must buy me . . .'

" The reign of the word ' comprare ' had begun. It appears that Don Pasquale had alleged that I had pledged myself to give numerous presents to the *ragazza*. And now, urged on by her mother, the *ragazza* was demanding these presents. I bought without wincing, but not with a good heart. All the clothes I had had made for her at the outset of our affair went for nothing in her eyes : they did not please her and she had worn them, it appears, only to avoid displeasing me. Now that she was free to choose she realized her old conception of smartness and I paid. She got herself up as a Parisian, just that. The words ' chic ' and ' chichezza ' were constantly on her lips. Where was the old black silk dress that had so moved me ?

" One evening she asked me to take her to the San Carlo theatre where they were playing *Siberia*. She had put on all her new finery. Particularly a very light serge cloak ! My money in her hands had taken such grotesque shapes that I blushed as at a joke at my expense. Whether it was the fault of the clothes or of the life of abundance which I had made her life, at all events it seemed to me that her beauty was slipping away every day. I mean, her *eyes* had become *stupid*.

" As we sat in our box I raised the grille under the pretext that I might be recognized by the people in the stalls : then I said to Angiola :

" ' Close your eyes.'

139

" She closed them. I looked at her closely.

" She looked like a little strumpet dressed up as a lady. I need not tell you that that was the end of it. I had to see it through to the end out of obstinacy. I insisted on pursuing the lamentable adventure. I owed the Cacace nothing. I had transformed the *ragazza* into a woman of the world : I had clothed from head to foot all the *ragazza's* little brothers and sisters : I had even newly dressed the immense form of her mamma, and had provided all the Cacace of the two Sicilys with Denaro : and I even fancy some of my Denaro had been sent to the *ragazza's* husband in Argentina. I was in a position to go without by your leave. But no. I wanted to see the end of it : I announced that we were going to leave for France and I took two tickets to Paris. To avoid the tears of the family I decided that we would go separately to the station. But I had a presentiment and I stayed on the platform. She did not come. I let the Rome-Paris express go and returned to the Hotel Bristol.

" I was not going to renew the affair but I wanted to know. I sent for a cab-driver who had often driven us to the outskirts along the beautiful white roads, by the side of which on the hillside the tea-gardens hum with music all the afternoon. The cab-driver promised to keep me informed. And he must also have told the Cacace. Through him I learned certain things. For instance that Mamma, who had been the widow of the late Signor Cacace for twelve years, had children of eight and ten, and had not married again. Don Pasquale was the husband of a sister of Mamma's and consequently Angiola's uncle. And this reminded me that one day the *ragazza*, having called Don Pasquale 'Zio' turned to me in confusion and laughed and told me it was a joke. Why had they concealed all that from me, and what part did the Zio play in the affair?

"I stayed for ten days in the hotel and never went out for fear of being stopped in the street by a Cacace. It is certain that they knew I had not gone. Then why did they not come and bother me?

"Finally my cab-driver brought Angiola herself. Her part in my life was ended. I had thought I should never see her again: she was now only a memory—and there she was standing in front of me. She came in an unreal fashion, like a ghost, like a portrait stepping out of its frame. We spent a couple of hours in my room at the hotel, unknown, apparently, to all the Cacace, but I could only drag out of her a confused and contradictory account from which only one clear impression was forthcoming: that not only had they all lied to me, but that they had all lied to each other. Thus Don Pasquale had sworn to them that I had never paid him a *centisimo* nor the smallest *roba*, though I had filled his filthy pocket-book with hundred-lire notes and had given him all the winter suits I had in my trunks. And upon reflection I seem to gather than Don Pasquale had done all he could to blacken me in Mamma's mind, and had spread the report among the Cacace that I was ruined and that I wanted to take the *ragazza* to France to exploit her. But why did he do that? Did he really believe I was ruined because I had refused point-blank to give him money? Angiola herself as she told the story had tied herself up in fresh lies, thought that I too was lying, and accused me of having given her a rival whom I had then concealed in the hotel.

"Yes. She would have gone with me to Paris, but Mamma would not hear of it. A pilgrimage they were to make together to the Madonna di Monteverginel kept on cropping up in her chatter. I wondered if she were passing through a period of religious scruples : not at all : that was plain to see as we parted.

"'Addio ! Gaetanino mio ! At least we will write to each other.' She wept. To console her I gave her five louis d'or which she carefully wrapped up in her handkerchief : and I had a carriage called and she went. And what do you think ? I found this letter waiting for me this morning at the poste restante in the Uffizi."

And the Marquis took one hand from the driving wheel and held out a rather dirty little envelope. I read :

Adorato Gaetano,

Non puoi credere come sono cattiva dache sei partito. Piango sembre perlatua lontananza. Ma spero che verrai più presto possibile eche saremo insieme e che non mi lascerai più. Ti facio sapere che io sono andata a perdere il fazzoletto e o perduto lire quaranta in oro dentro la vettura e cosi sono molto trista.

Vieni subito e scrivemi. Ti mando mille baci. La tua

per sembre

e così

ANGIOLA.

Cacace.

"Well," said Putouarey to me. "What do you think

142

of it ? You see, one never knows what the last letter is : a, o, e, cattivo, insiema, molte. And her hesitation between p and b. It's funny. La tua per sembre. Making fun of me, eh ? "

" I don't think so. But it is clear that she is still trying to get Denaro out of you."

" That's Mamma egging her on, the sly madre. Left to herself Angiola is rather disinterested. But what a series of snares is Italian life at a certain depth ! One would think they purposely complicate it with their lies, and that it is their way of living beautifully : to trick everybody and to trick themselves. And all those intrigues ending only in driving me away from them when frankness would have served them much better. There's no force in them at bottom with all their grand diplomatic airs. It's like their gestures : one can guess at a distance what they are saying. What ? I was in love like a boy : I would have made the girl's fortune. But no : they preferred to make a fool of me, wheedle little sums out of me, and when they thought they had squeezed me dry they threw me over. The letter amuses you ? Keep it. Yes. I shall answer it. Ma chè ? I can't leave ma poverina ragazza molto cattiva at having lost so much denaro in oro. But it will be the last time."

And then I, in my turn, told Putouarey the story of Florrie Bailey. But I could not speak of my proposal of marriage to a man whom Florrie would have considered a " good kind " of lover. I had to tell him that I had been Florrie's lover and that plunged me in a bewildering series of lies. I cut it short and came suddenly to the famous secret.

" What do you think Florrie Bailey's secret can be ? "

" She will lower her tariff perhaps."

Ah ! He is once more the rich man I love and admire, one who enjoys life carefully and methodically and does not lose his head, and pays more attention to the temperature of the wine set before him than to the life of a pretty woman who amuses him for a moment. I am confounded : how boyish is my stupid sentimentalism compared with his fine well-organized self-confident egoism !

I wanted to have my revenge and at Cesena I changed places with the Marquis, and drove the Voracious along at such a rate that he begged me to give him the driving wheel.

You drive like a cowboy, my dear fellow ! You are terrifying ! Ah ! He'll never kill himself !

(One to Putouarey, who since we have been at Rimini has never spoken of Francesca.)

SAN MARINO, ALBERGO REPUBBLICANO,
6 *June.*

I love the dim damp rooms of these little inns : the old paper with a brown background and little flowers, the furniture of mahogany veneer, long tarnished, and now sinking from weariness and ugliness into the floor. That tells us the hotel is something essential like the Hôtel de Ville, with always the same significance, whether it be the Rathaus at Bremen or the *mairie-école* in the smallest French village. And it is by virtue of this essential quality that the Albergo Repubblicano at San Marino now contains in Putouarey and myself, two of the most famous frequenters of the greatest palaces in the world.

It also contains a café-concert hall, and there the Voracious is lodged, being too big for most of the streets and we dared not leave it on the Pianello, the only place in the Città where it could stay with any comfort. It is probably the first limousine that has appeared on the Titano and all San Marino has come out to look at it. They talk of nothing but the Voracious on the Piazzetta, this evening, outside the hotel and in the chemist's shop.

We have even abashed the host of the Albergo Repubblicano, a ruddy Salernian, who serves us with all the charming manners of the South, his port swelling with respect in our presence. He insists on replying in bad French to the questions we put to him in correct Italian, and this evening he walked before us to our rooms carrying a lighted candle in each hand at arm's length.

He upsets P., who calls him "that officious Camorrist," pretends not to understand him when he talks French and shouts down the corridors to me :

" I hate the people of the Mezzogiorno who are not dark. Don't think they are fair-haired, my boy : they are only discoloured ! "

We have two rooms on the first floor looking out on a little street which goes steeply up and turns suddenly, and a little fresh empty sitting room with a painted ceiling. We dined there *tête-à-tête*, P. having refused to take a second meal in the big hall which serves as a garage for the Voracious.

" Too many filthy packs of cards there, and the smells

. . . Poor people, they lack amusement and the 'café-chata' is not often open."

The host served us himself with court ceremony, bowing profoundly at each order. The chief dish consisted in an indefinable substance which he calls " merlusse."

An old inn, all long corridors with absurdly high ceilings. The white walls, regretfully traced out by blue and green paint, are peeling. . . . As I walked along them grey insects hid themselves behind a portrait of Garibaldi. It is all so bare and dark that the warmth seems to be an intruder. And yet there too the fund of unexpressed joy, the confiding soul of Italy follows at our heels : something that strangely tells us : " So many centuries of unbroken civilization. . . . And still the stirring of men, and the little pink charcoal fire which has never gone out at the bottom of its brazen vessel. . . . Elsewhere time has shaped the countries anew, and elsewhere it may be better, but it is recent. Stay, be glad of the little that I offer : it is sure. Elsewhere, one is not sure . . ."

I should have liked to stay in Rimini. Yesterday evening I saw long tiled streets, with no footpaths, under the sheets of light thrown by the electric arc lamps, great squares surrounded with low arcades, and in the distance, the façades of Roman palaces (genuine and of the Risorgimento). But P. was in a hurry to be gone. He got up at six and began to study his road map : at seven o'clock he knew it by heart, at eight we took our places in the front of the Voracious and the chauffeur climbed up and went to sleep on the cushions inside. The Marquis let fly five notes from the testophone at a group of little boys who surrounded the car and we softly started off.

As we left the crudeness of a new suburb at a turn we found ourselves out in the country, "as thickly populated and cultivated as the canton of Geneva," said the Marquis, "and not at all like Tuscany. I mean in its aspect. Do you see what is lacking? The cypresses: for boundaries and borders they have elms. It is rich country, almost as rich as Tuscany: the patches of corn and hay surrounded with trees entwined with vines. And in spite of all it seems a little dry. The extreme end of a continuation of the plain of Lombardy, but creeping up the side of the rocks, and no doubt it goes as far as Ancona. I should like to see what comes after it. But really I don't like the country-side much: it's rather in a litter: nothing like the orderliness of the Tuscan country. Ah! The hill of Fiesole with all its medallions, pictures, terraces: and the Chartreuse at Ema, in the midst of its imperial guard of black cypresses! And the people: just look at their great rose and orange faces in their coloured kerchiefs: and all the women barefooted out of love for the Risparmio. The *ragazze* are pretty and plump, but with nothing like the slenderness of Tuscan girls. They remind me of the Sybil of somewhere, don't you know, in the Uffizi, in the Baroche hall, not the big one, the one on the right with her jolly calf-like head wrapped up in a sky-blue scarf. Hi! Look out! Diaminé!!"

With a jerk of his thumb he sounded the horn, and then went on:

"And they have a queer language, rather rough for anything Tuscan. The other night while you were writing I went all over Rimini and near the canal I got into conversation with a kind of general blackguard, newsvendor, rufiano. I told him I was going to San Marino and at once he remembered that he had a cousin who was a cab-driver and would drive me cheap in a good carriage and serve me well. Do you know how he said that? '*Chara ben chervito, chignore.*' I could have sworn I was at Volvi or the Tour d'Auvergne."

The road became more difficult and the Marquis was silent and I thought : " But he knows the Uffizi much better than I thought : and really his Italian is not so bad, for him to converse with a man of the people. It was his accent that made me think poorly of it : but then I too must have an accent. . . . And he drives very well. . . . I have really done well to throw in my lot with him."

We were passing a little pink painted house on which I read : " Caffé Repubblicano."

"Did you see that, Putouarey? We must have passed the frontier and are in your little circle ! "

"We passed it ten minutes ago at the bridge. And we are ten kilometres from the capital. I am deeply moved, my dear fellow, a new country entered, a State, in fine a country, with its traditions, a flag, postage-stamps. . . . And there are the first houses of Serra-valle, the second town of the republic after San Marino. We'll stop there. Why? To send postcards stamped by the office : it is most important for collectors. We have just passed a frontier, don't you understand ? "

"Well, we're still in Italy. Your Serravalle is an Italian village."

"Oh ! It is much more complicated than that.

You feel many things. It is strange that you have no excitement about little states. The toy-state means nothing to you. I collect them, that is to say, I amass all the official evidence of their existence : stamps, money, flags, arms, boundaries too. I already have Bolivia, Andorra, Monaco, Luxembourg, all the little German States, the Swiss cantons, Campione, Samos . . ."

We stopped in Serravalle and the Marquis plunged into the post office. A quiet village, white and pink, crossed by a white road : here and there the high grey front of a church, or an old town gate surmounted with a stone shield. A town, in fine, historically more noble than Liverpool.

"That is not all," said the Marquis, worn out with affixing two or three hundred stamps : "We must set free the *grillo canterino*. Yes. The one the little Italian count gave you, that sings so loudly in its little cage. Ma guarda ! Did you think I was going to leave it to the mercies of all those Swiss servants ? I brought it with me.—Baptiste, the little cage in the bottom case of the manicure box : ecco—we'll make it a citizen of San Marino. Are you coming ? "

I let him go alone to the end of the street. We set out again :

" A horrible thing has happened, my dear fellow. Yes. The cricket. I was holding the door of the little cage open by the grass. And, I don't know how it happened, just as he was coming out, the door shut to on him and crushed in his little chest. I tried to pull the door back again and the same thing happened : clumsy fool I am ! At last he fell down on the grass, on his back, with his feet all together : he seemed to be saying to me : ' See what you have done ! ' He had a great wound under his thigh and a drop of horrid looking water was oozing from it. I could have hit myself. I turned him over on his feet : he dragged himself a little way over the grass and hid himself under a tuft of mint. Poor little black prince with his armour so clean and fine ! I had one a year or two ago in Florence. And I often used to watch him eat greenstuff in his cage : his fore head rounded, his eyes sticking out on prongs, his mandibles functioning deftly : he used to look like a scientist solving a problem. There may have been something we could have done for yours. Ah ! I hope he will recover ! "

Suddenly, at a bend, the Titano appeared, rising above the plain and above the sea, solidly set on a base of brown earth. And above us, rising out of an island of clouds, the three peaks hung in the sky and their muscles of stone stood out in the light. The sky had been raised like the curtain of a theatre and that was what we saw : a promontory of the heavens.

" My goodness ! " said Putouarey, in amazement. " I've been seeing it ever since Cesena, but as a great blue-grey jagged tracing against a sky-blue background. Voracious, my boy, we are going to climb into the other world."

The clouds had melted. A great white cloud crept gradually from behind the high summit and seemed to emanate from the stone. And the rock appeared naked and unashamed in one quivering leap. High up, like paper boats on the top of a monstrous wave, one could see the three towers of the Three Peaks, walls, a bit of round roof. But that was nothing. What one saw particularly was the land piled up on the land, the land higher in the air than a bird : and the brow of stone pondering above all human preoccupation.

We had just crossed the Borgo, with its terraces, its market square lined with trees and their shadows, its piazza with dark arcades, its quays against the sky. One more change of gear—the Voracious eating up the road more slowly, but chewing it better—a cautious effort and we were climbing in the very shadow of the mountain, with the Marquis leaning over the driving wheel taking marvellous turns. At the corner we came out into the sunlight, and the shadow of the Voracious, for the space of a second blotched the plain five hundred metres below us. And soon, snorting with restrained force, we passed under the gate of the Citta. A severe, grey gate with a sort of machicolated balcony surmounted with a stone shield. The city of a period when life was more seriously lived than it is now, with narrow, steep, dark streets, fairly clean and fresh and I suppose, for eight months in the year swept by a cold wind that is no joke. The stone of the houses has been quarried from the rock and melts into it in the same pinkish-grey tint, as an ant-heap town is lost on a forest floor. And the Citta is indeed compact as an ant-heap, tight as a clenched fist.

" A little nation, but a great people," said Putouarey. " Look at the inscriptions there : ' We demand the right to vote. We demand universal suffrage.' They might as well give it them : there are not so many of them : it would not greatly complicate the accounts. If I could I would give them universal suffrage."

And the Marquis turned and reviewed his handsome bags at a glance.

" At least they do know what they want. Not like the people at Putouarey. To think that we are no longer in Italy ! and that in the air waves the white and blue flag of a republic. My poor Archibaldo, my delight must seem childish to you. You're not annoyed with me for having dragged you here ? "

" Not at all. This fresh light air is good after the furnace of the Aemilian plains."

I shall sleep to-night. Yesterday at Rimini I wrote until day feeling much too full of life to go to bed. Here it is like being on a great ship with a thousand portholes becalmed on the high aerial seas.

P., who does not keep a diary, is getting ready to go out. Arriverderci !

He thrusts his dignified impudent face through the opening of the door.

" Ciaò, bel faccin ! "

I am glad I met him. He drags me in the wake of his energy. And also I am finding him out much better than in our other two meetings : his curiosities, and his tenderness over the cricket. I must make him talk again.

San Marino,

7 June.

Spent the whole morning on the Pianello. It is a great tiled terrace with a stone parapet, looking out over a vast untidy heap of mountains : the Central Apennines with all their bric-à-brac huddled together ; stools, tables, desks and marble chairs, domes, great polygons of bare stone : the most commonplace of mountain ranges : cold without snow, and barren without majesty, mean and sour, the poor relatives of the Alps. To the north-west rises an enormous rock cleft with a great gap, the work of some vanished species, those who occupied the world before us and made a different use of it, an inexplicable gate, the terminus of some service of interplanetary communications. Our eyes are drawn to it, expecting something to come from the other side. An armed angel coming down the roads of the air to take his seat there. To the south on the horizon, a great cube of polished steel, ill-supported, leans over and rests against a corner of the sky. The bed of a wide river of grey sand, where there is still a slight trickle of water, takes in all the visible landscape in its pale embrace : and beyond, the air, the earth and the sea all become one mist, a dirty blue.

For a long time we walked up and down between the dark portico of the Palazzo Governativo and the little low post office with its grey tower and handless dial, its stone seat beneath the parallel lines of the standards of weights and measures embedded in the wall. A line of bare grey houses, with shutters of faded green, ends the square opposite the parapet. One house is a café. From early in the morning they cast a band of shadow over the flagstones, which get narrower and narrower until midday. In the centre of the Pianello is a fountain, old and grey also, supporting a new and conventional statue of Liberty.

"Given," P. told me, "by a rich German woman who received in return the title of Duchess of Acquaviva. Not a joke. One of the villages of the Republic is called

Acquaviva. And the Palazzo, eh? That's new too: but bearable, a recent descendant of the Palazzo Vecchio. Notice the machicolation, the tower and the shields and medallions set on the front."

Then, in the street which at the bottom of the Pianello goes between the low iron gates of the Palazzo and the line of houses, we discovered the Cantone, a little square of beaten earth, planted with a few acacias, with a stone parapet hanging over the side of the rock just above the little red roofs and little white streets of the Burgo, three hundred metres below where we stood.

" Look ! " said P., holding out his big Zeiss. " The Rimini diligence just leaving Serravalle. There in the patch of green crossed by a road. Ecco ! Astonishing that it should be able to come up to us here without leaving the earth."

Near us the wind combs back the hornbeam and brambles which clothe the rock, an east wind full of the scent of the Adriatic, with sudden leaps and shakes, impatiently, as though it were saying : " Come on ! " A man crosses the triangular piazza of the Borgo : it is like the movement of an insect across a sheet of white paper : he disappears in the little black cavern of the arcades.

" There must be a letter for me at the poste restante," said P.

Fifty paces and we were in the post office. And there was a letter for him.

" But it is your own writing, Putouarey ! Do you write to yourself ? "

" Always when I go from one town to another. It

154

makes me feel as though I were expected. And I like seeing my own handwriting."

I asked him what he could find to write to himself and I persisted until he showed me the letter :

" Have you had a good journey, you limb of obscurantism ? I am sorry to hear it. When will you break your neck in your 100 h.p. It is no good your hiding your real opinions beneath the stolen epithets of an independent republican. There is no deceiving the democracy. You are only a social parasite, a useless viveur . . ."

" What does that mean, marquis ? "

" Ma chè ? I didn't know what to write. Oh ! It is one of the charming things they said and wrote to me last January, when to please my wife and family, I stood for the legislative elections at Putouarey."

" Tell me about it."

" There is nothing to tell. It was a matter of finding a substitute for a conservative deputy who had moved up to the Senate. I was sick of the whole affair even before it began. However I held a public meeting to which I invited my opponent ; the socialist candidate, Rabot, the schoolmaster at Putouarey. I began by telling the electors that they ought not to delude themselves, that their vote could not alter the existing social order. That it was only a matter of procuring privileges for the people of the district : decorations, tobacco shops, scholarships, salaries, etc. That by the mere fact of my connections in Paris I was in a position to do more for them than my opponent if he were elected. That I felt disposed to serve them with all my power if they would honour me with their votes. And finally I gave them to understand that, if there ever came up any question of importance to the district, such as the concession of a narrow gauge railway, I should not hesitate to vote with the majority, even counter to the opinions I had advertised in my programme.

"It was clear and sensible. But, Madonna! They thought I was making fun of them and their republic and would only listen to Rabot, who gave them a lot of nonsense and trotted out all the commonplaces invented during the last hundred years by the disordered imaginations of the great dyspeptics.

"That was when I was accused of being a 'social parasite' supported by the right-thinking bourgeoises, the bigots of free-thought. For, of course, I had the clergy, the nobility (and common sense) on my side. But these good ladies were infuriated at not being received at the château. They said that 'since his marriage young Putouarey has gone wrong, he is never seen in the country and spends all his time in Paris on the spree.' To the good people of Putouarey I fancy 'the spree' means one of those pictures that one sees in the comic papers : Maxim's, a gentleman in evening dress with a woman on each knee, with empty champagne bottles under the table. . . . I suppose they see me like that. A man who leads such a life must be devoid of sense or knowledge, eh ? From that time on allusions to Maxim's and champagne glasses became frequent in my opponent's speeches. Poor Rabot! Poor little pedagogue. I should love to give him a night's 'spree' at Maxim's, myself too (with him, it would have amused me). So in his eyes I came to stand for the brute, the anti-intellectual, the eldest son spoiled by idleness and debauchery. At last he accused me of not being able to spell. A few more days of the struggle between progress and obscurantism and I should not have been able to read or write.

"On the day when he was elected I rejoiced. So it was all over, ended as it had to end. I had not a single vote outside the châteaux. And they came and hissed me in chorus at the park gates. I was happy. However there were some of the men I liked very much : Travaillot, the wheelwright, the curé's *bête-noire*, who called himself an anarchist, but with the finest head in the country, an open, honest fellow. I was beaten : the march of Progress was not arrested.

"'It was your wish,' I said to my wife who stood there pale, clenching her rather long teeth. 'Well, I'm quite pleased. Long live Rabot, Madame, and down with Putouarey !'

"And really I was very pleased that it was Rabot who had won the nine thousand francs a year and the free first-class journeys. If it will enlarge his horizon, and the life of Paris brightens him up—so much the better ! I ran to the bathroom and washed and douched myself for three hours. At dawn I was at the wheel of the Voracious on the road to Dijon. All day long I swept through the wide country along the Saône and the Rhone, and that night at eleven I lit my hunting pipe on the pavement of Cannebière : Good God ! There were still splendid days in front of me."

"And it was then you left for Naples ? "

"I spent a month on the Riviera, sometimes on my yacht, sometimes on the road with the Voracious. At Genoa I put the Voracious on the yacht and we set out

for Naples putting in at Portoferrajo . . . Ma scusa :
I have several things to do : visit the Palazzo, get a few
specimens of the rock . . ."

" And fix ten thousand postage stamps to as many
cards. . . . I'll follow you to the Palazzo."

We saw the little Palazzo of grey-pink stone with
its long windows opening on to the same aerial ocean,
the depths of which emerged into the dunes, the hills,
the dim confused vegetation. We saw the assembly
hall of the Council with the twin thrones of the two
Regents, the white urn and the blue urn, the balls which
served as votes. P. was moved by a portrait of Maréchal
MacMahon, a horrible red and blue thing, crude and
glistening.

We visited the principal church, the Pieve, in a mournful classical style, without conviction, in a pretty little
piazza from which one looks down on the roof of the
Palazzo.

" There was something better here ; a fifth-century
church : but they pulled it down," said P., who had set
himself to read the *Ricordi Storici* of Marino Fattori,
and before he came here, had made a good collection of
works about San Marino. The streets mount steeply
up between the tall houses of rough stone and the walls
where little gates open into the gardens : Via Bramanti,
for instance. We came back to the Piazzetta, following
the slope, and from there to the Bastions by the long Via
Omerelli, where the museum is, and a big college, a church
in the emphatic style of the Jesuits, a convent, palazzi,
and suddenly, behind the ancient stone of a parapet, once
more the abyss.

P. was so keen on seeing everything in his beloved

republic that I said to him as we were eating our merlusse in the sitting-room :

" You should become a naturalized San Marinian."

I had opened the flood-gates to the torrents of knowledge with which the Marquis was full. I had to hear everything : the conditions on which naturalization is granted in the republic of San Marino : the origin of the republic, its history, the history of its political status, its constitution, the Aringo of the Fathers of Families, the grand Consiglio, the Consiglio dei Dodici, the two Regents elected every six months, one noble, the other non-noble, and how in the twelfth century they bore, and still bear, in the pompous inscriptions of the Palazzo, the title of Consul. And the inhabitants of a certain Canton who for a long time have had no citizen's rights being regarded as a conquered race. . . .

" That's very funny."

" Ah ! Archibaldo, do not laugh ! It is all that is left, through the communes of the Middle Ages of the Roman Republic, this little piece of rock, this republic consigned to the heavens ! And the San Marinian army . . ."

" No, Gaetano, the Monegascon army is enough for me."

But I had to listen to a description of the uniforms and the composition of the Army : noble, grand, militia, etc. By the way, were there no soldiers to be seen ? Our ceremonious Salernian was at once summoned, and on our desire being expressed, he brought us postcards on which were depicted in colour various San Marinian soldiers.

" Ah ? There are none to be seen in the flesh,"

159

said the Marquis disappointed. " Do you sell these cards ? "

And off he went, spurred on by all his rich man's manias, stamp collecting, minerals, coins, cigarette packets, little flags . . .

" My dear fellow, if there are many people like you, in ten years San Marino will have become one of the chief places in the world for stamp-cases : the republic's coinage, instead of being used for exchange, will be sold as curiosities in the shops at three times their value, and the host of the Albergo Repubblicano will have become so skilful at fleecing travellers that San Marino will have become uninhabitable."

Back he comes with a blue and white flag in one hand and a bag full of pebbles in the other. We are going out to smoke on the Pianello.

8 June.

" Well, social parasite, are you still going to the devil ? You are never seen at home. Young Putouarey is kicking over the traces. Really I never have the pleasure of your company except when it is time for merlusse."

" Me ! It is you who won't go with me."

" It is quite an exploit to go up to the Pianella and when I get there I stay there smoking cigars and chatting with the carabinier."

" I have photographed him and made a note of his uniform. But his grey tunic with its red collar is not a summer outfit. It is very important. . . . Have a liqueur ? Senti padrone : c'è alkermes ? "

" Nelépa monsié."

" That's a pity : alkermes is delicious with water. Shall we have Strega then ? Va bene, ci da due Streghe."

" Biennemonsu ielaporte soubite."

I asked the Marquis what alkermes was.

" What ? You have lived in Florence and never tasted it ? I know what it is. You stayed at the Carlton and never had the courage to take the plunge into the life of Florence. It would have been much better to go and stay with the Assunta and all her nieces. The ragamuffins of the portico of the Uffizi of whom you have spoken so enthusiastically—I suppose you never dreamed of entering into relations with them ? I knew all that at the beginning of my European life : indolence and disgust. . . . You don't stay with the native because you are afraid of domestic insects. You must have your central heating and carpets everywhere : you must have the Palace and not the Palazzo : and it bores you to go and find your bath outside : you want it six yards from your bed."

" I can do without comfort. Here, for instance. And elsewhere. It is true that in Florence this time ——"

" But in Florence there are not only your museums : there is the life of Florence which is also worthy of attention. And encounters in the streets,—You passed the best by. And the opportunities one has, when one lives with the natives, of giving enough Denaro for everything to go off nicely and gracefully : The Florentine women, Archibaldo, are the finest in Italy. Their skins, the colour of the ripe corn, the plump little cakes of hot polenta which I hope you have tasted with more than a sip of your lips ? And its architecture, clean and without

effort ! like a new pea out of the pod.   The classic skin.
They always make me think of Virgil and the Abbé
Vernet who used to make me explain : ' Corpora lectis-
sima matrum . . .'   Ah !   How can one but love Italy
when one has held in his hands such lovely fruit.

" *Salve, magna parens frugum, tibi, tibi.* . . . I don't
know any more.   And the neck and shoulders ?   Have
you noticed them ?   The noble fragility, the brown burning
depths under the flaming crown of black hair ?   How
can you pass that by, all the lovely life which I adore
with all my heart, as with all my heart I lap up those sandwiches filled with sunshine. . . . At least ; have you ever
dined in a real Florentine trattoria ?   Have you ever
played lotto ? or waited impatiently for the Saturday
evening estragione ? . . . Good.   We'll go round the
Palazzo once more.   And do you want to see the law
courts on the right of the street which leads up to the
Pieve ?

9 *June.*

Went with the Marquis to the Borgo by the high road.
Walked for an hour under the arcades of the triangular
piazza we saw so small from the Cantione.   And drank
wine in a sort of trattoria set in the icy hollow of a cave.

The shops in the Borgo are not so poor as those in the
Citta and one feels nearer the great facilities of the
plain.

" I should like some coffee with cream *granite*," murmured P., finishing his glass of red Chianti.   " Do you
think we should find some at Rimini."

A storm was threatening the Titano and already we
could hear the thunder.   We climbed back to the Citta

as the first drops were falling, by the paved path which goes up almost sheer, hanging on to the side of the rock, and ends in a low vault at the end of the Via Omerelli. We returned there in the evening and stayed sitting on the edge of the bastion, watching the great towns with the flashing lights breathing afar off in the great plain.

10 June.

P. was disappointed this morning, he counted on seeing the Regents on their thrones in their costumes at a High Mass in the Pieve. He consoled himself by thinking that to-morrow, Monday, there will be a meeting of the Grand Council in the Palazzo.

This afternoon he succeeded in dragging me to the fortress of the Rocca, the finest of the Three Peaks. Truly the Citta is perched on the top of a wave of stone. On the ridge, between the quarries which never cease to ring with the full soft sound of hammers on the stone, a narrow road goes straight up to the austere gate of the fortress. It is a prison, apparently, and P. must have asked for permission to see over it. We were taken to the parade ground.

" Eight hundred metres above the sea. Drink the virgin air, bubbling like the water of a mountain stream. And look at the view : the coast where the Adriatic makes a little white movement and says something one cannot catch, and the earth terribly calm beneath the sky, like the jaws of a loaded gun. Yonder the Marecchia, dried up, throwing out its great road of grey sand to the sea. And how useless those roads seem and yet with all their windings they mount up towards us."

We came down again with all the mountains at our feet. We turned and saw the three towers standing on the edge of the abyss, little, grey, square, with their almost flat roofs of bricks, each surmounted with a little iron feather to remind one of the pun on *Penna* which means both feather and peak . . .

This evening we smoked our " best cigars " on the Pianello and went up to the Cantone where thousands of fireflies were shining. It was as though the air had suddenly allowed one to guess a great secret, and revealed its true nature of fire. Sometimes they would be put out and lighted again in the same moment ; and sometimes it was as if one had shaken out an immense black veil filled with gold spangles. In the hollow of a stone, on the edge of a road with overgrown stones, a glow-worm was tending his drop of lunar light. The sea wind, full of whisperings, was visiting the rocks and the leaves.

11 *June.*

As I was walking outside the St. Francis Gate, waiting, with several boys, one of the two carabiniers and an old woman, for the arrival of the diligence, the Marquis came and joined me all out of breath.

" Archibaldo, if you wish to see the San Marino soldiers now is your opportunity. The Palazzo is full of *gardes-nobles* in uniform. Because of the Council. Come quick."

We climbed up to the Pianello. Just then a gentleman in a black frock coat, followed by a kind of valet in blue and silver livery with a cocked hat passed near us, crossed the Piazza and entered the Palazzo.

" One of the regents," said P. " We ought to have

164

taken off our hats to him. We can go in : they don't
say anything to me."

(They are beginning to know him.)

A dozen tall fellows in sea-blue uniforms with orange-
yellow facings and stripes, with cocked hats of the same
blue with a bunch of blue and white feathers, and swords
at their sides, were lounging in the hall of the Palazzo.

"Archibaldo, have you never thought of the moral
utility of uniform, as a thing which makes us more visible
physically and conceals our personality more than any
disguise ? It helps us to dispense with any need for
explanation. Hallo. 'Bon giorno. Lei sta bene ? '"

"So you have friends in the noble-guard ? I suspected you were calling on the local aristocracy."

"Yes," said P., rather embarrassed. "It is Cevaliere
Landolfi. I didn't know he was one of the guards.
. . . Besides, they are nobles, all those fine fellows. My
peers. And yours ! I was forgetting that ! I have
been reproached often enough with my nobility. Not
only at Putouarey. So much so that really I need some
courage to keep it up—and that is really the reason why
I go on with it. And to think that there was actually a
time in my provincial days when I was proud of it, because it distinguished me from the bourgeois. Count
Aquibajo, do you know what nobility is. I mean noble
birth ? You know the French saying ' *Noblesse oblige.*'
Well, that is the definition of nobility : it compels you
to do nothing else. It used to compel its possessor to be
nothing but a man attached to an estate, and the vassal
of the man to whom the homage of that estate was due.
And it is not done with yet. It is as though we had no
names. The estate lends us its indestructible name which

will pass to others after us, either by succession or marriage. No hope of *making a name* for ourselves, it has been already made for us, too long and too complicated for us to know what to do with it, or for it to find a place in the modern world : a heavy suit of armour in which we have to fight the battle of life. You talk of the pitiful condition of the millionaires but there is something to be said for us. The commoners do at least have their names to themselves, applied to their flesh and blood and it comes to an end with their descendants. They fight with free limbs, unhampered by anything. They can make a name for themselves if they have anything in them. It seems to me so distinguished, when, in a room full of commonplace titled people, a man is announced whose identity is expressed in a simple name. I find myself envying him. He becomes at once the interesting minority, the elect of the elect. It is so true that when one of us rises by his personal worth to the highest ranks of humanity he at once loses his title : people say : La Rochefoucauld, Saint-Simon, Vigny. . . . But for us, the general run of noblemen, our nobility is nothing but an obligation, obedience, circumspection, sacrifice. That is why I cannot bear the d'Escarbogneas at home near us in the country : they have no idea of that obligation : their nobility does not make them heroic : but, like the parvenus who cannot get used to their wealth, they can't get away from the fact of their nobility, and one hears them talking about their bourgeois neighbours, who are idiotically proud of their money, which they despise. I have discovered the meaning of my coat of arms and coronet. . . . And my poor young brother, who was killed at twenty-three on Lake Tchad,—I have his

photograph in the uniform of a Senegal Spahi in my bag
—he knew it too, better than I, the obligation of nobility.
Glory ?   He knew it was not so !   A few papers published his portrait as a Man who Died for his Country,
in the Society Notes, and then silence for ever.   A café
concert bill-topper is better treated than that.   But he
tried to live and he did live, nobly.   And I too should
like to live nobly and do something better than chase
about Europe and waste my time.   Do you know what
I am sometimes on the point of doing ? . . . Yes.   I
have . . . a kind of vocation, even I, and I would just
like to give myself up to it.   But then : one would have
to give up all his other hobbies : and that would mean
renouncing the world to a certain extent.   It is hard
when we have everything in our hands.   O Jean, the
December sun on the Riviera, speed—the world opening
out everywhere, offering its valleys, its towns, its foods,
its kisses—and a bullet in the head by Lake Tchad."

12 June.

P. is happy.   Yesterday, after the sitting of the Grand
Council, he was received in audience by one of the
Regents (the non-noble as it happened), and he returned
quite excited from the interview.   This morning I said
to him :

" Well, what are we doing here ?   You have bought
all the stamps of the latest issue and there are no more
post cards at the stationers.   What are you plotting with
your friends of the noble guard ?   You know there is
no deceiving the democracy ? "

" You want to go," said the Marquis downcast.

" Not if you insist on staying.   It is fine : I have

nothing to do anywhere. But I should like to know when you think of going."

" I have telegraphed to my banker in France to send me some money. We will leave the day after the letter of credit comes. I've a few more post cards to send to-day : an old series I found in rummaging through the lumber-room at the grocery."

We sent them all over the place : P. to thirty young women scattered in five or six different countries not forgetting Angiola Cacace, and I to Stéphane, Cartuyvels, Tournier de Zamble, Maxime Claremoris. (Pity I don't know the name and address of the two men who shadow me for Cartuyvels. Perhaps they are on the Pianello every day, watching us.)

As we were smoking in the Cantone I said to Gaetan :
" My dear fellow. I've been finding you out, and I will frankly confess that I had misunderstood you until now."

" How do you mean ? "

" Yes. I have found in you many things which I never even suspected in our previous dealings."

" Capito. I knew that of course : and what you tell me pleases me. It was the fault of my hobbies, my way of finding everything amusing, and my gallant adventures. You used to think me a coarse man of the world. I felt that. The Duke of Waydbury and Prince Stéphane had the same opinion of me : a French squire rich enough to try to knock the corners off himself by mixing with the great Europeans : a local type, a café-concert Frenchman, a little provincial among you swells of the wagons-lits."

" No, Putouarey, no ! "

" Oh ! yes. Just as the free-thought bigots at Putouarey misjudged me. I remember your saying to me one
day : ' Well, every time you leave France, you progress
a little. I hear you lunch every day with the Duke of
Christminster ! ' "

" You are merciless . . . I meant . . ."

" No. It was quite clear. No offence. I too was
bourgeois and idiot enough to be unable to get away
from the idea of having the same tailor as the King of
England. And so many other stupidities. You were
so sure of the accuracy of your judgment that you never
for a moment thought that I could see your raillery. And
that was why I was not annoyed, and also because I too
thought you were different from what you are : super-
ficial sly, not yet up to the ways of life. It was excus-
able. I am thirty : there is seven years difference between us. Yes I know, it is very painful when one has
to go back on one's rash judgments, very humiliating.
But when it has happened once one doesn't do it again or
one is incorrigible."

" But, Gaetan. I never misjudged you so much as
that ! And it is hard on us swells of the wagons-lits to
be compared to the women of Putouarey. It is true that
I was mistaken, and your gallant adventures were responsible. You see, what I can't understand, in an intelligent
earnest man like yourself is the gross search for physical
sensation in inglorious intrigues—inglorious because they
are not even gratuitous."

" Are you sure that there is not a remnant of Puri-
tanism in you which is shocked when I talk of Angiolina
and sandwiches filled with sunshine ? "

" Anyhow it is a very clear impression : your intrigues

169

seem to me nothing but a waste of time and a squandering of energy."

"Oh. That's a very small affair. . . . And the 'search for physical sensation.' But you're right off the scent. . . . To begin with, this between ourselves, I am not a braggart. . . . But it is difficult to explain ! Your opinion is much nearer than you think to the opinion the ladies of Putouarey have of me. . . . How shall I begin ? . . . Ah ! You like the people, don't you ? You told me decidedly that you preferred the women of the people to the women of society. So do I ! You see what distinguishes us gentlemen from the bourgeois is that we know how to talk to the people : to us they are men and women like ourselves, with all our faults, and all our weaknesses, and all our qualities. We understand them. To the bourgeois they are machines, children who must be protected, and sly vicious brutes who are to be distrusted. At Putouarey the wife of the tax collector always makes her maid walk four yards behind her : she is afraid of the girl's being taken for her friend. That is exactly typical of the middle-class. Am I afraid of being taken for a pal of my chauffeur's ? People can see that I am a gentleman at once by my walk. And even if I were taken for a friend of Baptiste's, what would it matter ? He is a handsome fellow who has bested me on the sly in one of my affairs. Anyhow I am just like your American poet : I treat ' the savage and gentleman on equal terms.' Do you remember your nurse when you were a child ? You had negresses, over there, I suppose, a red Indian ? I shall always remember Marie-Bonne, a great virago from Sombernon in the mountains. She was full of stories and wisdom. How superior were these women of the people to us, more developed in every direction, seeing further and better than we, and full of all the poetry of the truths from which we pretended to turn away in disgust. . . . When we learned how to decline Homo and Dies and Mames, we thought we were very fine and we used to go to them to astonish them with our new knowledge. But they knew much more than we about far more important things, so that when we were with them our Latin seemed no great thing. When I was seventeen I saw Marie-Bonne again. I had finished my classics, and gone to Paris, but I had not caught her up. A few years ago I saw her at Sombernon. It was after my first travels : I was married, had lived—but she was still ahead of me. . . . She knows as much as life. . . .

" And I understood that it is useless to try, and that the people will always know more than we. . . . ' Physical sensation ? ' . . . Oh, no . . . it is you I am looking for, Marie-Bonne, and you I find, the Maries of my country with their lovely stories, their boundless wisdom, and their uncalculating gentleness, the trust, and into the bargain, the majesty of the People.

" Yes. That will seem to you a post facto explanation : rhetorical justification. And it would have seemed more probable to you if I had told you that I was out for a collection of memories of women, and nothing else. And there is something of that in it too. But it is above all a need of contact with the people, my need of Marie-Bonnes, my intrigues are hardly flattering to myself ? I have not always had to do with people like the Cacaces. My beard and I have been known to be appreciated. And isn't it just that I should give back

to the people something of what I have had from them ?
Knowledge of its heart and its life ?   My intrigue with
Angiola taught me more of Naples than I could ever have
got from all the novels of Madame Serao.   I remember
all the women I have known : the big Spaniards with
their orange skins, the Germans with their stifling kisses,
the Hungarians who are like the realization of some
ancient dream and the little Russian cocottes who swoon
away in Italian. . . . *Et mores et studia* as the Abbé
Vernet used to say.   Poor man he would be unhappy if
he knew the life I led.   He would never understand
either that it is a question of *mores et studia.*   He too
would think I was seeking a coarse sensation. . . .
But in reality I am a very zealous student of *mores et
studia,* and disposed to pay the needful for learning : and
if, in doing so, I give people like the Cacace a good time,
so much the better.   I should hate seducing girls
and upsetting families.   I prefer to help the poverini.
They are never very bad and it gives them so much
pleasure.

" Indeed I would rather spend a thousand francs on
the Cacace than lose a hundred at poker to my neighbours
the de Cudebœufs who can talk of nothing but the mar-
kets and pass idiotic comments on the leading article in
the *Gazette de France.*   Are there any men to whom a
woman is a distraction, or an amusement ?   A few brutes.
I tell you that to me they are a study, an austere and pro-
tracted study.   Like chemistry, but more complicated,
and demanding much less egoism.   Take that from me
and now judge me and my gallant adventures.   What do
you know of a country if you don't know the people, or
of the people if you have never lived in contact with

them ? Contact lip to lip—but I am shocking you again. . . ."

I wanted to tell him the thought that came to my mind.

" You are living like Montaigne and Stendhal, but you are greater than they and despise writing." But one doesn't say those things.

13 June.

Once again after breakfast, as we were walking in the strip of shadows on the Pianello :

" But, my dear Gaetan, how did you ever come to adopt this way of living ? How did you *kick over the traces.*"

" Don't expect me to tell you my life. . . . I can understand your curiosity. We men of the governing classes are as a rule determined by our class, we find life ready made : we are taken early and put through a sort of preparation, not quite but something more serious than having our feet bound, since we are put in blinkers and have nothing to do but follow the beaten track with our equals. In effect, you want to know how I became irregular. I say nothing of my travels : that are those of my class : we are even beginning to spend our honeymoons in Japan and the winter at the source of the Nile. My irregularity begins in my wife's absence and is continued logically by association with people in the Via Mazza cannone.

" Oh yes. I found my life ready made. My parents died when I was young and I was brought up by my maternal grandmother at Putouarey. She began by separating me from my brother with whom, till then, I had shared everything. He was sent to school in Paris and then entered at Saint Cyr. I was delicate, it appears, and my grandmother had ideas about the education of eldest sons. And everything was done in accordance with the programme she had mapped out. I grew up with my tutor, the Abbé Vernet, who cultivated my mind and my manners, and our groom Ducarouge who taught me to fence and ride, and took me out hunting. When I went to Paris to take my first examination the Abbé Vernet and my grandmother accompanied me. To read for the second I was sent to a school in Paris as a day-boarder : but the Abbé Vernet and my grandmother used to wait for me at the gates and Ducarouge used to go with me for walks in the Bois. Ah ! They did as they liked with me, drove me from school to the little provincial Faculty, where, in disgust, I deliberately got myself plucked in the law examination : then to the army, anticipating the call to the flag by a year. With her whole mind concentrated on the future my grandmother had arranged for everything. She came to live in the hotel in the town where I was quartered. Our cousins the Carancys happened to come and stay in the same hotel for a time, to see the town which is what is known as a show place. When my year of voluntary service was up I was betrothed to Marie de Carancy. I left barracks for marriage. The following year, within a few months of each other, the Abbé Vernet and my grandmother died.

"But I too had lived with my mind on the future. In going through an old chest of drawers hidden away in an attic at home I found the atlas I had as a boy, and I saw in it the imaginary journeys I had drawn over the

map in red pencil and the names of the towns I had under-
lined.   And in sketching out a journey in Italy I had
even put a mark of interrogation against the name of San
Marino.   I too had lived in the future and foreseen
everything, but unconsciously.   Only I did not know
that there would come a time when my life would be
given back to me and I should have permission to do as I
liked.   I cannot say that I was very unhappy waiting
for the time when my time would come.   But the dear
old lady and the good Abbé were sitting on me hard and
would not let me get up.   They were hatching me.   It
was a physical impression : in all the photographs taken
at that time I am round shouldered and stooping, and at
Stanislas I was nicknamed the Humpback.   They were
sitting hard on me but they were very light. . . . Besides it was a time of probation.   Even the friends they
chose for me were temporary.   I was waiting for the
time when my travels would begin.   The question mark
against San Marino on the map did not mean : 'Shall I
go there ?' but 'Is it worth while going there ?'   (I was
more reasonable or less of a collector than I am now.)
But. . . .   I remember :   I even made a journey to
Italy, during those years of probation, with the Abbé
Vernet.   Twenty-five days and a circular ticket.   But
it was the Italy of Putouarey.   I was taken there in my
cage : it did not count (though I saw a good deal through
the bars).   Those years did not count either : they were
not mine : my grandmother, the Abbé Vernet and Du
Caroupe robbed me of them, and, as I had been well
brought up, I let them.   They were my grandmother's
years :   really, when I look back on them now, I can't
see myself in them.

"My dear fellow, it is a delicate question. Proud and cold, yes, but you mustn't think the least ill of Madame de Putouarey : all the fault is on my side. It was a sad mistake. My grandmother chose a substitute for herself, another broody hen, but younger and more vigorous. And I behaved like a fool, like a school boy trying to seduce his mother's maid. I assumed a brutality, a masterful Don Juanesque manner which is not in my character. I am ashamed to think of it. . . . Fortunately, the following winter in Paris, a woman of our world, a school friend of my wife's, took me in hand and made me see reason. But the mistake was irreparable. And above all I had felt that I was free. There was an unforgettable night in February. I was alone in my room and I felt that for the first time in my life, I was alone. My turn had come. I trembled with happiness. Tenderly I kissed the portrait of my grandmother and the Abbé. I thanked them for having made such joy possible for me and I regretted that they could not share my luck. They were incapable of it. How they must have wept that night in their graves, poor old things. . . . All the work of their life undone to the very last stitch. But it was neither my fault nor theirs.

"Then I looked round me. At all the middle-class people hugging their money : and the nobles their nobility. I had been taken for one of the two : and cut to the measure of my class and province. But my turn had come and I was not satisfied : and everywhere the mould was cracking and giving to my sudden growth. There was no obstacle : *she* had voluntarily withdrawn to the room to which I had lost my right of entry since she had taken it for her own. . . . Ah ! swiftly . . .

other forms, other ideas, something beyond such imbecile satisfaction. Another air, other thoughts. . . .

" I once had a German governess for a few months. The next day, at lunch, I told my wife that I was going that evening to Karlsruhe, alone, to learn the language. She said nothing : besides, my mind was made up. That very evening I got into the express at the Gare de l'Est, and that was the first day of the Year I of my epoch.

" The following week I returned to Putouarey beaten. I had discovered that governesses are no use, and that one cannot learn anything without trouble. I was beaten but I did not despair. And I knew now that the cage was open. You should have seen me at that time, Archibaldo—during the year I spent at Putouarey. It was heroic. My days and nights : the use I made of my time : grammar, history, chemistry, picked up where I left it at school, and my long vigils, sometimes up till dawn, with a German-French dictionary and a cheap copy of Wilhelm Meister. Words. . . . With every new word I learned I felt that I had filed a bit more through the bars of my prison. I loved the words : I absorbed their life. Sometimes I could not tell exactly how to pronounce them, but I stored them up in my heart letter by letter. You will understand that it was not only a matter of Wilhelm Meister nor even of German literature and philosophy : but of exercising my mind, and, how shall I say it ? contact with other minds, and of having at last forced open the gates of the world of thought. And my bag was then packed ready on another table in my room.

" A whole year. And once more I took the train to Germany, to Deutsch-Arricourt : it was as though I had discovered a new sense : I understood what people round me were saying. . . . I entered my name on the Faculty of science at Berlin. It was a different affair from the idiotic examinations I had been made to pass, the substance of which seemed to be nothing but a systematic contradiction of the religious instruction I had, on the other hand, been given. . . . And since then, every day, or almost, I have been discovering new senses. My life interested me enormously. I rose, I expanded, I reached out in many directions. I had been sat on for such a long time. . . . One day a blade of grass crushed to the earth, took life, shivered and slowly stood up. I regained my childhood : sometimes it even seems to me that I am becoming good again. And perhaps one day, if it goes on, I shall end by becoming a faithful husband and a father who will know how to bring his children up severely.

" Basta. I have a letter to write. To a woman, a reply to this announcement in the paper."

And the Marquis held out a Roman newspaper among the advertisements of which I read :

Attraversando triste periodo, signora, giovone, simpatica finemente educata, prego facoltoso gentiluomo per piccolo aiuto. Riconoscentissima. Scrivere. A. X. 2.24. fermo posta.

14 *June.*

A blank day with no Putouarey to fill it with words. (He has gone in the Voracious to visit the Castelli of the Republic and I refused to go with him. It is too hot.) Went by the Via Omerelli and the bastions, then by the road to the little Capuchin convent. An enormous spider

178

was hanging under the portico.   Revisited the Museum and the Hospital.   Those two institutions owe much to strangers.   I read the list of donors : several names known to the great bank (London, New York, Paris) I contented myself with putting a handful of English sovereigns into the poor box in the chapel.

Turned over an anthology of contemporary German poetry.   Extremely sensual.   Every verse was a young houri with perfumed veils.

Thought of P. forcing the gates of the world of thought, he too.   Seven years older than I, like Stéphane. . . .

There is the little girl who lights all the street lamps in the capital : with one hand she carries her long stick extended, on the end of which quivers a drop of light and with the other she holds by the arm, her draggle-haired, sulky little sister who deliberately drags behind.

15 *June.*

This evening on the Cantone as we smoked our cigars among the fireflies I said to the Marquis :

" Even here, like the scent of a hidden flower, one feels the sweetness of Italian life.   But I suppose every foreigner feels it differently, each according to his country and character.   You, a Frenchman, must be very near it."

" Not so near neither !   We come to Italy with our French notions, without a qualm, just because of the *fratellanza*, and singing, like conscripts going to a bawdy house.   And then we perceive that Italy is not that, that the Italians are not all of the south, that the weather is not nearly so fine as we had thought.   Blue sky, love, carelessness, the reins of strong passions loosed, all

179

that I thought Italian was brought by myself from home with scraps of poetry by Musset and Gautier. They are much more practical and less easily carried away than we are. I wonder sometimes—oh ! blasphemy !—whether taken as a whole they have as much taste as we for pleasure and the fine arts. I don't know their literature. I suppose they have developed in another direction. Not excessively, I bet. Take their oaths for instance : how calmly they speak even the most horrible. It is we Frenchmen who finish them off with exclamation marks. And the melancholy and rudimentary debauchery of the chiassi is not exactly the love we expect to find. Love of money is the ruling passion. They often remind me of the characters in a classical comedy who, when purses were put into their hands, cried at once : ' Ah ! If you give reasons of that kind ! ' The Denaro justifies so many things in their eyes and they need so little of it ! And as for the great and famous Italian passions the best I have had in that kind up to now are words like this : ' Tu sei mio bimbo : tu sei mio piccino. Ma, mi piaci sai.' Not much, eh ? And after all I was pleased with that little. It was sincere and I did not deserve as much.

"Eleven already, Dio bono ! I'm going to bed. To-morrow if the money comes I'll pay some farewell calls and I want all these people to see the composed countenance of a French cavaliere."

16 *June*.

The letter of credit has come and we leave to-morrow. It is time. The Pianello and the Cantone are pleasant places, but sometimes one catches oneself wanting more room to walk in. A desire to leave the San Marinians to their political disputes, their dark streets, the fireflies and the wind.

P. has come back pleased with his calls. His eyes told me that all was well. Well, what? Ma chè?

"You should offer the government the crops off the Putouarey vineyards this year and ask in exchange for the title of Prince de Bouvino, Gaetan."

He laughed nervously.

From the Pianello we looked out for the last time at the red sun melting slowly in a vast brown-pink mist, when, one by one, the mountains sank to rest like a herd of fabulous beasts.

"Gaetan, tell me another gallant adventure."

"To shock you again. It is a side of life you don't want to see. At heart you are not really Europeanized and become only an honorary American; not for nothing does a man come from Swedish colonists in the Valley of the Hudson, not in vain does he have three Quaker great-aunts who were called: Faith, Hope and Charity."

"You are quite mistaken."

"Then am I to think you are still at the beginning of life and love? A schoolboy in love with the porter's daughter? My poor dear friend, you know perfectly well that love is not of this world. However, if you want a story, here you are."

"Do you know Birmingham? No? A great industrial town the geographers call it; and I take their word for it. I only know a little corner of it. Colmore Row, where my hotel was, opposite a gloomy church with a graveyard: the big windows of the restaurants and the banks on the other side of the street, reflected the turf and the graves, all among the trams, cabs,—dense traffic. Colmore Row and a few glass-covered passages where I spent my days. There is a network of them with scented branches and luminous blind alleys : under glass roofs, glass walls on both sides of a wide cobbled road —a kind of Italy. And behind those walls of glass are the fruits of the Antilles, all rare flowers, palaces full of toys, others full of good things to eat, grottos of raspberry ice, rivers of milk of almonds. And on the first floor, along the green balconies, the warm kiss of England— you know the slight bitterness and the taste of honey— always waiting for you on the edge of the cups of tea.

" To be freer I had taken a room over the private bar of a pub, near these passages. You must know that too : your heavy luggage in the best room of the best hotel, where you never go except to get letters, and your bag in a room at an inn, where you live ? I have become more knowing and now I go straight to the pub.

" Ah ! The girls I brought back to that room. No ' search for sensation,' no ! A few hours of conversation purchased, contact with other human beings, high knowledge patiently acquired. They were quickly at their ease with me. Neither time nor money wasted, nor energy squandered. There was not one from whom I did not draw some nourishment and learn something. I felt my power of mockery rapidly diminishing. I believe it to be the sign of complete intelligence to find nothing ridiculous. Poor girls, they understood the kind of man they had to deal with and they told me everything. The ' tender North ' as you say : a need of affection, a soft frailty, nothing of the kind here, it is the hard South. I soon got to the point where I could see the ridiculous and understand it so well that one had no mind to laugh.

"Ma guarda! What am I thinking of? I was telling you about the room over the pub and I had not even taken it when there happened what I am about to tell you.

"It must have been the evening after my arrival in Birmingham. I jostled into her at the corner of a dark street. She was tall, neatly dressed : in a long cloak over a dark dress, with a wide cloth cap. She said in answer to my excuses :

"'I am unhappy.'

"'What can I do?' I said. 'Are you hungry?'

"'No. Take me where you like.'

"I dared not take her to my respectable hotel in Colmore Row. I put her into a passing cab and told the driver to take me to a small hotel. He drove us about for nearly an hour and at last stopped outside a lodging-house near a little suburban station. On the way I said :

"'What is your name?'

"'Winifred. They call me Winnie.'

"'You live here?'

"She had arrived the night before from her own country : Wellington, New Zealand. She had come to Birmingham to find a relation, an uncle, I think. She had found on her arrival that he had gone bankrupt some years before and had disappeared, leaving no address. And she was stranded alone in Birmingham.

"Curiosity, perhaps a kind of sadism which a bourgeois, if he had felt it, would have taken for kindness, made me want to help the poor lost girl. I took her hand without thinking what I was doing. She clasped mine warmly and said :

"'Have I found a real friend?' and she brought her face close to mine.

"I understood : she smelt of whisky : she was drunk. But I wanted to see it through.

"I wrote Mr. and Mrs. Smith in the book of the little hotel, paid in advance and joined her in the room they had given us. She was kneeling by the bed, with her face in her hands praying. I stood and waited near a table. A glass of whisky which she had ordered was brought.

"'You'll make yourself ill with that whisky.'

"She did not seem to hear me. After a moment she turned to me with her face wet with tears.

"'Go out. I am going to bed. . . .'

"And as I hesitated :

"'After all, I suppose you may stay.'

"I went to the window and looked out at the night. The bed creaked.

"'I suppose you want to come in now?' she said, 'That was why you brought me here to have the satisfaction of dishonouring a poor girl who is utterly alone and unhappy and will have nothing to eat to-morrow if you don't pay her for the night : Well, what are you waiting for? You see how I am. It won't last long : you'll find me in six months wrecked by drink and misery : a bundle of rags to be kicked out of the way, a bag of bones from which the very beggars will turn. Better make good use of your opportunity, sir. You don't get a good honest, well-brought up girl every day. Why should you hesitate : no one will know, and who will blame you for it? Just acting, you're thinking, eh? A plant : a girl giving herself airs and making a fuss after letting herself be picked up in the streets ! '

" She raised herself on the pillow, gulped down a quantity of whisky and said :

" ' My feet hurt : this foot seems to have been hurting for years. I've walked such a lot these two days after all those weeks of keeping still on the boat. At night I've sometimes thought about the people they used to torture in the Inquisition. A silly pain in my foot ! My boot pinching all day, and going on next day in the same places, and going on at every step. Oh ! If I were strong ! Will you, sir, wash my feet ? '

" You may laugh if you like but I had no mind to refuse. She sat on the edge of the bed. She was really very young, and her life, whatever it may have been, had left no marks on her. One of those big fair girls with rather red complexions and with open eyes, of limpid green. . . . I got through with washing her feet fairly well. And then I put a wet towel round her forehead. I wanted to make her calm enough to listen to me and understand.

" Winifred ? I am sure you are not play-acting and you can count on my entire respect. But will you tell me how it all happened ? You arrived the day before yesterday : you heard of the ruin and disappearance of your uncle. What then ? Where did you spend last night ? You don't come from New Zealand without luggage. Where is it ? Excuse my indiscretion. But I want to help you and get you out of your fix, if I can. I suppose, to pull yourself together you went into a pub, then another and another and so on. . . . It is not your fault. To-morrow there'll be no trace of it. In any case count on me. Do you follow me? Do you hear me? I tell you : you can trust me.

"She looked at me but did not listen. She was following other thoughts and the look she fixed on me was full of contempt and disgust. And suddenly she began to cry in a deep voice :

" ' Thus hast thou abandoned me. After all the years that I have thought myself to be in the shelter of thy arms : in the green meadows, by the calm water. And now will not the Good Shepherd leave His flock to gather up the lost sheep? Ten thousand times ten thousand, but not more! I have no need for *you* to have pity on me, but pray for me to the Lord our God. Winifred. You'll remember Winifred ! '

"She hiccoughed. I said :

" ' Winnie, make an effort. Try to hear me. Do you hear me behind the wall that is keeping you in? Try and feel that I am your friend, that you can trust me and have courage.'

"I was almost shouting. She went on looking at me with those eyes so full of contempt, which I shall never forget : she seemed to see in me what I refused to see then, behind all my pity and tenderness—the base fear of being tricked, a look full of boredom too—so far above me ! And in spite of all there came back and back the thought : The delirium of a drunken prostitute. . . .

" ' Come and kiss me,' she said suddenly, in a sharp voice. ' Come on. Like brother and sister. I know you won't do any harm now.'

"I stooped to her brow, but she made a sudden movement and brought our lips together. Whisky gives kisses a taste of new milk.

"Her head fell back on the pillow on the coils of her bright hair. She was already asleep. And I stayed there going over every jesting word, intonation, but of course came to no conclusion.

"And a moment came when I felt worn out and ridiculous, sitting there in an arm-chair by the bed, a yard or so away from the basin in which I had washed the girl's feet. And the unpaid cab was waiting at the door.

"I wrote a short note, something like this : 'Dear Winnie, here is something to keep you going until five o'clock to-morrow afternoon. I'll be under the Great Western arcade. I beg you to come there. Be sure that you have henceforth *a true friend*.' I placed the paper on the middle of the table and a piece of gold on top of it. I went down without being seen and returned to Colmore Row.

"I had hardly got to bed when I had to get up again. I could not leave Winifred like that alone, in that room which anybody might enter. It was a betrayal : I was morally responsible for this girl, at least until the next morning. I went out and called a cab, but I had forgotten to note the address of the little hotel. I tried to find the driver who had taken me there. But I gave it up. Next day I was under the arcade of the Great Western. She did not come, not the next day, nor the next.

"However, I had set myself sedulously to finding the hotel, I was bursting with impatience. 'If her story is true—the sovereign will be spent by now—she will die of hunger.' Hours in cabs, walking, going over and over a cock-and-bull story, impudent jests to face, contempt to suffer. At last on the third day I recognized the house opposite the suburban station. I had to wait for the girl on night duty. She remembered me and Mrs. Smith. The lady went in the morning without saying anything. And there was the glass of whisky to be paid for.

" Nothing was found in the room ? ' I asked.

" The servant who had cleaned the room was sent for. I repeated my question. She looked sulky. I ventured to speak frankly :

" ' Listen,' I said, taking her aside, ' if you took the sovereign on the table, tell me. I'll give you five, but tell me if you took it or not.'

" She swore that she had seen nothing and that she did not know what I meant. She took the note I held out to her without thanking me : and now she stared me out of countenance as who should say : ' I wonder, after all, if you are an honest man.'

" A waiter brought me a piece of paper on a tray : the bill for the whisky. I paid. Their suspicious faces, all wide-eyed astonishment passed and repassed before me, surrounded me. I should know nothing, and I have never found out. . . . Ah ! the curtain that life lowers, noiselessly, suddenly, just when it was so important to see a little more. . . . A second's weakness in the cold dark water and I have felt the poor hands loosening their grip on me and a weight carried away in an eddy. . . .

" Archibaldo, I am going to sleep. To-morrow morning we start early."

" For ? "

" I am hesitating between Montenegro and the Principality of Lichtenstein. Anyhow, we shall sleep in Venice to-morrow night, don't you think ? I'll address my insulting letter to Venice."

188

Arrived here by the last express, leaving the Voracious at Padua to continue the journey to Trieste overland, where we are to pick it up again. The Marquis is afraid of its being " wrecked " on the boat.

We left San Marino this morning at eight.

We came the whole way in the inside of the car, picking up the country through the glass screens. We went down the familiar road, through the Borgo, and followed the turnings and slopes to Sarravalle. Below us stretched the Aemilian plain, the land of abundance where all the pleasures in the world beckon to us, telling themselves, as we came nearer and nearer, of our arrival with great still joys gazing fixedly as they watched our approach. We let ourselves sink into the boundless blue : we slipped smoothly along the parapets of the sky.

The Marquis was afraid of my having thought him sentimental last night, with his chaste story : and he made a great parade of cynicism, even going so far as to say that the sight of misery was one of the spices of his life. I capped his remarks with the same rather flabby hypocrisy :

" *O the delight of being cruel to the poor !* . . ."

(Yes. I feel in myself that fount of cruelty : I master it, I scorn it, but it is there together with an almost indecent pity which is closely allied to that kind of cruelty.)

" Gaetan, I have thought of an explanation of your Birmingham story. Something horrible. . ."

" Oh ! Tell me."

" Well : suppose the girl had really had five or six

months of—*mala vita*, and whisky. Suppose she really had fallen as she told you, on her arrival from New Zealand, but *six months* before, and was giving you, so to speak, a second performance of her fall, this time with words and all her feelings clearly expressed through her hiccoughs and the scraps of hymns and prayers brought back into her memory by drunkenness ? "

" Capito. Hem ! It's subtle and not so bad either. But it doesn't help me. I am sure she told me the truth. I had saved her. She slept for a long time. The rascally servant girl knocked at the door, had no answer, entered out of curiosity, saw the money and the note explaining it. She did not hesitate : with the meanness of prosperity she told herself that it was not stealing to take money given by a rake to a drunken woman of the streets. And Winifred never knew that she had been saved."

" The poor have no pity for the poor. Oh ! that servant girl ! A daughter of the people. All the same, what about the tenderness and majesty of the people. Marquis ? "

" That's no argument. Besides, what are the people ? You believe there really are classes ? Don't you think the division a very artificial one ? "

" But what does that mystic expression the People stand for to you, Gaetan."

" It's not easy to explain ! Potential ? Dynamic ? Ah ? Ohibo ! How do I know ? Let us say that the People means everything that is not mediocre. We are a species of moral eunuchs : they are fully developed human beings."

We had just passed the Caffe Republicano.

" Here we are back in Italy. How can we leave that great nation without tears ? "

" Oh, rot. I am taking away what I went there to find," cried the Marquis with a joyous grimace. " Where is my bag ? Yes, the big one with gold fittings. Cospetto ! Here it is. Oug ! "

He opened it and rummaged in his leather writing-case which has a delightful smell.

" Caro Archibaldo ! There are the patent, the insignia, the ribbon ! "

" I thought so. Sincere congratulations. How much did they cost you ? "

" Twenty-five francs at the Palais Royal. Yes : the insignia and the ribbon. I have had them a long time in readiness."

He saw my smile in the front screen.

" The patent ? Oh ! that was nothing of course."

" What about the registered letter ? "

" There was for something else. A handful of bank-notes I offered the Ospedale. Big notes."

" They could not do less than add to your collection of ribbons."

" Yes. I wanted it to pay for diplomatic privileges in France, and also to hear the Rabots say that I am decorated with orders as strange as they are foreign. . . . Fortunately I have other hobbies which give me more pleasure. My laboratory, my experiments, my retorts, furnace, and the bitter smell of it all. Do you know what I am doing just now ? Escaping from my laboratory. There is something in it that obsesses me, a problem which is at the back of my every day, of which, in spite of myself, I am thinking all day long. Among my hobbies I am like a Sultan in his harem : I do not know how to share my favours among so many beauties without making some of them jealous. And I am afraid one of them in the end will win and possess me utterly."

Through Rimini and along the shady road to the shore where, round a terrace of wood and canvas, we found once more the muttering of the sea and its eternal movement : the heavy waves lingered, gathered up their impulse, and with a great noise flung their bundles of foam on the darkened sands. Opposite us were boats with tall red sails wedged in between the sky and the water.

Set out again along the coast road, by the marches and the Pineda, swollen with fever. I love the sea pine : the bare tree stretching up and holding its garment of foliage at arm's length. So they offer themselves to the sea wind, ranged in long black troops, between the hard barrier of the Adriatic and the sky reflected in shreds and patches among the clods of red earth and the armies of reeds. A disordered formless country, which man has been compelled to arrange, uniting the wandering rivers, giving them a slope to their beds, building up the road with ramparts and fortifying the fields.

Lunched at Ravenna. P. arranged everything. He found the little cheap trattoria where he, Baptiste and I ate delicious things. He made the waiter reduce our bill by six soldi which he tried to overcharge us. Finally he discovered the best café under the arcades of a dazzling piazza, the sun's private property.

We wanted to revisit the Baptistery and San Vitale : the Baptistery is a bare barn of bricks, which contains all the mysteries of the sea, all the feasts of the Heavens,

Athens at dawn, and a thousand summer mornings. And imperial processions and great golden birds in an infinity of azure and ultramarine. . . .

"Archibaldo, to think that this little building, this low room containing all this : those marvellous pictures, and that gigantic tomb, unadorned, which seems to weigh so heavily on the earth and snaps its fingers at us from the depths of the ages! And what does it represent? A bishop preparing to burn an Aryan book on that grid, I suppose : and he is showing the four orthodox gospels arranged in the little cupboard. They used firmly to believe that fire was created to burn the books of heretics, and, incidentally, to cook the food of men and give us warmth. . . ."

We set out again.

"Take the palace of Theodoric," said the Marquis. "I was much interested in it on my first visit. I compared it minutely with the mosaic which pretends to depict it at Saint Apollinaire-le-neuf. . . . Do you know what Ravenna makes me think of? A sentence in our Catholic litany : 'Per gaudia tua. . . . By your Blessed Joys. . . .' I should be hard put to to explain the connection. . . . Yes, there is an unmixed joy in those oceans of colour, the wells of the mosaics. . . . It is one of the capitals of this world, that little town which has not even a tramway."

"Do you think Rabot would be sensible of the pleasure you find in Ravenna ? "

"Don't make fun of Rabot. Who knows ? Perhaps he will go there. . . . I am interested in his career. I feel that he has the will to get on and a studious mind. If only I could help him. . . . Oh ! I bear him no ill-will. On the contrary, Madonna, on the contrary : I would much rather be here than in Parliament."

VENICE. 18.

I ventured out on the piazza of St. Mark's, whence the sun has driven the German, French, and American honeymooners. It is no longer an annexe of Wilmersdorf and Passy. Merely a great Italian provincial town. In the white empty space the pigeons are playing at sending their shadows from the roofs and catching them under their folded wings as they touch the earth.

But the Merceria glares with all its shops at nightfall, in its narrow labyrinth. Encouraged by Putouarey's example I bought a thousand useless things (and a note-book in which I shall continue this diary to-morrow), and here I am once more with a dozen boxes trailing behind me.

Thought of killing Maxime Claremoris by sending him a box full of Venetian things : mirrors with many coloured glass frames, statues of laughing negroes, with green, yellow, red, purple and blue bracelets : all the abominable barbaric things which the touring bourgeois buy here.

" Those are the things you would have bought, Marquis, if you had not made the effort to free yourself you described to me. Think of that and you have a means of measuring how far you have travelled."

But really I don't see why I shouldn't buy some of them myself. Isn't there a virtue in the acceptance of ugliness ? Above all, in the fact of feeling neither disgust nor hatred for anything outside oneself ? To live and

194

love and work among those mirrors and niggers—what force, what affirmation of self, what a challenge to the world. It would be a perpetual escape from all surroundings. . . .

I must have a room entirely furnished with these things, and I shall invite Max to the house-warming.

BOOK III

Trieste, Moscow, Serghievo

BOOK III

Trieste, Moscow, Serghievo

AT SEA,
19 *June*, 190 . .

ON board the Trieste boat. It does not leave until midnight. I have two hours for writing while Putouarey is wandering through the Calli of Venice in search of adventures. We went and lunched early at the Casino on the Lido and spent the whole afternoon on the beach, lying on the warm sand (and when you plunge your arms into it, you feel its cool depths), and suddenly we realized that we were on the point of leaving Italy. Putouarey began :

" There is a good deal to be said for and against . . ."

" No, there is nothing to be said for or against Italy : there is simply a good deal to be said. I can easily imagine the kind of fool who would cavil at everything in a country and the other kind of fool who would admire everything. We are beyond that At heart I think Italy the pleasantest country in the world. But what reason can I give for my preference ? Also I must confess that, politically, the Italian nation does not interest me at all. But none of the nations in Europe interest me. So long as they let me come and go unmolested, that is all I expect of them, that and the abolition of the customs at any rate for trains-de-luxe and motor-cars over 50 h.p. The people ? I was going to say that the Italian people are the best civilization has to show. Idiotic. I like them and that is all. And now we are going to leave it all : the flagged streets which in three days harden the feet of travellers, the streets where behind the open green shutters fair faces watch you pass, and the hills rising up to the blue like the banners in a procession. We may have been slandering the country, we may have been deceived and taken the convenience of German life for high civilization. But we shall see the difference when we are in countries where that civilization is of a less generous growth : Germany, for instance, where the mind never exists outside books : England, where, in the public squares, we should never see the lovely nudity of the Neptune, or the David. Poor little clod-hopping natures ! . . . No. I am beginning to talk like Maxime Claremoris and like a fool."

" Ah ! " said Putouarey, with profound feeling in his voice, " I too love the Italian people. Two years ago I spent three winter months in Florence. I soon won the favours of my landlady's daughter, a splendid auburn *popolana*, with grey-green eyes (you know the type with a fine broad chin). Her name was Roma del Prato. (It was her grandfather, a fanatical Mazzinist, who wanted her to be called Roma.) Of course, at the end of a fortnight, when our intrigue was confessed to, I was on the best of terms with her family, and when I went to take ship at Leghorn, her mother, her aunt, her little sister, the maid, all wept in my arms. And they entrusted me with the greeting of all the Del Pratos to a branch of the family who had settled in Marseilles : a Francesca del Prato, who was married to one Giambattista Fanfani, who kept a cantina, in the Via Rossa at Marseilles.

" And upon my word, I nearly forgot the commission, for as soon as I landed in Marseilles I began an intrigue with the ayah some Americans had brought from the Soudan (my only black affair, and it was quite enough). One day as I touched a coat in my bag I found the paper on which was the address of the cantina, Via Rossa. I went instinctively to the St. Laurent district and asked my way. The rue Rossa was unknown. Of course I had to re-translate ! I was told where to find the rue Rouge at once. A common narrow ditch, deep, oozy and damp : one of those penitentiary streets where none of the seasons can make themselves felt, so that the empty pavement stares you out of countenance. I only discovered the Fanfani's Cantina by the name written over the door. It had no flag like the other Italian cantina in Marseilles, and it looked like a house that had been recently been on fire with the water from the engines still dripping down. Opposite, a horrible flayed-looking house spewing black out of its windows and opening on to the street not with a door but with the mouth of a sewer. It was a Greek inn, with a white inscription on a black board which said : Xenodokion Hellenikon. The tariff was not even a franc but a drachma a day. Oh, yes. They are our counterpart, the cosmopolitan of the poor. And people lived there as we live in our palatial hotels.

" As I entered, the bambina who was minding the

Cantina rushed up a staircase which I could not see. She returned, holding her babbo by the hand. M. Giambattista Fanfani, as soon as he heard my explanations, understood what I had been to Roma.

"'Cecchina, viene presto!'

"Then appeared Madame Françoise Fanfani, née Del Prato, a big fair woman caught in the honey of her hair. She listened and understood at once, and embraced me without ceremony saying, as though to excuse herself:

"'I am Roma's aunt. Is it possible that the bimba has grown into a woman?'

"I was adopted by the family. M. Fanfani asked me what I would take and warned me that it was his call. There was a moment's embarrassment. I had presence of mind.

"Gazzosa.

"A little lemonade would not ruin them. I felt that I had the respect and sympathy of the Fanfanis. There were great sentiments in that dark low room: hospitality and the bonds created by love, kinship, friendship. Signora Fanfani seemed to be proud of my relations with Roma. I was presented to her two little girls and they came up to me, and the smaller of the two was soon on my knees the better to admire my beard. The taller had her hair divided into four plaits tied together at the ends forming a kind of round handle, by which to hang the little creature up, you know, as one so often sees them in the streets of Florence. Ah! I was in Florence, and my heart remembered Santa Maria Novella.

"Then I went, Mr. Fanfani taking me to the Quai

de la Tourette. It appeared that he liked Marseilles and the Cantina was flourishing. We shook hands with a great feeling of mutual esteem. It was absurd, my dear fellow, but I was moved. Those good people ! I declare that I quite felt that I was something of an Italian myself ! "

And I too feel that I am something of an Italian, now that I am so near leaving Italy, on this boat where everything is already German. A gondola has just come up and two mandolins are strumming in it. And a jolly little woman's voice sings out with a slight tremolo above the tremulous music. Italy bids us good-bye from her hiding in the moist night. And I recollect a hundred lovely warm evenings in the narrow cobbled main streets of the provincial towns, flanked by houses so high that the evening turns dizzy and hardly dares descend into them. Men go by with their shoulders huddled under their cloaks. The little girls have bought a bagful of pine kernels which they pass from hand to hand, while they move on swinging their striped skirts round them. Ladies in black, accompanied by officers whose eyes shine under the peaks of their caps, take up the whole street. In the shop windows the smokiest of lamps shine like suns, and everybody talks so much and so well that one would think one was in a drawing-room sitting between two ladies.

TRIESTE. ADRIA PALACE.

20 *June.*

I am copying out (for I have lost the notebook I bought for the purpose) this attempt at poetry without punctuation which I composed last night at sea, in my

203

cabin, under a framed piece of cardboard which bore, in Hungarian, German, and Italian, all sorts of annoying and useless recommendations.

HOPE

The great desert with its thousand folds and the huge
Black spider of a palm tree in the stars
And the scraped banks where on the dust sleeps
The pale vegetable squid
And the gardens beneath the bluish air where the ship
Of the wind is stranded in the heart of the groaning·groves
And where clucks
In perpetual ecstasy
The gliding falling water while
Beyond the green lawns sings
A station, like a nest of smoking compounds
And the tardy forests of the mountains round a lake
And their silence where the blackbird drops his heavy cry
The pulsation of happiness and ripening summer
And the last dèfeats of the sun in autumn
When the last beams resist
At bay against the trunks of trees and the rest
Are already slowly dying in the dark grass
Ah well sweet Hope is sweeter than that
Hope that sorrounds me with a warm confidence
I shall not sleep at night   And my eyes
Will once more see the spot of dawn grow and the pool
Of dawn slowly fill heavens and sea.

(It is not quite the thing, but I shall work at that poem again.)

I am glad to be in Trieste again, the capital of the Adriatic, as Italian as Venice, but more within our reach, with something crude, new, rather disquieting to us coming from towns where existence, made easy by the customs of the ages, turns and slips noiselessly on its well-oiled hinges and rails : Florence, San Marino, Ravenna.   It is snowing pigeons in the squares, between the great blocks of palazzi built of a dull yellow material : and the mixture of the Italian names of the streets, the Slav-names on the shop fronts, the German inscriptions on the monuments, and the Austrian uniforms, bright blue in this light, summarizes the political situation and takes us in thought to the South, towards Taranto, Bari, Patras, where in great new empty squares immense new empty cafés offer their windows to the incursion of the sea-wind. Ah ! How far it all is from Bond Street !

One sees handsome Viennese go by with their pale delicate faces fringed with well-trained whiskers cut high : Montenegrins too accustomed to the national uniform to be at their ease in European clothes, and their war-like faces seem rustic under the black hats which swallow them up.   I went down the principal street, which is no doubt the best lit in the world with a pink electric light.   The hotel also is of a mixed civilization : great corridors tiled Italian fashion, Viennese rooms, with the sober decorations and the black and white which reminds one of cuneiform writing and the signs in music, and the maids are too pretty and too polite to be anything but Hungarian.

Putouarey is dragging me to a circus.

Friday evening, 21 *June*.

A sensational entry to-night.   I have received precious confidences from P., which have somewhat estranged me from him by making me see in his character an element of disorder and folly.   Another lost illusion.   I felt that

Putouarey was so cool in his handling of life, so direct in his appetites, taking, without even troubling to stoop, the flower of the world's pleasure : I thought he was so firm and so full of certainty that I was ashamed in his presence of my own sentimental weaknesses, my unreasonableness, disgusts and timidities. Nothing could ever induce me to commit the smallest lapse from Self-respect : and now suddenly I find him a prey to a horrible scrupulousness.

It was as we were leaving the circus. We were going on to supper, for I was hungry. I ordered soup and cold meats. It was half-past twelve. Viennese time. The Marquis cried : "But it has been Friday for half an hour : I am fasting." When he had arranged his meal with the waiter, he seemed to want to excuse himself.

"But, my dear Gaëtan, it is quite natural. I am an agnostic, but I go to the English church every Sunday because it is the correct thing to do. I don't see anything distressing in your observing certain religious forms, especially as it distinguishes us from the blatant vulgarians whose vulgarity consists in eschewing the correct thing. Besides, even if one is not faithful in big things, one may as well be so in small things," I added, smiling.

"You tell me that ! Archibaldo, I have something important to say to you. As soon as we get back to the hotel. . . ."

"Well ?" said I when we had reached our sitting-room in the Adria Palace.

Putouarey looked as though he would have liked to escape.

" H'm ! You need not say anything, Marquis."

" You will despise me."

" Much less, you may be sure, than I despise myself."

" Well now, Archibaldo. Suppose the myth were true ? "

" What myth ? "

" The prayers we are made to say, and—all that."

" Before you go any farther, let me speak to you frankly. We have both traduced many things. We have avoided the myth, simply because we belong, without knowing why, to two different sects. But indeed I wonder if anyone can really believe in it. Think of modernism, the Esperanto congresses presided over by your bishops, the miserable opposition to Socialism, our religious revivals, the Salvation Army, and one wonders what is to become of it all."

" If only you could convince me. But you are beside the question : all these blemishes, all these absurdities, all the Esperanto congresses, don't prevent the truth from being true. And what if the myth were the truth ? Ah ! my reason tells me no, and no again, a thousand times no. But my education . . . I am very unhappy, Archibaldo. I assure you. Yes, of course, I don't believe. But I doubt, and my doubt is in favour of the myth. See how I have lied to you : for instance when I told you that I was shocked because Angiola of Naples used to put pious pictures under our pillows. I said that because I thought I must put it to you in that light, as a Protestant by label and an Agnostic in fact. But putting those portraits of saints in an adulterous bed was fidelity in small things : it was better than nothing. You remember the woman who thought : ' If only I can touch the hem of His garment . . .' There is no moral difference between Angiola and myself, who, in all my vagaries, have never parted with my scapulary. Habit, superstition—oh, yes ! . . . but my doubts have never left me either. I have wrestled with them, believe me : I have read all the books which are regarded as most dangerous : Renan, Haeckel, Nietzsche. Haeckel's hypothesis interests me, but it is only a hypothesis, another explanation without proof, all mixed up with Prussian jokes about the wives of Henry VIII. Huxley is another explanation without proof. There is no scientific basis to it —just like the myth ! and at bottom they go back, even those which are considered the greatest and most novel, to Aristotle and Plato. It is not enough, and my reason by itself and the evidence of my senses tell me more about it than all the censored books in the world. I am a man who likes things clear. God does not answer my appeal. So much the worse. I will do without Him. But all the same—and my old doubts return stronger than ever (and I have never had what is called fervour) ; if the intellectual world were superimposed on the material world, with a whole hierarchy, species and places, as in a plate on which one has taken two photographs, so that it shows a piece of lace or someone sitting by a table appearing through the middle of a great street full of trams and people ; suppose intellect and mind were independent of matter and constituted what we call Heaven ? And suppose we carry in ourselves a more complete, more perfect and more real world than that which surrounds us ? Our impotency, our dislike of imagining the beyond ? But then you must see how we turn in disgust from the realities which surround us, the fundamental facts of this life : digestion, birth, death. But why argue ? I can't help it, nor can Haeckel, or anybody. I am just like the heroine of the Birmingham story I told you, which you found so dull. Winifred. She is myself. Oh ! she really did exist, but I saw myself in her, feature for feature. And remember how I have played the roué for your benefit : even in my irregularities it has not been as I told you : no, there has always been a thought of the myth strangely mingled with my adventures in the streets. A need of practising charity, a hope of satisfying the hunger for love that I feel in myself. And then to be able to help another creature, one fallen into the depths, for a moment to bear the burden of her life ! I have consoled them, I am ashamed to confess, cared for them, tucked them up in my bed. In my room above the pub in Birmingham, for instance Lilys, Ethels, Connies, poor fat docile creatures who asked sadly, 'Must I undress before you ?' What a slavish thing to say, eh ? Sometimes they were dropping with sleep, and then I undressed them and very gently put them to bed. Without doing what Winifred called 'harm.' Oh well ! So much the worse for me. I would not go to bed. And then hard at work over the mysteries of sulphur and chlorine : sulphur—and potassium, that is our emblem. My dear fellow, it was a small theory, but it was good to think that a woman was sleeping there, in shelter, a few steps away from me and that I was standing between the world and her. It was nothing : it was only the poor charity of Marie Joseph Gaëtan Fontbon, Marquis de Putouarey, the little brother of fallen women. But, my friend, sometimes the Devil was too strong and I succumbed. Say something, tell me that you despise me."

"Not at all. I envy you those nights of toil near the lost child whom you had taken in your charge."

"Ah ! That is the good side of it ! But you can't imagine the baseness to which it leads. I am a man who goes chasing through the streets of a town, at night, looking for women, all the while saying his breviary, praying not to find any ! Oh, yes, I ought to despise the morality of the bourgeois. A nobleman with a high notion of honour should take and leave. Certain disciplines excuse certain irregularities, and if one is a man of honour one can run after a drab, for society is not injured by it, and, apart from the offence against God, one is no less a man of honour. But I can't argue like that : it's no good. It reminds me of the pig who felt that he might grow angels' wings ! If it were true ! If it were enough, with your mind firmly fixed on the absolute, to let such unimportant things pass without touching them, if it were enough to enter into the Omne-Intelligence, where everything one wills is possible, and everything is known and consummated, and life is an eternal reign in boundless light ! Foolish, isn't it ? and stupid in a world like this when everything we see is organized for mortal life, and nothing for life eternal. Archibaldo, I owed you the confidence. Yes. Even after what I have told you, you were mistaken about me. You saw me as a cool-headed, deliberate man, with no anxiety, too much so indeed. Well, you must be satisfied : you know my anxiety and its nature ! Well : you won't talk about it ? Never ! Let it remain between us. Yes, I am going out. One of the equestriennes is waiting for me : the little fair one in blue tights. Oh ! It's impossible to cut the appointment, but I will be prudent and shan't stay long. Back soon."

At first his story made him look smaller and more ridiculous to me. I was not expecting it at all. Now I know and I pity him for being tormented by all that theology, and yet I wonder if my own curiosity, although it seems to me to be much higher in degree, is not of the same kind : the need of being at peace with oneself, and the hunger for the absolute. . . . Ah ! If that was it ? No, no. Is there no one in the world who has any certainty ? Or, at any rate, is happiness, the faculty of enjoying all the things of life and the mind, the privilege of coarse natures ? I had already begun to learn from Putouarey, I was beginning to yield to his influence and encouraging myself to develop everything in me that is at all like Putouarey, and suddenly, the abyss yawns at my feet, a soul which knows its own dirtiness, and in its efforts to escape sinks only the deeper. And can that be a religious soul ? The purest thing there is ? I can speak out. My soul also sees its own dirtiness, and it does not seek to escape, and it gloats over it, and its crust of mistakes, appetites wherein it suffers, and baseness keeps it warm. Already the vermin have built their nests in it. Oh, well, suppose I am dirty, at least I know all about it !

Saturday.

The Voracious arrived during the night and this morning Putouarey, the chauffeur and the Voracious have embarked on the *Graf Wurmbrand,* which in a couple of hours (it is ten o'clock) will land them on the quay at Zara. When he got up the Marquis was beginning to hesitate : Lichtenstein ? Montenegro ?

" You'd better go to the best place for adding to your collection of ribbons."

" That is exactly what I don't know. I knew a Montenegrin Prince at Stanislas. If only he is at Cettinje ? Bah, let us go to Montenegro. It's very hilly and I doubt if I shall be warm there. Come on ! "

It was my turn to hesitate. In an instant I had seen the German boat going down among the Fortunate Isles : Lussim-Piccolo, Spalato, Sebenico, and Ragusa, and beyond them, when the little white steamer is no more than a dove's feather lost in the black gulfs of mountains and waters, the ascent into the Tsernagora, the country of chaos, arid as the moon, where one could well believe that the earth had reached the year Ten Thousand and that there were only a few pockets of moisture left in the dried crust of earth : all the little fields like a carpet made of rags sewn together. Then the rest at Cettinje, the great Slav air, the feeling of being crushed by the sky, the beauty of the little green plain, where the few trees and the turf comfort the man of the plains, who finds in it a colony of his own country. . . . But immediately the abundant life of Vienna invaded my memory and I thought that after buying a lot of useless things in the shops of the Kohlmarkt, I could go and see more of Servia and Bulgaria, which I once passed through in the Orient express and can only remember by vast melancholy fields of roses (with an even still more melancholy smell, after an hour of it) and mountains harsh and bitter to look at though they conceal a very delicate life : on the little stations I saw young boys and girls dressed in charming costumes, going along with great painted carts, with solid wheels, as I imagine the chariots in the Homeric poems.   And amid the great menacing savagery of the country, new, bright-looking towns, with pink roofs and sunny white walls.   And I remember a cavalry regiment : blue and red, in the streets of Nisch, neat and shining like lead soldiers taken out of the box for the first time.   And how charming I thought Sofia as I saw it from the train, veiled in white like a baba from Little Russia.

" No, Gaëtan, I am going to Vienna."

From the deck of the *Graf Wurmbrand* we watched the Voracious being lowered between decks.   When it was lashed and wedged up, I called the chauffeur, gave him a tip and said :

" Baptiste, you know the Montenegrin roads are very dangerous : sharp turnings, steep gradients, and the sun on the stones is very dazzling.   Please see that the Marquis does not drive himself : he is so nervous."

I felt full of anxiety about Gaëtan.   Round us family parties from Gratz and Vienna were settling down. The siren hooted, drawing up as it seemed all the noises of this world and shaking us to our bones.   I watched Putouarey's face.   What ?   Was this the man who had confided in me and laid bare his most intimate life ? Surely there was no room for that in his handsome, proud, mocking face, with its black beard bristling out ! But there was no trace of study in it either, or the nights (sulphur and potassium) spent over chemistry books. How splendid is human nature that it can contain such folly, such balance, and such contradictions !   I accepted

Putouarey as he was, and I felt that, in spite of his oddities and absurdities, I loved him. We felt inclined to embrace. I didn't really, I did not dare !

From the quay I watched the *Graf Wurmbrand* cast off. The Marquis was on deck, waving good-bye.

" In Scotland at the end of August. Eh ? Or for the grouse shooting at Worley's."

" Perhaps. And you'll have the ribbon of Saint Machin de . . ."

The siren sucked up our voices. And soon the Marquis and his handkerchief were only a creation of my imagination. That was how I parted, with neither pleasure nor grief, from that honest man.

Returned to the Adria Palace. The idea of visiting the Balkan countries had given me the desire to learn, with which I am still sometimes possessed. Books, particularly grammars and dictionaries, called to me insistently. Already my hands were making ready for the movements of carrying them, opening them and turning their pages. Shall I begin with Servian or Bulgarian ? Would it not be wiser to make a real start with modern Russian ? I wasted a couple of hours in the Trieste book-shops in looking for a book of Tolstoi's or Dostoiewski's and a suitable dictionary. I could find nothing but a Tschek book and a small dictionary. At last I remembered that I had only read the two first parts of the Divine Comedy. I bought *Il Paradiso* in an edition with a few niggardly notes, and plunged into it at once. And I should still be at it : but that as I was going from my room to the dining-room I met Gertrude Hansker. We recognized each other at the same moment.

" Oh, Archie ! "

" Oh, Gertie ! "

It is flattering to be seen with this beautiful young woman with the auburn hair. She is as tall as I, and though she is twenty-seven she has never worn corsets. With her wide smile she shows that she has all her teeth and she gives me the measure of her strength in a vigorous handshake : I gathered at once that we were to continue the little flirtation we began in the spring of last year at the Tennis Club at Cannes. When I asked after Mr. Hansker, who is a great man of business somewhere in the States, she told me she did not know.

What was it I wrote some time ago about women, apropos of a café concert dancer ? That they blind and impede us ? Some such nonsense. All that vanishes before Mrs. Hansker's smile. Other women may be so : a very heavy drag on a poor man's life,—matter surrounding him on all sides, the Woman sitting and sewing and singing like someone shut up for ever. But Gertrude Hansker, of Santa Ana, is an Amazon who can ride astride for ten hours at a stretch. I have been told that, three years ago, the shopkeepers of Bristol used to go up to Clifton on early-closing days to watch her galloping like a cowboy over the downs. She is not a limitation but a conquest hard to make, and once made, difficult to keep. She is so beautiful, so free and so terrible that she could do without being rich. Impossible to humiliate her, as she presents to the world her calm daring adorably girlish face. Poor Florrie Bailey, with a true idea of her own baseness ! And that adventure with a dancing girl was so small a part of myself : it is as though someone had taken my place. Now that Gertrude Hansker has come back into my life, and I feel that she is disposed to listen to me, I see the story of Florrie Bailey as even more absurd and incomprehensible than it seemed to Cartuyvels. I renounce it utterly. And, gazing into those big, wild eyes like ocean birds, I forget it.

We exchanged our news. And what had happened to the Andes and Pacific Company? And why had I not been seen at the polo tournaments in England with Lord Molland and the Duke of Christminster? And what an idea to sell off all my houses! And was I intending to leave Europe.

" You are so unsuited to America, Archie! You are quite European, and continental! Do you even remember the years you spent over there? "

So we chatted as we lunched at the same table. And round me I was conscious of the envy and admiration of all the men.

" Archie, do you mind talking French? "

She lays great stress on the " tu " and that is why she wants to talk French. I shunted and directed my thoughts (as far as possible) into the language of Molière. My daily writing and conversations with Putouarey have kept my French from getting rusty.

" Yes. French works look solid, rather heavy, but serious, very luxurious, and with the grand European manner."

" Just look at all the idiots staring at me : it is maddening."

" I can understand them, O young white bear, O fair lily of Ireland ! "

" Archie, be careful : don't you see the man looking at me in the corner over there? "

I turn round. . . . Ah ! We are in a Germanic country. And it is as though every reasonable creature were telling me to pluck the fair lily of Ireland and take the young white bear to my arms. " Poltroon if you don't."

In Gertie's presence, secretly, I examine myself. Could I, after such a long time without polo or golf or regular long walks, keep up with her ? I remember how good it was to feel her walking by my side with her long supple stride in the sun over the elastic turf of the Lawns at Brighton. It was before anything had begun between us. As now she was in white from head to foot, and the rather stiff stuff of her skirt made a pretty noise and the yielding thin stuff of her bodice showed something of her arms and what was not covered by her high-cut chemise of her firm throat and bosom. The thought of all she could give me oppresses me, over-whelms me. I know of no more desirable possession. The moment when her strength and her pride are hum-bled, when the Amazon feels that she is a woman in the embrace of a man, will be one of the finest moments in human history ! What a conflict with the angel ! What a noble burden for my arms !

She has come from Vienna, driven out by the summer, and she hopes to find a little cool air in sailing about the Dalmatian Archipelago. Her yacht is moored at Pola, and the day after to-morrow her motor-car is to take her to it.

I showed her round Trieste, which she did not know. Went on foot down the long Via Giulia, etc. . . . Then to Miramar. We sat on a bank which shook every now and then with the long black trains. The sea was fading away in the sun. A desire grew in me and left no room for any other. An exact desire which made me gauge my companion's body with my eyes. The instinct in me thought. I am thinking of the child, of the mingling of our lives, of the gift of my life as I wished to give it her, carefully, seriously. And I carried my thought on aloud :

" You know, Gertie, as old Whitman says :

' " That which has been so long accumulating in me . . .' "

She turned her face aflame with warmth, measured my strength, my youth, my chastity with a long look and then turned away with a heavy sigh.

Ah ! I should have said nothing : words were superfluous. I understood why women set so little store by language : all the essential moments of life can do without it. Until that moment I still had my lucid and well-pondered desire to join my life to Gertie's. A divorce properly managed would soon rid us of Mr. Hansker. That night I paid Gertie the boldest compliments. As we came downstairs (how beautiful she was in a black dress cut very low) I murmured in her ear Petrarch's lines :

" Gli occhi sereni e le stellant i ciglia."

I saw then that she had noticed with annoyance that I was not in dress clothes. Though she has no moral prejudices, yet she is the slave of certain conventions. Once again, obedience in small things ! It was only distressing for a moment. At once her presence, the warmth, the odour she exhaled, brought back my sweet desire. Ah ! you tuppenny poet : how could you put the woman from you for a moment and talk of boredom and captivity? The best use you can make of your life is to spend it by her side. Your wealth was made only to adorn her and make her happy: your strength was given you only to defend her: your tenderness, only to love her. You might have followed Florrie Bailey from town to town, then another, and then another, and in the end you would meet this woman whom you must not let go. Once, in Russia, I read *Sapho*, a novel by Alphonse Daudet. It tells of a young man, very ordinary, who spoils his very ordinary career for a grisette. Ah! how right he was and how wrong was I to judge him severely when I was seventeen! The author dedicated his book: "To my sons when they are twenty." I suppose he meant to advise his sons to do as his hero did, to smash an ordinary common-place selfish career and give themselves utterly to a woman? And so in my enthusiasm, as Petrarch was not sufficient, I began to recite the dialogue of Roger de Collerye between Beau-Parler and Recueil-Gracieux:

> " Honour to the ladies."
> " It is right."
> " It is their due."
> " At all times, etc. . . ."

" Ah! Gertie, was it ever better said? And behind it all, the chivalry of the West, sword in hand!"

Too many quotations, and I hasten to change the subject. But the thought of this woman still fills me. Oh, lovely arms! Does she know it? She washes and dries them, and that is all: and I should feel it the height of happiness if I could hold them in my hands for a second: her arms prisoners and her lips defenceless.

And then I feel full of respect for her. And questions like these come to my mind, questions which it is impossible to ask :

" Tell me, is it not true that women are weak, and timid and full of coquetry ? Surely you are only pretending ? Pretending to be afraid, to want to be protected, not to like serious things—and all to make us prize you, to leave us something, the illusion of being something : like a learned man among ignorant people, who for fear of humiliating them, says nothing. You belittle yourselves to be one with your children."

She has just been to my room to ask me for clothes : she is going out dressed as a man. She would not let me go with her. But I made her promise that she would not leave till after to-morrow. It seems to me that if I had insisted I could have got more than that.

Sunday.

Went with G. to church. Pleasant to sing the hymns standing side by side. I followed her voice, which she did not try to hide from me, through the throng of other voices :

" Rock of Ages, cleft for me . . ."

The whole physical intimacy revealed in her voice. . . . G. has a certain deep note which rings out in brief moments in her low chanting. It was fresh and white and innocent. The Devil alone knows where she took my clothes last night.

A great surprise as we came out. A group of sailors who had come in after us were standing near the church door.

"The crew of a yacht," said Gertie.

At that moment the sailors clapped their heels together and all saluted me at the same time. They were the crew of my old *Parvenu*, sold by Cartuyvels to Bernardino Valls, ex-President of Montanera, where he got rich. He soon changed the name of the boat, a name which the N.Y.Y.C. made some difficulty about registering : "Libertador" is so ordinary ! I wonder if the crew have any regret for me. I felt some pride in the salute of those good fellows from Devonshire. And it is quite possible they think I am ruined, or in less flourishing circumstances.

"Let us go and see the yacht," said Gertrude, " let us see if anything has been changed. Your winter garden in the saloon was a treasure, with the fountains and the fish—the axolotl with their red ears—and the sandy paths and the heaths and the gramineous plants. Do you know Valls ? "

"Go and see the *Parvenu* ? My dear, I would rather go and ask that policeman to tell me the meaning of life. No, with your permission, I'll go and telephone to my manager and tell him to buy everything back : villas, palaces, houses, automobiles, yachts collection. We'll buy back the *Parvenu* : we'll give Valls whatever he likes, enough to get him elected President of another Republic (he appears to collect Presidencies). And we'll go on board the *Parvenu* to join your yacht at Pola. What do you say ? And so I shall be able to welcome you to my own place. And then : ' Come live with me and be my love——' "

"Archie, don't talk nonsense."

"Why not ? Hansker is nothing to you. You have

been his wife ? For a few days, wasn't it ? Oh, Gertie, last night, I did not sleep thinking of the child, with my lips impatient to kiss the flesh born of us two."

Once more I said what it was useless to say, and she walked on by my side in silence, not ashamed, but erect with lips pressed together, showing, with the approving testimony of the sky with its silent cataracts of light, that nature dispenses with words.

" Gertie, all that wealth, all that vast treasure is not for me, it is to respond to the great treasure in you, it is for the child. Shall I telephone to Cartuyvels ? "

" To-morrow. I will stay to-morrow. Let me go home alone. It is so hot. . . ."

I should have gone with her. Or rather why did she not say : " Follow me." A quarter of an hour passed and it was too late.

At one stroke all the sadness in the world filled me. It was not impotence of the heart, but a need of flying and hiding myself to taste my despair. I did not think of Gertrude Hansker, but of certain philosophic doctrines, vague, and narrow, impeding our smallest movements. For instance, this idea that men are only of value in the mass, leaders of civilization are only instruments, and that great artists are but the expression of a time and a race. But what of those who have lived without saying anything, with personal interests, such as money or family affairs, the thousands of dumb creatures ? Yet what good are they ? To make earth ? What a waste ! One soul spoiled after another. And you, O Truth, why are you not in evidence ? Poor ideas, one needs to be very young not to see at once that they are less real than the mist of an evening three thousand years ago. . . .

But I exist, with the roots of my soul deep in immortality. I remember when I was a child how in my bed I used to laugh, wordlessly pondering my eternity. And I will not be dragged away : the world shall not do as it likes with me : I will not fall, unthinkingly, into the snare of marriage, like anybody—like everybody else, because a woman has pleased me and I fancy I am not displeasing to her. A couple. A charming young household. Ah ! I am disgusted with that kitchen of life. . . . And yet how far I shot ahead of all my duties when I thought of Florrie Bailey. . . . Was it that in my heart—I knew it would come to nothing.

When I examine my existence during these last few months I am astonished : nothing has happened to me. And yet I asked only to meet adventures : I invited them. Henceforth delivered, without ties, absolutely free, to do everything and go everywhere—what ? My life has been less varied perhaps (surely) than the life of Putouarey's chauffeur during the same period of time. For Baptiste, also, has lived in Italy, even as we, and who knows how many people he has met, how many things he has learned, what ideas he came to about the buildings, and works of art, the life of the country, and what love affairs the handsome fellow had in Naples, in Florence, and even in San Marino ? My wealth and independence seemed to promise a hundred romances of high adventure, and this is my diary : hours spent in hotels, visits from friends, letters, and at last, at great expense, a miserable intrigue with one of those women that come to you at a nod.

But with Gertie came the opportunity to change that slow, dull existence, and at last to bring into my life an element, if not of adventurous romance, at least of bourgeois high comedy. And once and for all to escape from my life. But no, I prefer to let myself slip back, the risk seems to me too great : and I am already thinking : "Besides, she is married : and then she is too independent : I shall find other women later on." And I was not deceived by my instinct. I was thinking less of a romantic love-affair than of founding a family. What : could I never see a young woman's shoulders without thinking of founding a family? The need is there, always ready. Good : it will do another time.

Gertie saw at once, at lunch, what had happened to me. In my disgust with everything I should have liked her to show a little irritation. She seemed quite indifferent : " Ah ! You don't want me any more ? Very well." If only she had seemed to be a little sorry. No. " I am not playing any more."—" As you please " . . . What a fine marriage I am missing : a woman with ten million dollars !

The memory of the group of the Sabines in the Loggia de Luigi has just reached me with remorse. There were males who once at least ventured something to have women and children : the father bleeding in the mud, the mother pleading and weeping, and the terrified prey clutched in an arm that will not let her go—the other arm holds a sword. Perhaps I should have done that. But . . .

I wonder what the young Roman did with his living booty when he got home. In spite of everything the circumstances would favour him. To see at her feet, with sweet suppliant voice, the savage brute who, a few hours before, was slaying and roaring would be enough to move the young Sabine woman. I am sure they got on very well together after a very short time.

Ah ! There is no excuse for me : I know that I am cowardly and disgusted with what Nature and Gertie expect of me. And it is no good my telling myself that women, even virgins, have treasures of indulgence all ready for us, I cannot force myself to take the final step.

I am trying to find out why I object to marriage with Gertie. I have tried to say to myself : " What, so soon ? Before you have had your share of adventure ? Putouarey could make an end and go back to his wife, with his international collection of letters and locks of hair. But have I lived ?. It is false, absolutely false. I do not envy Putouarey his collection of letters. And besides, I have certainly lived : twenty-three years and three months.

I think I have found my real objection : marriage with Gertie would not be a real marriage. She has her own life, as I have mine, in a different moral country. Solitudes divide us. Certainly a day would come when we should go yachting separately. And what about the child ? But she is not thinking of the child. She wants an intrigue to pass the time. That and strawberries in champagne and ices and the hammock under the deck-awning in the morning wind. . . . And in the evening on the divans of the dark cabin, the love of a young golfer who in the twilight of the senses gradually awakens the slow desire which comes to nothing. . . . In fact, a liaison between two worldly people.

And I won't have that. Everything drives us to it : example and all the books for ages past, are full of such things. But I refuse. I say no once and for all to such adulterous counsel : I will have none of that trickery. I renounce all unfruitful love.

I can only admit two schools : either sensuality practised as an art, with specialized slaves and all that one reads of in Suetonius : or marriage, the perfect realization of the promise given me by Nature when I awoke in shame at puberty. But adultery, that half measure, that commonplace literary thing. . . . The whole world may go into it, but it shall not have me.

(I wonder why I never formulated these protestations before. The assent I gave to stories and novels of adultery has never been sincere : I ever found it hard to conceal my disgust.)

But no doubt it would be impossible for me to make Gertie love me enough to make her be a true wife to me. And that is where my heart fails me. For at least in this life of mine where nothing happens to me I do have the illusion of being free, of being able to send my thoughts as I like over all the places of the inward universe, and, in fine, to have great adventures in the region of ideas. I remember an impression I had one day in Hamburg as we were leaving the hotel to go boating, Tassoula and I. She was in front of me as she went through the door : and women were then wearing very clinging skirts which reached only to the ankles. A moment's nausea as I felt that I was tied to that. . . . But she turned quickly, laughing and showing her even teeth under her heavy lips. Yes : even with the Amazonian Gertie it would be like the day whose brightness conceals the sky, like the luminous tunnel of summer. No. I shall get out of this intrigue and go and see the stars again.

And my riches shall not catch me again either. And yet the temptation is strong. Is there anything in the world more beautiful than wealth ? It seems to materialize the spirit and to project into the life of the streets the inward splendour of man. A motor-car, for instance, is as beautiful as a thought, all transparencies and reflections : glass, varnish, brass : and beautiful women inside and the chauffeur with his coat fringed with gold braid and the arms of the family, and near the chauffeur a little girl with long legs like a mosquito, wrapped up in soft rich coloured stuffs. The wealth which takes us everywhere, with little cares and delicate attentions : no noise, air, cleanliness, a smell of clean linen and fine leather, so that walking has become only a health cure. All natural forces are at our service : to take us up, and carry us, put us down, and help us. That also I have given up : the impediment of bourgeois luxury, the anxiety of a household. Another evasion and a gain.

This afternoon, in the smoking-room as I was pretending to read and watching Gertie, I thought of a scene last year on the Riviera. The whole troop of us were coming back at night from Monte Carlo in a car : rich young men from Chicago, *Porteños*, South African magnates, and a woman dressed as a man, Gertie herself. Little bourgeois men who had come to spend a fortnight in the South, people who had only two or three thousand francs between them and death, had lost everything that night, and we were returning with our pockets swollen with bank-notes, and Gertie with a bag full of new hundred-franc pieces which she amused herself by pouring down fat Rufus Wandeler's neck to hear the piercing shrieks he gave. As we passed through Nice one of us proposed that we should go and visit a mean street which had been mentioned in the local papers in connection with a murder, a few days before. We all went there. It was not at all what we expected to find : the street was dark and empty and all the houses were in darkness. The one we entered was the poorest of all. In a room haunted by the ghostly flame of a candle we found two women lying in an iron bed with grey bedclothes : a fat bawd bloated with flesh, and a tall dark woman whose bosom was as though furrowed by her ribs. They had raised themselves on their pillows and with their eyes still stiff with sleep they watched us come in. They soon smiled when they saw the gentlemen come in with their white shirt fronts and tried to rise to the level of the occasion. They were visibly wondering what grotesque and obscene sight we should demand of them and if they could debase themselves enough to satisfy us. But it was quite enough to see them like that : the two females of the human species in their filthy cage. . . . At once the fat woman said as if by way of excuse :

"I can't take off my nightgown."

"Why ?" asked Gertie, moving towards the bed. "Why not ? Take it off at once."

"But, my little gentleman. . . . Ah ! It is a woman. . . . No, madam, I can't."

And she explained that she had recently had an operation and had a scar : that it was too ugly and would disgust the gentlemen. But Gertie would listen to nothing. She had taken hold of the nightgown by the hem and was trying to raise it above the woman's fat yellow knees, and the woman tried with both hands to prevent her.

" Has anyone a pair of scissors ? " said Gertie, turning to us. " Ah ! I have a pair."

She took out her gold case, the knife of which had a little pair of folding scissors, opened them, and began to cut the nightgown. Then the woman began to struggle and storm at her. One of us said :

" You'll hurt her."

She had done so : the woman's thigh was scratched and bleeding, and Gertie was roused to a fury and raised the scissors to plunge them into the flesh. We drew her back and dragged her towards the door. Before she went out she turned and threw her cigarette on to the bed, and the two women got up from it screaming. She was already quiet again and did not say another word until we reached the steps of the hotel at Cannes.

And now to see her innocent profile bending over a book, so childish that one expects a lock of her hair to slip from her shoulder and suddenly hide the page : the absorption and sweetness of a big fair-haired girl at rest : clean and neat, of good breeding : ah ! what a wife for a prince—and I can see her in that room with its quivering dim light, scissors in hand, stooping over that horrible bed. Is it possible ? With those proud, tender eyes, a defenceless schoolgirl, all attention, bending over engrossed in her book ? Is it possible that she even knows that such hovels exist ? And that she deserved the insults of the fat bawd at Nice ? . . .

And, as on that night, I cannot help regarding her as the symbol and résumé of the troop of us, my peers, kings, the asbestos king, the petrol king. Gertie's brutality seems to me to be that thing that is concealed beneath the ceremonious awkwardness of that world, the world where

I had the right of entry, and was so little seen. Oh! I know they are well-intentioned nice people, as far as they go: nice people preoccupied with a fear of not being taken for gentlemen who take a great deal of trouble to show that they have been well brought up—even going so far as to raise their glasses to the hostess with each new fill of wine: good people bristling with politeness, larded with civility—quite different from the young aristocrats against whom you may jostle in Loch's narrow shop, as they are waiting, standing, while their hats are being ironed. People who, at heart, would find nothing odd in the visit to the slums in Nice (I caught Roger Wandeler placing a thousand-franc note on the mantelpiece as he left the room). . . . But if one of them happens to be weaker of will or richer in temperament, then it is a bad look out for anyone who has the misfortune to be weak and poor and naked. . . .

"Do you remember the fat woman at Nice, Gertie?"

"Accidente! My dear boy, you interrupted me in the finest passage of *Pigs in Clover*. I suppose the book was written against rich people who have no social conscience. Have you a social conscience? I don't even know what it means and don't want to know."

"The only thing I know is that I detest Merchant-Princes."

"But you are one yourself, Archie. You can't help being one."

"Oh! well. I am ashamed of it. That's all."

She went and fetched a review from a table. How she misunderstood me! But I admired her tall figure and proudly compared it with the little Italian women I had seen in the streets of Trieste and a line of Statius came into my mind :

Latias metire quid ultra
Emineat matres :

What other Merchant-Prince could have so aptly found an appropriate classical quotation to fit a fact in actual life ?   No.   There is nothing in common between them and me except the scandalous wealth and grotesque royalty : the guano king. . . . As if all royalty were not grotesque . . . and all domination—and the only way of being perfectly dignified that of the absolutely correct and unknown gentleman who goes on foot to his bourgeois Liberal club and lights a moderate priced cigar on the pavement of Dover Street.   And very soon I slipped back into the slough of despair.   And with blanching face near screaming with horror, I saw that I was on the point of living through an old dream : all the conditions were fulfilled : the smoking-room was just the same as that old dream and what we had said, and our gestures, all the same.   And now Gertie would go and open the window and say : " There's a storm coming."   And indeed she went to the window, opened it and said :

" There's a storm coming," and she closed it slowly, exactly as she did in the dream.

Possibly I was transposing the scene into the past.   But this much remained true : that I was the same as I was years ago.   I have not added a cubit to my stature : the same old chime rang the hour in me amid the same disillusioned sadness : all my reading, all my travels, all my conversations, ideas exchanged and received, impressions, all had left me the same.   In spite of all that had passed through it, all the travelling shows, the village has remained the same, with the same poor old houses gloomily staring at each other in the empty square. And I was just beginning to construct a theory : dividing men into two classes : those who are capable of development and those who are incapable. I belong to the first : Gertie to the second. I saw her immutable and I thought I was advancing. . . . Ah ! to have done with all that and ask someone for an explanation and a way. . . .

However it has all led me to-night to write in a few minutes the dedication of my *Dejections* :

To Gertie H.

I bring thee all my soul,
With nonchalance, my nullity,
My meagre pride, my paltry flame,
My disenchanted misery.

Thy unworthiness know I,
But am I worthy to be loved ?
I know you think yourself so sly
You know I think myself unmoved.

I have plumbed enthusiasm
You have felt and still enjoyed
My apathy you don't believe,
Your gaiety in me has cloyed.

And in our love no mystery :
Let us be serious or gay,
Remembering that there can be
But strangers here on earth alway.

We think that life is good, but tell
Thy heart triumphant and beguiled
That no one cares about us—well,
No, not ourselves, my dearest child . . ."

I left Trieste last night, immediately after I had finished my diary. I knew there was an express to Vienna at 12.30. Left the hotel without telling Mrs. Hansker I was going.

Slept little. Here comes the sultry morning with its new awkward light over the half-wakened fields and roads shaken by the purposeful train making its way into the heart of Europe. And near the window where slowly the new day pours in, on a varnished shelf, the kettle is boiling in my tea-basket. And once more I feel free, and I say to myself that I have got out of it cheaply, and that if my vanity is a little injured, so much the worse for me. And incidentally I have avenged the fat bawd at Nice.

O Concha and Socorro, a little thought for you, hidden sweetness, pure hearts, a brief thought in the bitter morning of Central Europe. I am alone, and feel so jolly, looking down at my sweet smelling leather slippers, with my Dalmatian trunk on the floor, the heavy copper ash tray, the mirrors with the initials W.L. entwined, and my body which I love, and a Muratti from which rises a long ribbon of blue smoke floating towards the half-open window, dancing to the rhythm of the train, hesitating a little and then melting away in the keen air which the sun will soon sweeten. . . . Ah ! I ought to have said good-bye. It looks as though I had run away. Well, so much the worse for me, again. The express taking me with it is excuse enough. O little German landscape, I love you, and I am going farther. It was cowardly : and perhaps I have hurt her. Oh well : so much the better, I too have suffered.

No. It is no good. I shall never again reprove myself. Once and for all let it be understood that I am righteousness itself. I stretch myself : I dismiss moral passion for ever. I renounce the captaincy of my soul. Never more shall I work. Praise be to God. I love singing hymns : they make me think of a real home to which I shall come in the end : a dull and sleepy country, like the district round Yarningdale in the Midlands, where the station platforms have flower beds in summer.

I abdicate my interesting personality. I feel in myself secret hereditary qualities which are awaiting their turn : my father's sensuality brooding and talking over its memories of certain rooms in Valparaiso : my mother goes over her accounts and profoundly enjoys the sensation of being seated : she too sometimes thinks of her gay past in Melbourne, and the French naval officer whose signed photograph I found one day in her drawer. . . . Never again shall I make an effort. My money will carry me on from day to day. I give up all thought of climbing the Himalaya which I felt was in me. I do not want even to be conscious of it. I will sit by the roadside just where the ascent becomes difficult : the white turning with its green borders is enough for me, and the view of the country at my feet, the plain where the hand-to-mouth people live, all those who are satisfied and my colleagues the Merchant-Princes. I understand why I used sometimes to turn back. I thought I was measuring the distance I had gone and in reality I was with all my strength longing for mediocrity. The hidden me wished to return to the vague dreams of childhood, was afraid of appearing before the impartial reason, did not want to be dragged into the midday brightness. I shall be once and for all the Merchant-Prince, the Distinguished Sportsman, and the Wealthy Amateur of whom the society papers speak. I will be interested in everything that interests those people. And to abase myself I will even share their ambitions and desire success like any other vulgar soul. And I should be lying if I were to say that I have not thought of it before. I know why, when I love only one town in the world, I do not live in it : because it is hard for me to pass unknown in the streets which should be ringing with my name. Yes. I have thought of it seriously. London—as a naturalized Englishman ! I am too rich for a political career : but firmly to establish my family in the only country in Europe where it is still worth while, and to hide my red hair under the coronet of a Baron of the United Kingdom ; with the name of my Scottish estates for title—ah ! I have even imagined the scene and the robes which Lord Barnabooth of Briarlea would wear at the King's Coronation.

But that is not going low enough : it is only a desire for a kind of covering, as a reasonable man will legitimately desire decent clothes. There are even more vulgar and inert souls who do not even desire success. Outwardly one might confuse them with those who know the vanity of success. But there is nothing more different : they are at the bottom of the water. Oh ! to live as they do, on the philosophy of a health resort, the metaphysic of the Riviera ! I will belong to the majority, one of those who live on the margin of themselves with their backs resolutely turned to the Central Africa of their souls. In fine, I will be like everybody else ! And lower ! I will share their tastes, their points of view, what they call their ideas, and their political opinions. What noble struggles for the cause of humanity ! And, of course, no class-spirit. With what zest will I attack the idea of God ! (Shall I be able to keep serious ?) I will even end by being proud of my money : I will even end by being pleased with myself.

And how I shall enjoy, years afterwards, visiting the fair deserted state, the park where the avenues are obscured by the upstart weeds. . . . I will say : " That is the way that led to metaphysical speculations, the road of the musicians and painters, the royal road of Poetry where formerly I too . . . And the path of Science up which one climbs on all-fours. I came near a feeling of great certainties, and morally I was sure I could march straight on towards the grand detachment. Anyhow, I had risen above contemporary thought : I contemplated its origin and marked its infinities. I was no longer the slave of my time : I was no longer subject to the truth of the newspapers. I knew that there was something else : I had found the sacred breasts once more and drew my nourishment from them. O great foster-parents I went to you, and little by little I knew and understood you. And from you to me came uprightness and purity of spirit and intelligence and practical sense and republican example, and filled the measure of my mind. Even when I deserted you I felt you all round on my horizon, and you were the hard blue mountain in the upper air, veiled with clouds from whence all waters flowed down. The lazy life of the plains soon wearied me and I rejoiced to know that you were there, inexhaustible wells of fluvial dews, in depth as the height of the Amphora. O my resplendent Athens, my Capital, I am going to leave you and lead a café-lounging life in these provinces. . . ."

Well, I am going to begin at once. Tea whose aroma leaves a smell which is like a taste of honey and pepper : ten o'clock, as I see by a station which we burst through leaving it groaning and wounded : hymns filling my mind with a familiar rather sad harmony : a wise little prayer in my heart in spite of myself : speed : landscapes : money squandered : love offered though no one wants it : vagabondage : little stirrings of kleptomania ; long hot baths : too hot : scents and memories : my lost soul is yours. My hand smells good : my flesh clean and warm, and a memory of pure tobacco. . . .

All these thoughts have come to me already and my hand has had that smell before. I am finding old days that I had forgotten in myself : they gaze at me and turn towards me so that I may recognize them. Yes, here we are, with our boredom, our useless labour, the old blunders, and still suffering vanity : your nullity and weakness clearly felt, and the street noises coming through the open window. . . . The world does not even stop to contradict you. And what have you to say yourself ? You leaned over the well and because of the reflection and the rippled water you thought it bottomless. But take a stick and you will feel the earth at once ; and as that will annoy you to have found yourself less complicated than you thought, you will take refuge in the arms of death thinking : it is a fine thing to be alive.

And now, as I have ordered, my wagon is being coupled on the Berne Express. I am going to see once more the deep valleys filled with fresh leaves, the German winds blowing over the rivers in their summer sluggishness, and the scrambled eggs mixed with the cinders of the Berlin—Vienna express. A thousand times the branch of an oak-tree waves in the warm air and holds up to the sun a symbol of victory. It is enough. It is nothing : an invitation to which no reply is given, and the moment passes ; the distress of having given pain to a person whom one does not love : the intelligence which would like to be able to accept more : vanity reappearing under another mask : the action already done, the words already said : the old pity for the fool who affirms and cries out against the established order and loses his temper : the eyes of love which look out once from the eyes of some person, and already her face is turned away : the silence of the poor every day dying for us : the murmuring of people praying for us in convents. . . . Ah ! It is nothing but the little naughtiness of living. . . .

PETROVSKOIÉ. (GOVERNMENT OF MOSCOW).

Sunday, 21 *July*.

Through this window by which I am writing I can see nothing but three silver birches holding up their handfuls of foliage to the grey sky in a false light. What a huge sky ! I ought to be used to it again after being here nearly a month. And yet on the least thing reminding me that I am in Russia I am astonished and become sentimental. First the double windows and the sky tearing holes in the foliage of the birches, overflowing the barriers and woods of the park, and taking in its sweep the princely villa and the whole empire. An Empire that matches the sky : as soon as you pass the frontier, everything is bigger : the railway, the roads, the provinces, the horizons. It is a greater Europe, a Europe tidied

238

up : with space to spare : a field for demonstration and experiment. Seen from here the rest of Europe seems to be made of the coloured blocks of wood of a puzzle, a holiday country like the Swiss Cantons.

This is the Empire *par excellence*. An expanse, pure and simple : a country in which Putouarey and his dealings would be out of place : out of place and absurd the French roguery and the Boulevard spirit : out of place and ridiculous the bourgeois morality of the Protestant north, all the people with their pure lives and proper books : even the Minervian genius of Italy would be out of place. And from the red-cabbage fields of Eastern Pomerania to the China Sea in a hundred thousand post offices are a hundred thousand portraits of a Czar in hussar uniform.

These last few days I have been wondering why the villa is princely, what distinguishes it from the villas built here by the Moscow millionaires, which form a neat little town with silent streets which are too wide between gardens which are too new. It is not merely the yellow and black sentry box and the sentry in front of the gate. It has a greater regularity in its lines : the railings which always seem to be freshly painted with the points freshly gilded : there is nothing too apparent : and it is the same thing as the house opposite, but better. I can imagine it in winter with its red face under a heavy hood of snow : in the twilight it is like a heap of glowing charcoal under ashes : and the princes' sledges stop by the steps in a shower of tinkling bells.

Russia and my adolescence. . . . Oh ! when I was in this country with a face in which all men could read, and my breaking voice, and my desires blinding my eyes.

. . . How little was I master of myself and how unconscious even of my slavery! How poor I was! Or, rather was not that taciturn, desireful little beast, my real self with his unhappiness in not having his desire, suspicious, timid, deaf to the ideas in books and indifferent to the experience of old men?

A few days ago, I saw myself struggling through those old years, to pass through that dull forest of desires, to break in the lazy obstinate young brute. That was my real self, the little isolated brightness seeking its way, under the ground, to mingle with the great light of the universe. And now I am wondering whether it was not only ideas got by heart, and concessions made to life which have supplanted my real nature? My nights of tears in the castle at W., and in a certain room in the Hotel Prosper at Kharkov, the boundless appetite for thousands of vague things: liberty, action, travelling. Ah! I have had all that. I knew I should have them sooner or later, that it was only a question of time. The unhappy naughty child had to be satisfied first before the other could grow out of him: and here I am. You, small boy weeping in a hotel room in Kharkov, see: I am not ashamed to come before you: I have done all you bid me do: and I bring you much more than you asked: I bring you a little wisdom. But I hear you say: I don't want it. So much the better: he is satisfied: therefore he is dead. And I stand in his place, with my face turned towards the new sun.

I remember how insensible I was then to the sights of the world, times of day, colours, seasons. There was only one great night for me, or rather a kind of tunnel with the whole day shimmering at the end. I was blind to my own self. And now under Stéphane's influence I am beginning to look only into the inner world. But I have another light. I jot down here my conversations with Stéphane, or rather what Stéphane says to me. For I am once more absorbed in another man's personality and my thoughts are made out of another man's thoughts. I thought when I saw my dear Stevo again that I should have a lot to say to him. I imagined his surprise and wonder when he saw the progress I have made, the ways I have travelled, and the positions I have conquered. Perhaps we should meet also in the region of morals : perhaps I should be able to help him to journey in it. But at once I felt that he had long known the road which I was inclined to believe I had discovered. . . . I thought : " I left him amusing himself in Berlin : then he went to the Royal Jubilee festivities : then on a military expedition somewhere in Asia Minor : he has led a pitiful life in restaurants : official functions, and barracks. And during that time I have reflected." And suddenly he comes back into my life, settles down and dislodges me from every one of my positions. He even takes from me the expressions and images I had invented to describe my moral discoveries before I could use them. If only he prized the discoveries of which I was so proud as I prize them, but no : they are commonplace to him, stale stories.

I listen to him and remain overwhelmed in his presence, dispossessed of my imagined wealth already big with the new thought he lodges in me : and, having nothing more left me, really, than the ultimate generosity of not being annoyed with him and of listening to him with all my might.

And yet the way in which he came back into my life . . . At one of the last German stations before the Russian frontier. At dead of night on a too brilliantly lit platform, suffering from being up so late, a group of old generals in full uniform respectfully salute a young officer in a grey cloak, a tall fellow with a long sharp face under the short peak of his cap. He returns the salute, standing erect with his heels together and climbs up into the saloon next to me. A servant follows him. I wait until the train moves on and then I run to the door of the saloon.

" Porfiri, tell your master I want to speak to him."

" But sir. . . . His Highness has spent the whole day on horseback after ten days manœuvres and reviews."

" Let me pass, Porfiri," said the young officer, coming out of his sleeping compartment. " I recognized your voice, Archibald. You have surprised me in the practice of my profession. I hope you have reached a state of mind from which a prince's profession looks no more ridiculous than a grocer's. Not, not your hand, my boy—Russian fashion ! "

He took me by the shoulders and smacked his lips against my cheeks in turn. He smelt of Turkish tobacco and horses.

It was I who spoke first the day after our arrival in Moscow where we spent a night.

" So many things to tell you, Stevo : and so many questions to ask. Or rather only one question : what is there behind all the festivities and sorrows of the world, and behind history and everything we see ? When I left you, delivered from that intolerable weight of possessions, and went to Florence to be alone, I thought I should find an answer in myself, I thought I should find the truth : and I have been alone and have thought a great deal. Sometimes I saw so far ahead that the words would not follow, refused to follow, and took fright, like Columbus's crew. But I did not discover *terra firma*. I'll lend you my diary ; you'll see what Sargasso blocked my path.

" But first I had to destroy everything that the experience of others had constructed in me : the morality and ideas of our preceptors. One day I saw that their morality was bad and their ideas were false. They had inoculated me with impurity, and every now and then a little of it would come out on my face. I was continually on my guard. Even now when I least suspect it John Martin's way of looking at things or your father's supplant my own.

" Everything, or almost everything we learned is false. Indolence, which according to them would be so dangerous to me, has given me a taste for work and reflection : my wealth which was supposed to help me, has been a hindrance and so on. Take an example : do you remember how they used to warn us against that they called parasites ? I used to imagine parasites running to me from all parts as soon as I was free to go out into the world, and surrounding me and flattering me, laughing at my jokes, exclaiming with delight at my reading of my own poetry, applauding all my whims and sharing my dinner and amusements. That was how they were painted for me. When I was free, at twenty, I was rather afraid of the thought that they would come about me. Well, I have not seen a single one I have even had moments of solitude when I have longed for them to come. . . .

243

What a gross conception, what a twopenny coloured picture : the young man in dress clothes flinging handfuls of money into the streets with a jostling herd of worldly young men and cocottes after him ! I am ashamed for John Martin and the Prince."

"You are wrong. We have had parasites or at least they came to us. Do you remember the young men at Thérapia in the Embassy who came under pretext of showing us the low quarter of Stamboul and whom we invited to supper at the club in the Pera Road ? They were parasites. But you saw how quickly they left us. In the end they did not even nod to us, and yet we were quite disposed to welcome them. But you see, we bored them, you by reciting your verses, I by talking of my studies. That spoiled the suppers we gave them. You see we did not deserve to be inflicted with them : they fell away from us like dead lice. Our preceptors did not lie to us but they did not know much about us. Remember again what they told us about gambling. Last year, as I was going through Monte Carlo, I went into the Casino and stayed there until I had won some thousands of francs, but that was all I could stand : through an open door I could see the sun on the myrtles, the faint pure light, decanted and filtered for the winter visitors. . . . Yes. They were wrong : all their advice had no meaning for us."

"And I had to bear the burden of their mistakes. They wasted their time and made us waste ours. And here I am just as I was seven years ago, in the same dining-room in the Slav Bazaar, with the noise of the fountains rising above the chatter of the diners. In spite of everything I am the same shy boy, impressive and hard and unhappy.   I mean, I am no more certain of anything than I was then."

" And you were coming to ask me for certainty when I met you ?   Because I am seven years older than you, my poor little brother, do you think I have any certainty and have arrived at some conclusion. . . . Ah, yes, I am certain of something. . . . I will explain it to you later. . . . Come and smoke a cigar under the Riady. They had not finished building them last time we came to Moscow.   What a child you were !   The Red Square must remind you of your first cigarettes.   And St. Basil, what a fine box of bricks : a boarding-school of holy little girls in their robes of Paradise.   You see, I am watched too.   Those two moujiks lounging outside the door of the hotel, pretending not to be following us. . . . Let us go into the Kremlin and don't forget to take off your hat in the violent draught of the black gate.   Here is the children's room with all the toys in disorder : the pith and the germ : understand if you can.   Napoleon did not understand at first.   You know the room he slept in : I had exactly the same room in a little pre-fecture in France ten years ago.   He must have seen things clearly by the light of the candle we lit for him. Then he saw what a terrible position he was in : he knew that he was before his time !   He was intelligent : he did not insist. . . .   Let us go to the Riady now.   You see we have all the modern inventions, wide streets, trams, electric light, big shops, bottles of rare wine, jewels, toys, perfumes, all the comforts, all the good things of the West, like loot heaped up round the Kremlin.   We have all that because it is amusing and convenient, but you feel that it does not really belong here.   It is temporary.

Europe lives by it : but we are all beyond it in every way. We have another kind of thought, another idea. Look at our sky. In the west our cities soil it with their contact, communicate their activity to it, or, above the confined stretches of country it looks desperate. But with us it is at home, and all day and all night the Empire contemplates it and that is our other idea. And at the same time life goes on its ordinary way : and there are fat commonplace women in the little towns where the tailors' shops are known by the headless men painted on the white walls, and that is our good old Russia. A country whom you can approach. Don't you admit that you love Russia ? And there are glasses of tea at the Filippow. Porfiri must be waiting for us with the car. . . . Here is my summer ' Voracious ' for going and coming between Moscow and Petrovskoïa. The two big sabres in front ? They are to cut the wires our revolutionaries have been stretching across the roads for some time now. My cousin Constantine's chauffeur had his head clean cut off last month on the Oraneinbaum road."

PETROVSKOÏA,
Sunday.

To church with Stéphane. A little new church, a little bride in white with a tall golden hat, and chains and necklaces of gold, standing very erect at the end of the unduly wide avenue. And on our return, in the billiard-room of the villa, Stevo said to me :

" I read your diary yesterday even and last night. I saw that you have not lost the need of society which we used to have seven or eight years ago, and I no longer have ; what queer people we used to consort with. Anybody would do : French barbers in Kharkov, little cigarette girls at Pera (with their nails stained red) and all the frequenters of the embassies : German officers with old French names and French officers with vulgar German names and little Slavonic princes looking like young peasants in their Sunday best : in their European uniforms and waxed moustaches. And old Prince V. with his memories of Saint Cyr and the great days of the Second Empire : he used to wear his Western education as he wore his decorations : so that it suddenly hit you in the eye. . . . And now here are you with your Irish æsthete and your French squire. Congratulations ! The others were better than that. For after all the world of the courts may be stupid and insignificant, but the people there do at least have good manners and a kind of philosophy in spite of everything : a way of giving importance to little things and of treating big things as though they did not exist : a need of disinfecting and sterilizing everything. . . . There's a certain amount of humbug about it. . . . The King is an officer : the Queen a hospital nurse. Politics, religion, the arts, are not their affair, fortunately. Their business is to hold reviews, to entertain their colleagues, to open hospitals and bazaars. They are good little bourgeois people : but models of what good little bourgeois people should be. They are steady and keep in their places. And if they ever lack steadiness then the King disappears and the Queen falls to the gutter without any transition. They cut no sort of figure and never create any talk. That's why I love them. The great middle-classes may have their Nietzsche, their Rodin and St. Francis of Assisi. Who can deny the superiority of a Maxime

Claremoris or a Putouarey to almost any of the men whose names are in Gotha. Poor old Gotha, which is only taken seriously now by old-maids and anarchists. It is your Claremoris and Putouarey who cut a figure in the world ; the vivid and aggressive rich middle-class people. And that is why I abhor them.

"I cannot tell you how it has happened, but I have gradually broken away from those people. But I became one of them through the education I was given, the books we read, and all the ideas I greedily absorbed to raise myself above my princely condition and escape from insignificance and Gotha. I am their equal in fact : and now, I confess, I am disloyal to them and am a renegade. Every now and then I come across one of their books and am at once filled with nausea. What a dirty little well-fed contented world ! I am very glad to be out of it. What a queer society it is, what a queer period ! Their perpetual need of self-satisfaction : their boundless self-indulgence : and how they infect everything with the moral and intellectual diarrhœa ! Their mean debauchery, which they call paganism, their fear of death and their idle pastime they call religion. And their criminal prodigality. You know the horrible expression they use : eating money. Read the novelists who have written for them and depicted their manners : it is repulsive : you should see the squandering of Power. They have eaten enough to build three Empires like the Roman, enough to change the whole face of the Earth. I prefer to think of their being attacked by a general paralysis. Even the people in Gotha, sterilized and empty in soul as they were, shared in their degeneration. The poor grand-duchess of . . . I did not know her personally, but they have just published a volume of literary filth she wrote. She could not rise to the fine education of the great middle-classes, but she had secretly acquired the slight veneer of letters and æsthetics possessed by any little provincial school-girl. She was twenty years behind the intellectual and artistic movement of the country over which she reigned. My dear fellow, it was pitiful : they ought never to have published it. Of course in the Court-world, it was considered very well thought out, and I never said it was not : what was the good ?

And behind the middle-classes are the People. A nice lot they are this time. A lot of candidates for the middle-classes, a lot of aspirants for a fat belly. Slippers, what ? Back to fire, belly to table, the ideals of Béranger and M. Prud'homme. They wanted their comforts first. What do you say to that, you frequenter of the big hotels ? Oh ! my little soldier's bed, and the nights under canvas, and a man's gift of himself to his work, with cold hands and feet and burning head ! Ah ! If they would only be quick and overturn the last obstacles put in their way. They will triumph inevitably. I wish they had already triumphed and one could at last begin the great revolution. No, I don't hate them ; I should be on their side if I had to take part in it. But I don't belong to their world, you see. It does not even interest me. I have turned to other things, I am a man of a new age. Talking of your diary, you would have done well to read Dante again while you were in Florence. You would not have written one Sunday evening, a certain sentence about misers and prodigals. It was in the Inferno already. There are books which it is necessary not only to have read, but also to know. A small number of little books which are above fashion and periods, and would be enough to support and restore a whole civilization. I am not speaking of the doctrines they contain, but of the soul that dwells in them.

"You are astonished at the change in me, brother? You don't expect me to believe that you didn't see it coming? But I owe it chiefly to my Kharzan expedition. You haven't been reading the papers these last few months. You don't know that I am the massacrer of Kharzan? The Western journalists have dubbed me that and I can't be ashamed of it—which proves that I am sunk deep in crime. You thought it was a military expedition. It was a war. Kharzan is a province situated at the extreme south of the Empire, and has nominally been part of it for forty years. But bands of brigands terrorized the country and were its real masters. I was ordered to put an end to it. In a month it was all over; a regular Roman conquest and I did it alone : war, roads, organization of the public services. Whatever the Western journalists say about me there are still regions in Asia which need such treatment and an acquaintance with martial law. I shot down a handful of self-styled patriots who had been tyrannizing over Kharzan for years. I did exactly what the regicides of Europe want to do. 'Tyrants, down into the grave,' the phrase came into my mind when the rifles of the firing-squad rang out in the dykes of the fortress at dead of night. I was out to finish the marking of a road and I brought to bear on it all the knowledge I had as a brilliant scholar at the Constantine School. I had no remorse. Those patriots were the most revolting characters I have ever come across : they tried to come to terms with me and betray the country they were pretending to defend. I have proofs of it. I have not published them : and in France and England they are considered heroes and martyrs. I have got those proofs carefully put away in the archives of my palace in Petersburg. They will be of interest to the future historians of the Empire. But the shooting and all the things I did down there were not of my own choosing. I had to do it, or everything would fall to the ground, and that country which I had begun to love with all my heart would return to what it was in the middle of the nineteenth century. I saved it.

" I went there desperate, feeling that I was incapable of doing anything, convinced that I was going to cover with ridicule the government which dared, in spite of my youth, to send me to conquer and organize a country to which I had never been. I went there telling myself that on my first failure I would find some means of killing myself. And you see I have come back to face the insults of all Europe, proud, mightily proud, of what I did down there. Now you can go to Kharzan and take Claremoris and Putouarey there. I have won a new region for life, enlarged the domain of man. Before that I thought I should never be anything ; much pride concealed by a false modesty, and beneath my pride a great doubt of myself. The smallest joke could hurt me, the most involuntary show of disdain could plunge me in despair. If they were right, I used to think : suppose I were at bottom only an absurd little person ! Like any other provincial bourgeois I needed consideration. But now I accept criticism of all kinds and am the first to laugh at myself when I have done anything to deserve it. In Asia there is a whole district which will one day call me the 'Father of the Country'; a country to which I have been what Hercules was to Argolide. And all traces of the Hydra's blood will soon be blotted out."

"Stéphane! I am in such need of comfort. I am as you were before your expedition to Kharzan. A humiliated creature with no self-esteem. I am just as I was at fifteen when I tried to astonish you and said ridiculous things to you which made you blush for me. Not so long ago either. Nay, I was worth more when I first came to your father's house straight from America, as a little shy boy, in deep mourning, a little savage who knew nothing but the Spanish of the negresses, little English and no French. Do you remember how long it took me to learn not to call you Estéphane? The only progress I have made is to discover beneath the thick crust of vanity of which you speak, abyss on abyss of doubt and nullity. And I class myself with those whom Maxime Claremoris called the Ignavi and Putouarey dubs Piccadilly Johnnies. What is there to distinguish me from them? Is it, as I sometimes believed, merely a little better knowledge than theirs, of useless things, or having read the classics while they have only read the novels of the day, and passed into the world of darkness, mines and blast furnaces in which the Greek drama take place, and walked beneath the painted ceilings of Ovid? No, a million schoolboys know as much as I do. Once when we read Flaubert's letters I used to say: 'the Idiots.' Now I dare not. Stéphane, tell me that there are no Ignavi."

"Oh, yes. There are Ignavi. And the proof of it is that there are small towns, what are called Provinces."

"You remind me of the waiter at one of my clubs, who used to say ' the country ' in talking of Manchester. There are not only superior men in the big cities."

"No doubt : but there are superior men only there : or in cells in the desert. There must be inferior organisms : everybody cannot be all nerves and brain. Besides the Ignavi are quite well-meaning, they recognize their inferiority. But don't think there is anything to be gained by consorting with them. It is a waste of time : you would not change them and you could not take their advice. They will fall away from you as the parasites did. Leave them to their small lives, their petty nature, their poor vanity and their small finenesses (for they have them also). Dante defined them well ; those who live without glory and without praise, those to whom the world leaves unheeded : *Non ragionar di lor* . . . You know the rest."

" It is easy for you to talk for you have something to make them respect you. But imagine what they must think of me if they knew my private life. You know what they make of the little they do know ; the journalist who marvels and yet sniggers with contempt at the scandalous figures of my income. If they had read my diary, and knew the story of the dancing-girl, they would die of laughing."

"No : they only die of old age. And though you desire to hide the story from them, that alone condemns them : but do not insult me by being ashamed of it before me. And at heart you are proud of it. (I wanted to talk to you about it : it has given me a better opinion of you.) You keep the memory of it as a thing too precious to be shown to any chance comer. Oh, yes, ' my great stupid schoolboy,' you are proud of it, and quite right too. It's the greatest act of faith you have yet accomplished. You have done nothing better. You have shown that you do firmly believe in the possibility of salvation for all men. Even for the Ignavi as long as they are of this world. That is the meaning of your dancing girl story. And it is perhaps worth more than my conquest of Kharzan. It is a pity she refused to let you follow her."

" I should not have gone with her without marrying her. I have a horror of irregularity."

" Say rather that you are cowardly in the face of adventure. And that adventure was worth trying because she was so far from you, socially and naturally. Contact with reality would have done you good : you felt that—too late. Woman is a great reality, like war. I know : reason rejects them, refuses them, denies them. We were brought up to live in dreams and theories and we cry out when life strips us of our dreams and reality proves our theories false. A young man leaves school with his measure ready made, his foot-rule, and he is distressed because things are always larger or smaller than his foot-rule. Reality teaches him to divide his absurd little rules up into ten, a hundred, a thousand parts if necessary. That was how my war matured me. I should not say that if it were not true : unless it was obvious before that I was mature."

" But I am still waiting for that time, Stevo. I have done nothing. I am of no use : I am only a collection of possibilities which I have a thousand reasons for doubting."

"It is just that in you that pleases me. All kinds of fine things which I never suspected have grown in your soul. How wonderful, O Lord ! is the transformation ; the ugly little sullen schoolboy suddenly grown up and uneasy : the fine adolescent in flower ! I can easily tell you your qualities : they are such that you will not loose them on their being shown to you. You are humble and patient. That is shown in small things. You do not think much of yourself : I mean your merits are in your own eyes contestable. You are eager to hear yourself contradicted, and if the truth beats you, you prefer its possession to your own comfort. You reject nothing off hand. You do not despise your childhood. You eat the food that is set before you, and, if you don't like it, you are not annoyed. You do not lose patience when they take a long time in serving you. You put things back in the places where you found them. Do you even believe that you deserve to live ?

"In fine, like myself, you do what you can to be a man. There is no other valid expression. Your ' ought ' and even ' duty ' have no meaning. Duty was the name the bourgeois gave to their own cowardice. I have lately been reading some of Nietzsche's books during the Silesian manœuvres. He had great gifts as a romancer, but his Superman is still-born. The very name makes me think of all the modern commercial clamours and all the products which cannot bear the name of a substance because they are adulterated. And ' we Europeans ' ? I am one of them if they will include the country postman, and the market-woman, and even the Piccadilly Johnnies. But I am afraid it is only an academic group. Anyhow the word Christianity would include more. And at bottom there is only that: the humble, patient Christian, like you and me, striving to realize if ever so little: and the inert Infidel who gets in his way. And beside the word Man vastly surpasses the word Superman. There are so many things that the Superman rejects or overrides, even Man himself. Why leave the unhappy brute with simian eyebrows, the glorious son of God, behind?"

On our return from a walk to Moscow on a warm rainy evening.

"To go on with my criticism of your diary. Now I want to talk to you about what I dislike in it and your faults in general."

"I prefer that. I need someone to take me to task. But don't fall into generalities again as you did last time. It is so easy to talk about Man and Christianity in connection with nothing in particular. I am surprised that a tribe of general ideas has not been drawn up like a table of logarithms. By considering the equivalents one would make a remarkable reduction in the dimensions of such an epitome. While I was listening to you, in spite of what you call my humility, I felt my mind disagreeing with your ideas."

"I will think over what you have just said. Yes. What do we mean by Man and Christianity? That's it."

"Words from the bourgeois vocabulary, I suppose."

"Just listen. Take your wealth, that is where the shoe pinches. When a man like Putouarey says: 'My money,' it goes without saying. It is just the bourgeois vocabulary. He is not proud of his money, because he is used to it : but he cannot imagine himself without money. He does not know whether he likes it or not, he is possessed by it. If he wanted to describe a poor man he would show him as a bourgeois who lacks something : money or the things that money give : education, instruction. Take the literature it produces : the most bourgeois of all : their pity ! No it would offend me if it could reach me. Others are proud of their money. 'And who can blame them,' as your dancing-girl said. Not I, certainly. And then you, Archibald Barnabooth, are ashamed of your money. You speak of it as some simple, sensitive men speak of their slight physical defects, laughingly, as if to excuse themselves. You introduce yourself saying : ' It is grotesque : I am the richest man in the world : but that does not prevent my being endowed with normal intelligence.' Do you believe that your wealth is such a monstrosity ? But every ordinary young man who receives a thousand francs a month from his family might think himself an American millionaire. Did you ever think of that ? How is your life different from that of a wealthy undergraduate ? They have everything that really attracts you. The only difference is in the price they pay for it. Your racing-stable soon bored you, but they have never wasted their time on even wanting one. . . ."

" Stevo, you know that at bottom it is a question of vanity. When I hear anyone say : ' Merit without money climbs slowly,' I blush for shame. In the race of life I am like a man placed two yards from the finish. His dignity insists on his allowing all the rest to pass him. I have been given too much start and it is unjust."

"Then you should kill yourself."

"I have thought of it!"

"Fool! But what do you mean by 'climbing' and 'the race of life?' It sounds all wrong to me. When I see a man who has started with nothing, and has by his own merit become somebody, and goes about everywhere with the assurance of being somebody, and the clamour of his fame and his decorations, I want to gather all the naughty little urchins like myself round the triumphant great man and dance round him saying:

'He has succeeded, the idiot!'
'He has succeeded!'

"And if ever I think I have done enough to think myself deserving of the smallest honour, I hope I shall be done by in the same way! And admitting that it is desirable to 'rise in life' and become somebody, do you think money can help? It would be easy to show that the contrary is true, and that merit, overwhelmed with riches, rises slowly, and that money crushes and drags down more souls than poverty. . . . But you must see that you are as much above good fortune as bad. Or if you are not, so much the worse for you. Do get rid of your shopkeeper's preoccupation. Stop being the rich student who is kept from working by his money. Fortunately money no longer means what it did a hundred years ago. The most important things have ceased to depend on it. Little by little we are breaking away from it: we no longer love it for its own sake. Anyhow, we no longer belong to it: we belong to the spirit: the spirit can do more. We great gentlemen of to-day detest money."

258

"Quite so. I hate money. I did not dare say so."

"You hate money and yet you squander it? Don't you feel that we ought to have as little to do with it as possible? But you let yourself be dominated by it: breathlessly run after it through the streets, from shop to shop, instead of being its master and using it. I have been through that. I know what a chase it leads us. One of its exponents has expressed his opinion in verses which deserve to be more known:

> 'The rich have indeed a noble privilege
> Which every intelligent man must envy them
> And which justifies the pride of gold:
> That they can repel or keep at distance
> The base, repulsive details of existence. . . .

Pretty, isn't it? And what is one to say about the 'noble privilege'? All the possessions of which you so bravely rid yourself under Cartuyvel's very nose! 'Keep at distance' is charming. The idea that a man, or, more horrible still! a woman, performs in my bedroom certain duties which I can do for myself rouses indignation and shame in my heart! No, wealth, on the contrary, brings nearer to us 'the base and repulsive details of existence' and steeps us in them. Look at our luxury. It clings to us as the mud through which we walk sticks to our boots. It is no good wiping our feet, or brushing them or scraping them, it sticks, and we have to take off our boots to have them cleaned. Ten times have I made a clean sweep as you did, given away my travelling things, my cigar-case, my shaving-case, my English clothes, my absurd collections, my walking-sticks: and ten times I have bought others to replace them. Money was too strong for me: I always gave in and indulged my weakness.   Kharzan cured me of that too.   I was surprised to find that one could do without a solid gold cigar-case : I discovered that an ordinary brush, if it is hard enough, did quite as well as a silver-handled brush, and I learned that it is not so easy to lose a rough walking-stick as a bent cane with a horn handle.   I saw that there are many things more beautiful than those that money can buy, and that those things also were within my reach. One has no desire left for the things in the shops when one has done what I have.   I'd got beyond money.   I refused to give it my allegiance.   I reckoned up the time it had made me waste : the power it had made me squan-der.   And, as you cried out when you thought of another kind of squandering : ' Ah ! how beautiful is chastity ! ' so I thought that economy is one of the most beautiful things there is.   I assure you I spend only what is strictly necessary, and I wish I could contrive to spend nothing.

"The money I accumulate shall be turned to good account in Kharzan : they need it there. . . .   But that is not all : I must practise economy myself !   O poverty, it is you I love.   Contempt, sickness, tribulation, you are the treasure I have always desired.   What, other men suffer, are misunderstood, everywhere driven out, imprisoned, and I am to have no share in their sorrow ! Let some of it be given to me.   I shall be content. Brother, you do not know, I have a secret sore. . . . Don't tell anyone !   Don't tell. . . .   It is more precious to me than anything in the world."

I was looking through the windows which the sunset was filling with colour.   The rain had left the distant green roofs of the village, and the fourfold lines of the railway gleaming.   And slowly there spread over the world a Mediterranean of a delicate pale yellow with silver shores. Stéphane was also looking at the sky, and he suddenly said to me :

"The roads will be dry to-morrow. We will go to Serghievo."

SERGHIEVO.

Battlemented walls surround enormous buildings, a dozen churches with painted and gilt domes, a high tower three hundred feet high, inhabited by forty bells, immense sheds, gardens, parks, long glass-roofed galleries, libraries, a seminary, theological schools. And beside the monastery is the town which has grown on it, like a disease, with inns, traktirs and slums.

The gate of the holy city is surrounded with shops selling holy relics. It was to be expected. Pilgrims come here from the borders of the White Sea and from the heart of Siberia, gilt ikons, lamps, statues of Saint Sergius : a barbaric bazaar which I cannot see without disgust. It is obscene : the Pompeian pictures in the museums at Naples are not so indecent. This makes me blush and sickens me.

"It is no good concealing anything," mutters Stevo, who seems to anticipate my thoughts. "Or one would have to veil so many pictures and statues. It would be another waste. . . ."

The abbot : a portly old man with a red face and soft blue eyes, drove us in a carriage across his little state. Long low buildings containing prodigious wealth. We only saw a part of it : coffers, chests, glass-cases without end in galleries which smelt stuffy. Necklaces and chaplets of pearls, crowns and tiaras encrusted with precious stones, robes of cloth of gold covered with jewels, armour, a thousand strange objects, rich and rude, which made me dream of the old military Russia, of the files of convicts tramping through the snow in Siberia, and long trains of artillery running at a gallop over wooden roads. One expects to see even stranger things : remnants of forgotten Empires, the books and sceptres of kings unknown to history and the secrets of Asia. But on closer inspection one saw nothing but ugly and useless holy relics ; ugly as the feelings which inspired the donors : cowardice and a bargaining spirit. And they are all old and faded : the cloth of gold chasubles are only dusty old clothes, and the jewels are covered with a film which the light can hardly pierce, all falling into a yellowish light.

" Stevo ! How lovely are the jewels in the Rue de la Paix ! Oh ! a brooch representing the American flag in diamonds, rubies and sapphires ! Something bright and brilliant, something new ! A dark green leather motor spirit-case with gold stoppered crystal bottles : don't you think that would be pleasant to Saint Sergius ? "

" Surely : you are in the tradition of all these pious donors : they offer what they like best. Only the monks would have to be intelligent enough not to refuse your present."

SERGHIEVO,
7 *August.*

I had seen many monks going and coming along the galleries and cross the courts. But to-day I saw the Saint.

The Abbot had invited us to visit the refectories of the monastery. We had been there some time when a rumbling noise told us that the monks were coming down for the midday meal. Their footsteps rang out on the stone steps and suddenly the first of them came in : three little girls black-robed, with their hair waving under their high black head-dresses : the three Graces disguised as petty friars ! Others appeared : a pale face, lofty and calm in expression, and behind it pink faces, laughing eyes, Diana and her companions with their hair flying. At the sight of the Abbot, who was standing in front of our group, leaning on his long black stick, their beautiful eyes were lowered and their laughter stifled. But they had seen the astonishment on my face, and their lowered eyelids let slip a smile full of mischief. Linked arms were parted, the supple bearing was stiffened a little, and each, in passing the Abbot, made a slight genuflexion. Then they went to their places, stepped over the benches and sat down in silence. They quickly recognized Stéphane, pointed him out, and gazed at him. I remembered that Stéphane is now one of the men of the day in his own country. Familiarity and habit had almost made me forget that he is a Prince and handsome. He looked at them in his turn. Several of them blushed and others scolded them for it in low voices. But the young monks kept on coming in. The noise increased, and at the corner, surrounded with the purest faces I have seen since I left Florence, appeared a large pallid head that twitched and shook : the man was a cripple and his neighbours were pulling his hair and jostling him. Suddenly from the bend of the staircase a hand shot out and pushed him from behind. He missed two steps and pitched forward at our feet with his chin on the stone floor. He lay for a second with his eyes closed, and then got up, bowed to the Abbot and went back to his place, smiling. His body seemed to be dislocated with every step he took.

The men came in afterwards and finally the old men, and when we left the refectory I turned. A group of lovely nymphs in a fury were surrounding the lame man. They were accusing him of having let himself fall on purpose to show the Abbot the cruel treatment he had to put up with. They were all shouting, bending over him, with their hair hanging down over their shoulders. And the most beautiful of them was tearing at his ear.

Above the refectories a great court to which the Abbot took us was filled with a thousand pilgrims who were sitting round long tables of white wood, eating, waited on by lay brothers. They were eating in silence, with their heads near their plates. Each of them was like a bundle of rags, a bag of dirty linen. From a platform a monk was reading the Gospels aloud to them, in Greek. As the Abbot came in the monk stopped: the pilgrims got up and turned towards us and knelt. The Abbot blessed them with a grand gesture accompanied by a few words in which I recognized the Greek words for Father, Son, and Holy Ghost. A thousand voices answered him in one dull sound. Then the pilgrims began to eat again: they seemed to have come there only to eat. The men were stuffing themselves without looking round. A few women turned their heads covered with dark shawls towards us and looked at us.

"The people," murmured Stéphane. "Our people. . . ."

But my thoughts were elsewhere. I was imagining, hour by hour, the life of the lame monk. How pale and haggard he was when he came in ! And then, after his fall, the peace in his eyes and his unforgettable smile. . . . Where could he find a moment's quiet ! Even during the religious offices they must torment him, more than ever during the religious offices. I had understood the whole thing. Every face had told me its story. I looked at the Abbot. Did he know ? Did he understand ? His big red face, framed in soft white hair, had a little, round, almost absurd nose, but it expressed neither stupidity nor weakness.

As we were going out, Stéphane, who most curiously reads my thoughts, said :

" Oh ! you love him too."

" Whom ? "

" The Man of Sorrows."

Moscow : Slavianski Bazaar.

14 August.

The day before yesterday an august personage announced his intention of visiting the villa at Petrovskia. Stéphane wanted to keep me : he would have presented me. But that is just what I want to avoid. In my summer cruise on board the *Parvenu* I have always kept away from the Baltic and the Norwegian coasts, and even during the unpleasant period when I was drunk with worldly vanities I insisted on leaving Stéphane, and here I am at the hotel of the Slav Bazaar, all alone and a little at a loose end.

I want to spend to-night in noting down our last conversation. Later on I shall like reading it again.

Perhaps I shall say to myself one day as I come across Stéphane's words which seemed to me so rich in experience and beyond my years : " How young he was ! "

It was in the smoking-room after dinner. He was finishing a " Rothschild " and I was smoking a cigarette yellow with age, discovered in an old box on which were the French and Russian flags entwined and the name of the cigarettes : Phélix Phor. Stéphane was walking up and down and talking, and I was looking at him from the rocking-chair in which I sat. He looked a great big man, in a smoking jacket, with his hair cut short and his face well shaved. A long brown face, with deep-set eyes, a nose in one straight line with the brow, a prominent chin, the whole reminding me of the face one half sees under the helmet of Pallas. I see in it again the features of the young man of twenty-three to whom I used to tell the great discoveries I made when I was fifteen. But so many other things have left their marks on his features : his whole sentimental life, of which I never knew much, his marriage (apparently a simple diplomatic affair, though it may have changed his life) . . . I have heard it said by people who do not know that we are friends, that he had a " civil family " and " unofficial " children. Is it true ? He has never spoken of it to me. And that is not all : many other aspects of him are unknown to me : everything to do with his profession as a soldier, his engineering knowledge: like countries in which he has lived for a long time and I have never even visited. He knows all about me : he knows all my intellectual and moral baggage. I know that he remembers all the stupid things I have said to him, and has guessed many of those I have only thought.

266

Sometimes I feel that he is thinking of them : suddenly his eyes will remind me of some old story that I would like to have forgotten. Clumsy imitation of him : absurd revolt against his influence : things deliberately concocted to astound him : hypocritical attempts, dreams and plans for the future in which I never doubted my superiority to him. He has remembered all that. And I have not yet the strength or the audacity to criticize him in my turn.

"You are going," he said, "without the thing you came to me to give : a formula : or at least the fruits of my experience. But there is no formula, and my experience is uncommunicable. Or, rather, there are formulæ, but they are the most useless and trivial wares to be found in the market. There are the gross formulæ which the middle-classes all buy : respect for the social order, moral notions, Duty. When they are richer they buy better ones : Honour, the morality of the Holy Fathers, Stoicism. That corresponds to the jewels their wives wear : provincial jewellery, jewellery of the big shops and jewellery of the Rue de la Paix. There are better formulæ still : esoteric doctrines, the simple life, Tolstoi, Nietzsche : signed enamels and jewels. And they are as useless as the common jewels : they adorn themselves with them, but they do not use them. All their lives they wear their formulæ, as savages wear rings in their noses : and all their years they live without even trying sincerely to make some agreement between themselves and their formulæ. They would not even if they could. Try to live according to the precepts of Epictetus. I keep my place : let them laugh. But we know that it is bad taste to wear such gewgaws. One can keep a few of the most curious and costly at home to have the amusement of looking at them from time to time. But take care to have nothing to do with people who have a lower morality than your own. You see we have come back to the Ignavi, the Inert. Imagine a man like Benvenuto Cellini in a little town like Madame Bovary's. Don't think the good people of Yonville would be afraid of him. No. They would think him ridiculous with his love affairs, his boasting and his art : and all Yonville, even down to the fowls, would hound him out. They are the many, and Cellini would soon have understood that he had nothing to do among them. But why should I even need to tell you to keep clear of the Ignavi ? If you are not like them you will be inevitably separate from them, in spite of yourself, even if you liked—as is unlikely—being with them. No, I have no advice to give you. I have nothing to say to you which could be of any use to you. Every man has been set apart, every man has been valued.

" And yet I will tell you what I have seen, as a traveller describing the countries he has passed through. It will only keep you a moment and you will forget it at once. But later on, perhaps, when you suddenly recognize the country round you, you will remember the description I gave you of it.

" A man is born and his difficulties begin. So many obstacles to surmount, so many eliminating tests. Childish illnesses and the education people try to give him : the bad habits of this ungrateful age and his parents' lack of understanding : poverty, mediocrity, or wealth : sexual diseases and marriage. There are some who sink and care not to rise. One man has his physical trouble : another his household. That is enough for them : they are content and ask no more. The little flame which carried them so far will suffice henceforth to lead them to the grave. But in others a more vigorous flame reaches up to higher things : resistance does not exhaust them ; not content with defending themselves they attack. They know all the fights which the others sustain, and they want to meet with more violent struggles. They accept joyously what all the rest receive with a bad grace, and everything that the rest repent of having accepted. They accept illness and go out to meet love. They take everything ; they bear parents, wife, children with them ; such things cannot bar their way. But they want something else. They arise from passion and the home. Woman cannot bring about their fall : they take her in their arms and go on marching towards the light. For they have something to give to the world, and they will give it, in spite of the world, in spite of themselves. The others were models for novels and comedies : but these men get the better of Clio : they leave private life and enter public life.

"And what have you to give to the world ? What fruit is there forming in your heart as I speak ? Have the Greeks and Latins we read together sowed the seeds of greatness in your soul ? Have you done with the Germanic herd ? They go in shoals : they cling to their princes like mussels to rocks. Has the imperial idea taken root in you ? You know that what your country wants is a Porfirio Diaz. Do you ever think over what they write to you from there ? "

"Thanks ! am I to be what they call a *politico* ? "

"Yes, one does not know whether it is a beginning or an end. I do not know your country. If I were in your place I should want to see for myself. To see if

269

there is no way of helping them. To help, to be of some use, to do good to others ! nobility comes entirely from the gift of oneself. Ah ! we nobles, brother, we nobles ! What made you pick up that count's coronet from the gutter ? Let the world never lack noblemen, and I will answer for it. You may change their names, but their essence remains. There will always be dukes at the head of the armies, marquises on the frontiers, princes in control of the republics, and counts round the sacred person."

"Well, Stéphane, my prince ? Let my lord command me."

"You do not depend on me."

"To whom then do I owe allegiance ? "

"To what you love best. But you do not yet know what you love best. And I cannot tell you what it is. I know what you do not love and that is all. You do not love this World. I don't mean the world depicted in novels beloved by the vulgar bourgeois : ' The Duchess made a sign to the Marquis,' etc.—the world of clubs, racing stables, and pigeon-shooting, all the abominable vulgarity of the rich from which you have broken away : you were too good for that. I mean the World, what Satan called All This in the temptation : ' I will give you all this . . .' And you refuse. You are a deserter : you have turned out badly, according to the world. We had only to reach out our hands to take it. Pleasures, positions, honours, were ready for us. And we would not have them. Too easy ! or too late ! When you were sixteen you dared not dream that a woman like Mrs. Hansker would give you to understand that you pleased her. At twenty-three you found her and would not have her. It was not sullenness, nor was it boredom. It was the desire for something better. Others may have Mrs. Hansker and her money, others may make brilliant careers and die loaded with honours. They will do so for us, in our stead : we will give them power of attorney. We have better things to do : a higher ambition leads us on. We have passed by so many things already. I like the man who rises from whatever small beginnings : a peasant's son who becomes a schoolmaster, the shop-keeper's son who becomes a doctor. Their effort, their rise is very touching : the little step they take brings them nearer the light which we have reached. I know there is no great merit in my being there : for generations those of my blood have gorged themselves with all that the world has to give. That is why princely and royal families have produced so many ascetics and saints. But what do you want me to say about you ? There is a thing called nobility and suddenly among men comes one who finds himself clad in it.

" I have ceased to ask questions. I know nothing, I am ignorant, but at peace : I know what I love. It took a long time to know it, to understand the cause of the distress that went with me everywhere. . . . Fool ! I have always loved the same thing ! It lay concealed behind all my loves, and nudged me in the midst of my joys ; it waited outside my windows, and even with women I was thinking of it. Ah ! you know what I mean, and I need not pronounce the most holy and most execrated name. And you will explain all by heredity, you will think of the clause in the Holy Alliance in which Europe is called : ' The Christian Nation. . . .' No doubt it was my illustrious ancestor who dictated it under the inspiration of a mad German woman and a few Visionaries ! But I will not answer any objections. I love. And no doubt I have had to wait until I am over thirty to feel both utterly alone, and alone with him, and to understand that it was he who marked me out and waited for me.

" There is nothing and we are utterly alone. There is no cause, personal interest apart, which is worth a paring from one of my nails. There is nothing worthy of respect, as I have told you : and sometimes, for the fun of it, I long to outrage the flag I serve. The bond between men is a convention of the writer of comedies and novels. What would our friendship be without him who is the best part of it, and the pleasure of being together for an hour or two ? Everything may slip away from me, but he is left to me. You are not listening to me. But he listens. He has gathered up all my tears, shared in all my joys. No doubt I am pleased to have carried out what I undertook, and I applaud my success. But I know that it is more enviable to have failed, for he who loses all finds him. I found him. But that part of my experience is more incommunicable than all the rest. If I were to tell you : ' There is the truth, the only truth and the life '—you would not believe me. You know that I have always avoided talking of my love affairs and what people call fortunate adventures. Don't expect me to tell you about those which were not of my choosing and are a humiliation to me and a condemnation. I was only yielding to the appetite within me. See : the greatest and most assured are silent : the stigmata on the brow and finger on lips. One does not talk of one's possessions. And I possess love. And that is why, as I told you, I wish to serve. I must ultimately help him.

I will not have the power of love which is in me, which is himself, left unused. It demands to serve. I must deliver it : I must do something for him. I want to serve and I shall never weary of it. If to-morrow the revolutionaries seize power and do not kill me I shall go to them and say : 'Do not waste me. I used to build roads under the old order : you can use me now to break stones.'

"He too is an economist. Economy and love are perhaps two names for the same thing. And look you, there is just one title and one function, which have been left unused for a long time, for exactly two centuries. I have not placed my trust in kings, but why should I despise that function ? It preserves a place where any day a truly great man might appear. The name may change, but the august, pure conception of the spirit will always be necessary, and every earthly good can come only from it. Good-bye. I am going to welcome the Emperor of the East on my knees."

BOOK IV

St. Petersburg, Copenhagen, London

BOOK IV

St. Petersburg, Copenhagen, London

I HAVE been here four days and am glad to see again the wide horizons of Petersburg, the broad river, like an inlet of the sea, vast squares and the little pointed paving stones.

Yesterday and the day before I went for a long drive in a magnificent droshky : two big black horses with red and silver harness, and reins held and driven by a coachman like a round peg-top in his enormous cloak and little hat, with a fourfold cord of orange silk. We never go at a walk, we leave the world behind us : borne on by two wild beasts. The town expands and reaches out in all directions and seems to multiply itself : and the river rejoins it, leaves it, goes round it, passes through it, *ad infinitum*.

To-day I have dismissed the droshky and am keeping to the district near my hotel, between the Grand Morskaia and the galleries of the Gostin Dvor, the heavy and barbarous aspect of which I love. In spite of the summer heat there is movement on the Prospect : but Society has gone away. Soldiers stop suddenly, clap their heels together and salute an officer going by. In front of the

277

Roman Catholic Church there is always at certain times the same crowd of people going in and out, and loitering, breaking the parallel lines of the people going by on the wide pavement. To-morrow I shall go and see the little humpbacked bridges of the Fontanka.

I am recovering, gradually breaking away from Stéphane's influence. I am trying to extract some kind of doctrine from what he said. But I soon see that it is impossible. Often he said what I was already thinking and it seemed to me that he was talking instead of me, explaining my secret inclinations, expressing my highest aspirations. Then again he would exhaust me and leave me disgusted with his ideas: everything he had said would appear false, artificial, forced, inhuman. No good to me.

At first I applauded him: here at last was someone making a clean sweep, opening the windows, insisting on seeing clearly. I would take part in his explanation, and help to dislodge and destroy the lie. But no: he had merely breathed on the dust and swept up the crumbs and in their stead put back the old things: one day Dante, another the Hero of Carlyle, and another God, and finally the police. I would rather have those toys of painted wood, the gold of the ikon near my bed, the mournful colour of the palace opposite.

Ah! I understood well enough, economy, Service. To cease to be self-indulgent, and to cease from sterile self-criticism, and stiffen oneself up and use oneself utterly in some real action. But—what action? I should have to force myself, by an effort of will, to anticipate my own maturity. Is it impossible? It would not do, it would only be a pose. What should I gain by restraining myself? My body lives a respectable, normal, decent life, why should I not yield to my instincts and most natural impulses ?

Once more I patronize the shops. After all, is Stéphane sure that I was not created expressly to enrich the shop-keepers of the Nevsky Prospect ?

I went into the Hermitage and came out quickly : it is enough to make me hate Rubens, Guido and Raphael to find them here.

I am thinking a good deal. I am looking towards a new life. I am on the look out for a social position. I made a bad start. The life of a multi-millionaire had been arranged for me and I put up with it : the experience was worth the attempt. Then, when I saw that I had no taste for that kind of life I got out of it suddenly and awkwardly. I wandered blown this way and that, hesitating between the different counsels of my different friends. But I am weary of their talk. I do not wish to identify myself like that with every one who talks to me : I want to get rid of my trick of agreeing with the people who are near me, as if I were afraid of displeasing them or wanted to flatter them. I will dare to hurt them, even Stéphane.

I want a peaceful, easy, retired studious existence. I will live in one of the great capitals so as to be in direct contact with civilization. A quiet neighbourhood : but not the most aristocratic neighbourhood. A house equipped with all the latest conveniences : but not big enough to allow of my giving receptions. I am hesitating between London and Paris : Kensington and Passy. But, as for the house, I am already arranging it.

Outside, nothing shall distinguish it from the neighbouring houses. It shall be commonplace, even rather ugly, but respectable, with a rather pompous flight of steps and electric lights to inspire respect in the trades-people. As for the inside, that is much more difficult : and I have several schemes of decoration for every room. I am hesitating between one of the classical French styles and Chippendale and Serrurier. I am also thinking of asking Francis Jourdain for furniture for the winter garden. The purely practical part occupies my thoughts even more : especially the bathroom, twice as large as the bedroom (a mere hospital cubicle, white, tiled, with no corners), and it shall contain a little piscina with run-ning water, and a bath for sea-water which I will have sent to me from Bexhill every morning, like last year, if I settle in Kensington. I am even thinking of the electric-bell pushes and the electric lamps and ventilators and all the study fittings. Most often I incline towards purely practical, almost scientific, furniture, carefully avoiding every artistic consideration. A roll-top Ameri-can desk, a special arm-chair for work, and bare wood tables and chairs ; glass, marble, china, surfaces easily washed : as much air and light as possible. And then a great hall in the middle of the house, bright, with pleasant colours, and a monumental chimney-piece, a few very good pictures, and arm-chairs waiting to give comfort. Sometimes when I come back to the study I am seized with a desire to set out at once for Florence : in an antiquary's shop on the Via Maggio there was an old orange-wood desk inlaid with mother-of-pearl (big, light, lace-like leaves of it). I don't think they can have sold it after I left. But here the shops in the Prospect are keeping me busy.

Stéphane's influence has lasted hardly any time. It did not deserve to. I don't deny that he has found an answer to the most terribly pressing questions of his youth, and has found peace and discovered a reason for living and doing. But I should feel cramped on that summit of his. And he is wrong : I love the world : after my fashion : beautiful things in luxurious shops, streets where the ordinary daily life goes up and down, palaces, old houses, the gentle faces of old towers, new churches in festival costume, all the tangible reality of history, all the past that I can find out, all the future that I can foresee—I sit somewhat aloof as I do not wish to mix with it : so I shall see and enjoy more. If I too had my part to play I could not keep my attention free. And I don't want to miss anything : I want to feel the continuity of things, I want to see the fruits of time ripen. And, ultimately, I want to close my windows against all the clamour of the streets and not to worry about reading the stuff the newsvendors hawk about.

Resumed my long drives. I love setting out in the early morning, the swift horses, the driver's coolness as he sits stiff and motionless in his enormous high-waisted cloak : and the width and beauty of the roads : and returning at a fast trot about midday to the huge serious city, kindly and busy : all that exalts and fortifies me.

Let me see. Life is offered to me in a tolerably beautiful light and I am regaining confidence. Until now it has only been a time of attempts and preparations.

I have still before me, say, thirty years of physical and intellectual health. I must turn those years to the best account : not fritter them away—as Stéphane would say. But how ? Without hesitation I reply : in pleasing myself, above everything. It is useless to try to force myself, and to trick myself and to set myself a " duty " in which I shall fail every day. I know that I shall do well only what I take pleasure in doing. But I must first have that house. Peaceful surroundings to which to retire and reflect, and, with visits from a few chosen friends, apply myself to some work of my own choice. At the end of ten years' reading, research, experience in the life of a capital, I may perhaps be worthy of being useful to something, and Stéphane will be obliged to admit that I am right. Oh ! I have a great desire to apply myself like a good pupil and humbly to learn. But I must have that house.

I am thinking of going to Sweden. Two years ago I saw some furniture there, and printed stuffs and papers of a very charming freshness and rusticity.

ST. PETERSBURG,
29 *August.*

This morning, as I was returning to the left bank of the Neva by the Trotsky bridge, my carriage ran into and upset, at the corner of the Champ-de-Mars and the Millionnaïa, a cab containing a moujik and a woman of the people.

I had time to see the cab properly. A moujik driving attracts attention : the poor do not take cabs except on the great occasions of their lives. These people were in their Sunday best, and at once I thought : a wedding :

when I saw that the man, one of those fair-haired Christs one sees so often here, was sitting up very straight and carrying a box on his knees and weeping solemnly, without moving his face. The baba was sitting bent down by his side.

Then the accident happened: their driver tried to avoid us, turned too abruptly; one of their wheels went up on the pavement near the Marble Palace, and they were already upset when my driver with a simple " brr," almost whispered, stopped the rearing horses.

I got out: but what could I do? I saw the man get up, and help the woman to shake clear of the cushions which had fallen on her. No one was hurt. Their driver, protected by his clothes, was the first to get on his feet. The moujik at once went up to the box which had been flung against the wall of the palace: and at the moment when he picked it up I saw that it was broken and that it contained the corpse of a little child. The woman arranged the swaddling clothes and covered up the little pallid face, on which the features were already beginning to be blurred.

My driver helped them, while I held the reins, to repair the damaged wheel. Then they set off again. It had all happened without a cry, without a word. Just as I was on the point of saying a few words of excuse or consolation I was stopped by the moujik's look: evidently there was nothing to say.

And as we came out into the Dvortsovy Square, which for the moment was empty, a battalion of infantry, coming out of the arch of the Grand Morskaia, suddenly gave a thundering roll with its drums as it came in sight of the Winter Palace.

I am returning to my diary after leaving it for more than a month. I will begin by noting down what I have been doing in the interval.

Three weeks at Stockholm. The Grand Hotel contains everything one can desire in one's own home. I contrived to have a regular life there, orderly, without contact of any kind, among books and flowers: sometimes going to the National Museum next door, sometimes to the vast places of pleasure adjoining the opera. I began once more to love that bright great city : the living water between the quays of soft pale grey stone : the gardens scattered over the waters : and the decent easy existence : the respectable and respected intoxication : the uniforms, black and yellow, dark blue and gold, light blue and white : and the pretty provincial dresses of the ladies in the stalls at the opera. All the comforts of German life without the vulgarity of their great industrial cities. Bought several pieces of furniture which I have had sent to the Yarza girls at Leamington to wait until I have a house in London.

And one morning my boredom returned. Not with the old tearful crises, or the passionate despair and savage need of happiness, but in dull, heavy sadness, a disgust, an intolerable weariness. " The heavenly gift " of the poets (" It is only one of the names of grace," said Stéphane) ; and it is indeed a gift of Heaven, the gift of Apollo ; I look for physical causes of my depression : lack of exercise ? a too regular life ?

I left Stockholm thinking to go straight to Copenhagen. But a sudden impulse made me get out at

Hessleholm, whence I went and spent a week at Finja, on the edge of a pretty little lake. The inn, as clean as a new doll's house, with its little square windows, the white wood floors strewn with pine needles gathered fresh every day, the comfortable bathroom, and all the conveniences of civilization combined with a country-side apparently far removed from the great centres, and the country itself all pleased me at first, and would have kept me longer but for the increasing cold and my unconquerable boredom.

And yet I had fine afternoons spent in driving through the country in a high brake drawn by two superb horses which I drove myself most of the time. A grave-looking country, with long fields, pine woods filled with a majestic darkness, where on the outskirts the last flowers of the season were opening, and farther on, inside the wood, hordes of enormous toadstools, red, pink, golden, grey-green : and on the plateaux over-looking the lake grey and pink flats stretching away to other forests which filled the horizon. But everywhere one is conscious of the presence of man : white- and red-painted fences surround the fields : and here and there a shepherdess, reading, would raise her head and give me an old-fashioned bow. The men also would salute me : great big fellows in gala dress : black buckled shoes, white stockings, golden-yellow satin breeches, a short light blue or pink waistcoat. Often I regretted being unable to have a better acquaintance of these fine people with their respectful and independent manners : they attract me, as the Tuscan peasants attracted me. (I used to love to mix with them on Fridays on the Piazza della Signoria.) I feel that they have a serious and sensible conception of existence : a certain way of respecting the conventions, not because they are afraid of them, but because they know that they facilitate social relations, because they make use of them. They are well-brought-up children, and I should like to have met their fathers (the priests and the schoolmasters).

Ah ! I felt that I was beneath them from every point of view. Never was I so cruelly tormented with contempt for myself, disgust and shame at my past life, distress at the thought of the future and the emptiness of my life. In fine for nearly a year I have been watching the formation of the man I shall be some day. It began when I tried to live by myself and for myself : and it is still going on. As far as possible I shall have noted down from day to day the phases of the transformation. I re-read my Italian diary in the inn at Finja on a rainy day when the tarnished lake was suffering and restless between its mist-drenched banks. It was painful reading and it often made me blush. So many sentences that— already !—I would not write now. . . . Exaggerations, naïvetés, little useless lies, little scraps of malice sewn together with a white thread ! And yet I tried not to deceive myself : to see my life directly and not through books I had read : and to leave a matter unexplained rather than admit an explanation drawn from my literary memories. Often I have been near to striking out a sentence which did not ring true, a ready-made expression which did not correspond with my real thought. I needed courage not to alter anything and to leave the document intact with all its puerilities, its too intimate confidences, its confessions of weakness : my only consolation has indeed come from it. I was beginning

to disown my diary : I saw into it clearly : I criticized
it ; sham feelings, the last traces of the ungrateful age.
I noted all these things and in that way measured the
distance I have gone. I was no longer the young man
who had written those pages : I had laid all that aside :
" a sadder and a wiser man."

But how far had I yet to go ?

Monday.

I drag my usual and domestic despair round the streets
of Copenhagen. The emptiness of my life : my complete futility : the world is irreproachable : everything
in the universe is for the best : I alone am bad, I alone
am wrong. . . .

With such thoughts I walk along the Ostergade and
stop to look at the shops. I love the Danish book-
shops : they seem to combine everything I would like
to know in a neat pretty form. The Danish words have
a fine rare quality : a more aristocratic German, a less
familiar English : a language adorned with all the
dignity of the literary idioms, while its orthography seems
to have been fixed by great humanists in love with Greek
and simplicity. A desire to begin seriously to study
the Scandinavian languages. And then, what's the
good ?

I am still thinking of the young countrymen of Finja.
To be one of them. Who knows ? That might suffice :
to be a well-brought-up child. We are so little by ourselves : such a mixture of instincts, atavisms, influences.
I doubt even if the thought I have just written is my
own : and even that doubt has been taught me. Yes :
to obey, to take orders from Cartuyvels, put myself

under the wing of a sort of preceptor like Putouarey under the Abbé Vernet's : or I might enter one of my own banks as a junior clerk (but I have not even the technical knowledge they demand). Stick to the education I was given ? But so many facts had proved its inadequacy. . . . Ah ! and while I am thus debating with myself, my life is going its own way, going on like a story to which I am listening, and my destiny determines for me every moment (those heights and depths of myself were fixed from all time) and, without knowing it, I " do " the disease of which I shall die one day. (No doubt the most serious thing I do.)

I often go to the Tivoli Gardens where I love to drink in the sadness which dwells in pleasure resorts, especially in those of the North. The grand palace (a German seaside casino) is now occupied by a colonial exhibition which is touchingly meagre. I sit on the benches of an open-air theatre and listen to German and Swedish " Parisian soubrettes " singing Tyrolese and Swiss songs. Sometimes from one of the restaurants a man is respectfully carried to his carriage after being found drunk under the table. It is nothing : only the northern sun, kirsebaer and iced Caloric-Punch.

And I like sitting apart at a table in the Chinese pavilion, by the artificial lake, in the middle of which rises an island with stucco rocks painted brown and yellow. A sailor with a tricoloured waistband invites you to go in a gondola : " Vuole, signore ? " I make no reply. Italian words which would come easily enough in Florence refuse to serve me here. Sometimes I go to the Panoptikeum, where the characters of the Dreyfus affair, stuffed out in their faded uniforms, linger among the heads and hands cut off the most celebrated criminals in Denmark. Above the leaves the tower of the Raadhus changes slowly from golden yellow to reddish brown in the sunset sky.

I return to dinner at my hotel, in the Kougens Nytorv, a melancholy dark square, too big for the town, for the theatre which it surrounds, and also provincial : for instance, two electric lamps, one green, the other red, which mark the entrance to a little restaurant, are the only attempt at gaiety in its dark emptiness.

Met Maxime Claremoris this morning in the Oster-gade. I did not recognize him at first. His big fresh face, clean-shaven, rather childish, was, as it were, weighed down with sadness and bitterness : his kindly grey eyes had lost their gaiety. I had to run after him to catch him.

" Pilgrim ! my dear Pilgrim ! what luck ! where have you come from ? "

" Prison. Yes, for having put a sign saying ' Gen-tlemen ' on an indecent statue of Bismarck. My dear fellow, it was quite a reasonable mistake. They treated me as a madman. But I got out of it very well : two Prussians wanted to shoot me offhand. In the end I spent two months in the Lutheran cells."

I tried to take him towards the Tivoli. But really he seemed quite convinced that I would take him to a " low resort " and reminded me of our evenings at the Savonarola. We stopped outside a foreign bookshop the windows of which were filled with the latest novelties, German, English, and French.

" Look, Archie, at the French books : Anatole

France's novel, *Sur la pierre blanche* : and then, alongside, a bunch of clap-trap called *Ames de grues*, *Luxures paiennes*, *Flirtons*. That's what the Danes read (though less and less—have you noticed how the French territory in the windows of the international bookshops is shrinking ?). That's what Europe reads as French literature, while Laforgue and Rimbaud pay to have their books printed, and they leave the publishers only to fall into the boxes on the quais. . . . It is Gambetta's fault. He found France most favourably circumstanced for the development of the fine arts—and then, oh, damn ! it is too idiotic : you can say it for me, you know the formula."

I turned to him, offended. But I saw that his nervous laugh had changed to a wry face and that he was choking back sobs. A few yards farther on he suddenly left me.

COPENHAGEN,
7 *October.*

This morning early Max came into my room and said :

" I have come to ask you for something to eat. I am expecting a cheque from my banker and until I receive it you will be obliged to feed me and to listen patiently to the insults with which I shall overwhelm you by way of proving my ingratitude."

He stayed all morning lost in thought, and soon after noon I took him to the Tivoli. Suddenly, as we were sitting outside the Chinese pavilion, by the lake, he began to talk.

" I don't know what you are. A rich man, not so

horribly idiotic as most representatives of the race, because you are young and not yet sure enough of yourself to see that at heart you despise me or to dare to say that you prefer the official artists to those whom I used to defend in the 'Pilgrim.' Patience, that will come. . . . A tolerable rich man, in fine, who shares with me the coarse pleasures which are within his reach : dinners in the big restaurants, motor drives and yachting cruises . . . but what do you think of me ? A buffoon, a Bohemian, a madman, who, after all, perhaps has 'some value as a critic of art,' and at least has been able to 'make a name for himself' which is almost as worthy of respect as the possession of much money. And at heart, I feel that there is something else . . . I think you will understand what I feel I must say to you. And if you don't understand, it doesn't matter : for the moment I would talk to the post.

"I have had enough of this constant sneering, my paradoxes, and the polemics of the *Passionate Pilgrim*. The slating business is too easy, it is within the reach of too many people : it has taken the place of the madrigal and minor court poetry. And it is also perfectly useless. I have understood that for two years now, also that it doesn't amuse me any longer. I ought to have admitted it sooner, that is all.

"Yes. The little flame has flickered out. The little that I had to say has been said. You will know that great dryness of heart and that supreme lucidity on the day when, in some city or other, in the throng of people going by, you coolly say to yourself : ' I see now that there is nothing, that life is a wretched swindle, unworthy even of our curiosity.' The sudden, complete, the callous renunciation : the disgust with the work you have begun : the scorn of the work you have done, the reputation you have gained, the life you have lived : and in front of you a few empty decades in which to do the actions of a living man, and to contrive somehow that the other men living at the same time shall not see how you despise their efforts and how indifferent you are to their failure and their success alike. I have reached the very bottom.

"But I started well. I swear there was no other ambition in me than to make known and defend against the neophobes the works of art I loved, which I felt as though I had done them myself. My poor parents never understood me : that a son of theirs should have it in his power to become the biggest wine-merchant in the whole county of Cork and give it up light-heartedly ! I made them suffer, poor dears ! When I left for Italy the first time, without telling them, and, my dear fellow, borrowed the money I needed from a woman of the theatre. . . .

"I have known heroic days when I have dined on a Constantin Guys or a Piranese drawing : and nights of toil when I have felt very near the great masters whom I had set myself to interpret. It was my great period, when I was working without any thought of success and had no doubts. Then one day, and from then I date the beginning of my moral decadence, I saw that I had become notorious : people were talking about my work, the articles in the *Passionate Pilgrim* were being quoted in other young reviews, and then I had plagiarists and imitators. It was success : I was flayed alive in the big reviews, and in the newspapers my name was already treated with the ridicule which precedes what in our time, which is not over nice, is called fame. Even now I sometimes receive from certain backward or provincial places articles in which the whole accusation is begun all over again, and I am called mystery-monger and madman, and in proof of my lunacy, my finest passages on the Italian die-sinkers are quoted. At last there came a time when I understood that, without intending to do so, I had raised myself above the social condition of my parents. Until then I had thought, like them, that I had turned out badly, and I was sincerely sorry for it.

" Another day the idea that I had once travelled in Ireland for the firm of Claremoris & Son struck me as entirely comic and romantic. The people who were round me at that time would have laughed too if they had known that.

" Came the article by —— which made me known to the great public, when I was already weary of the pleasure of notoriety. The following month the same critic published in the same way a poor effusion of the same tiresome kind. And every day I was compared to frauds, illiterate idiots, shams, people who did not know how to look at a picture and have never really seen a single one.

" But what did it matter ? Gradually I broke away from all the things I had loved best. However, I persisted and undertook fresh work. For a long time I had known and understood that art is still the only bearable form of life : the greatest delight and that which is least quickly exhausted. The satisfactions of the heart can only be found in the family, and even then they are

rarely to be met with.   Art at least never refuses itself
to our love.   On the other hand, I insisted on not abandoning my researches : they gave me the illusion of being
useful to something, of earning my living, of contributing
to the common work.   But I had always regarded them
as an inferior kind of activity.

"I have become conscious of the vanity of all that.
The work done this year, which is alive and discussed
and approved by the fortunate few, and loved by young
people, will in fifty years be only a curiosity to smile at.
The examination of its sources, the lapse of time, will
reduce it to a very small and unimportant thing.   It
will be dissected, classified, docketed in the catalogues
of the specialists.   Look at the books of the past : those
poor empty books left with scarcely even a memory
of the perfume they once contained.   Ours will meet
the same fate.   And even if they do not perish in the
course of years they will become mere philological monuments.   They will meet the fate of mummies shown in a
museum, where they are hardly even regarded as dead
men.   I shall perhaps live a little longer than the mass
of contemporary art critics because I have been acknowledged later, because I have had the official critics and
the mouthpieces of the middle classes against me.   And
afterwards !   I am not even sure of that.   And why
should my work be worth anything ?   Because I took
pleasure in doing it ?

"I have gained a lot, haven't I ?   Why did I not
resist the instinct which drove me to write ?   Why did
I not keep to myself my sensations, my ideas, and my
enthusiasms ?   So that some day some rich amateur
half crazy with idleness, or some young critic intent on

making a brilliant career, might take me as the subject of a big book, dissect my work in accordance with a method which knows nothing of the very essence of art (every method is gross), rummage in my life, without sympathy, perhaps even without intelligence, seeing, for instance, in the actions I did against the grain the indications of a serious passion. . . . So that, and this is the supreme absurdity, a memorial plate should be put on the wall of the house I was born in, in Cork, the only town I could not live in, of which I cannot even think without distress ! I have gained a lot : I was violent, disinterested, sincere. I laid myself open to attack. In the great mass of works done in the past those which have no value still cut the best figure : their nullity protects them against criticism, or perhaps those which have obviously been written with a view to success. The lives of their authors are examined, and admired if they were able to turn their fame to good account. They at least have not been duped. The respect in which they are held is extended to what they leave behind : after all, they were reasonable men !

" Oh, well ! I want to do like them. I have no choice : suicide or that. Do you know a rich woman, widowed or divorced, who would like to marry a man ' with a name ' ?—a rich, very rich woman, none of your lower middle class. I have looked about : I have gone into society : and I only go to the museums now in the hope of a fortunate encounter. I want to be comfortable. Until now I have been dying of hunger, in spite of my fifteen thousand francs a year (a large sum, of which my parents were very proud), I had my review, my travelling expenses, and my gallery, which I was continually reopening. Always in debt : always some unsatisfied desire. I have had enough of it. I want to spread myself, to have a comfortable home, my motor-car, servants, and no longer always and everywhere to have to put up with second class. Only on that condition will I accept life. Seriously, there are days when I am so tired that, when I cross a street and a tram comes gliding full speed towards me, I feel inclined to throw myself across the rails. I should have done it before now if I had not been afraid of not being killed outright : suppose the soul were to be left, if only for a second, jammed in the half-open door ! I ought not to tell you that. An accident might happen and you would believe . . .

" You would believe what you liked. What does it matter ! And do I really set that much store by money ? I have tried everything. I became a fervent Christian in the middle of my youthful irregularities and my family were staggered by my conversion. I have become indifferent. I have considered death closely : well, no ; it is not for me. Ah ! my old good will ! No. There is nothing, there is nothing, there is nothing ! And I am not even afraid."

8 *October*.

My turn to talk this morning, in our rooms. I tried, not to console or encourage Max, but to make him understand that he had my sympathy : and that I have known crises like that through which he is passing. I told him timidly of my friendship for him. " I have little to give you, Max, but there it is."

" Thanks, my dear Archie ; and I have confidence in you. I give you credit for a few childish tricks. I know that your heart is good. You will be an easy and indulgent and not impatient friend. You will not be crusted over with formulæ : you will not measure your esteem by my success : you will not doubt me if you hear me criticized : you will not boast idiotically of knowing me if I am praised in your hearing. You will not laugh at me if I fail and if I fall ill or sink into drunkenness or bestiality. You know what I am. And you are still ready for intellectual adventures : you will still change your opinions : and still change in yourself. But what can you do for me ? I tell you : I have touched the bottom. I shall go on living and travelling : perhaps I shall even go on writing. But henceforth my point of view is changed.

"I shall go back to Italy one of these days. It is a crime to watch the autumn in the North. Can't you see that Nature is afraid of dying here ? The wounded, bleeding gardens are waiting for the mortal stroke, and only the spiders, the terrifying six-armed gymnasts, live in these wet laurels. In the towns the Greek buildings, burned by the years, hide their black domes and colonnades in the mist. If you stay a little longer you will see what becomes of the Amalieborg, and the Thorwaldsen museum by its Stygian canal, the terrible Thulean Acropolis. Down yonder I shall find the reddening vines dancing their rounds round the plain of Lombardy : and in Florence no other sign of the season than a golden crown on the black-and-white front of San Miniato. Oh! I long to see cypresses on hills ! *Tutto il mondo è poese,* but Tuscany is the country of my love. How can one live anywhere else ? "

"You see, you do still cling to something."

"True. But no longer with the old warmth : it is with a look backwards and hands slackening their hold. Or else, in utter despair as I am, what is life plotting to ask of me now ? "

In three weeks I shall leave Europe to go and live for a few years, perhaps to settle finally, in a country in South America which I do not know though it is my own country. All that is left me of it are certain childish memories which have been transformed by reading. Old Lolita, faces of Indian and African servants, recollections so distant, so intimate and so faint that they escape me just as I am about to catch them in the net of words. This morning when Concha spoke to me about the preparations she is making for the *Noche-buena*, an old palace in my memory, long since closed and forgotten, was suddenly reopened and for a second I saw the lighted halls, golden thrones, the gleaming crib, the Magi round the Most Pure. . . .

I am going without any pleasure simply because I have had enough of this, cannot live in it any longer and must make an end. But I see nothing in front of me. I have given up imagining what my life there will be ; I have been too often disappointed. I merely want to set down here, not even the reasons for my departure (reasons too profound to be expressible), but what has led up to my resolution and what is to precede my departure.

From Copenhagen I wrote to the Yarza girls to tell them to leave Leamington and go to London to wait for me. I told them when I should arrive and they came to meet me, and I found them on the landing stage at Hull. After a week at the Ritz Hotel I settled in the simple comfortable house of my desire and the Yarza girls took the house next door.

London took possession of me again : so much so that I was surprised to find myself saying, as Maxime Clare-moris said of Italy : " How can people live anywhere else ? " Tea-time, the fogs, the days well poised on the four meals, the familiar sights, all at first helped to soothe my soreness and to calm me. The Sundays gave me the nourishment of silence : and the empty square (the key of which I keep in my American desk) lent me a little of its correct, respectable, reserved boredom. For ten days I had the illusion of being at last at home.

I soon found myself in an entirely different world from that which I had frequented during my first stay here. I had asked Max for some letters of introduction, and so I got to know a number of his friends, that is to say, I divided my time, away from home, between a few bourgeois clubs in the West End and the studios of Chelsea. And the old story began again. I had to get out of the way of a crowd of fools and gross people who would have trampled me underfoot without seeing me : provincials who had come up to the capital the year before with the intention of conquering it, and thinking me a newly-arrived provincial, took upon themselves to give me advice. Commonplace people who, knowing that I was rich and in touch with the industrial world, supposed me to be ignorant and stupid, looked at each other when I spoke and corrected in asides what they took to be my mistakes and blunders. Cunning fellows who advised me to back theatres and revues and to buy their friends' books and pictures, and flattered me so idiotically or so hypocritically that I was ashamed for them. Some of them, knowing that I wrote, proposed to help me to "make myself known"; and a middle-aged man, who had never read a line of my work, one day brought me a slim volume of his verses dedicated "to the exquisite poet, Archibald Olson Barnabooth. . . ." Impossible to explain their mistakes to them: since they are unconscious of them, and since they never saw me.

One day I returned to what I used to call "my world." I saw at once that I no longer belonged to it. I blushed to see old men treating me with deference, and great noblemen, with daughters to marry, insisting on my going to spend a week at their country houses. I returned to Max's friends. There at least there were four or five minds akin to my own: men who had gone the same road as myself: who were where I am, or have gone farther. We are interested in the same problems. We exchange our intellectual coin. What I brought—and "my world" knew nothing of it—passed currency with them. Several of them showed that they appreciated me. When my verses appeared (published in Paris by X. M. Tournier de Zamble, with the title of *Poems by a Wealthy Amateur*, preceded by a preface in which Xavier-Maxence had mixed gross flattery with an irony which can no longer hurt me) I offered copies to my new friends. They liked several of the poems and told me so without mincing their encouragement.

But the crowd of fools was poisonous to me. I was constantly wondering whether, behind their welcome and show of esteem, there was not an ill-dissembled mockery or a tricked-out flattery. I was always on my guard:

I used to watch their faces : I would turn suddenly or watch them in the mirrors. If an older man than myself made way for me, I would cast about for some reason of etiquette for his doing so. A flattering allusion to my *Borborygmes* would fill me with distrust : the memory of a compliment would torture me for a whole night. Were they treating me as they would have treated any-one else ? Sometimes I wanted to get up and say : " Do you really, frankly, regard me as one of yourselves ? "

But my real life was not there, nor even at home. I had fallen into the habit of going in to see the Yarza girls early every afternoon.

Time and circumstances had parted us. Concha and Socorro were only bound to me by their loyalty, the loyalty of two weak creatures towards the man who feeds them and, though from a distance, protects them against the harshness of life. We had got to know each other again. I saw them as they are, no longer through the fancies of my twentieth year, when I surrounded them with a poetic mystery and a vague exoticism which was in very bad taste. In their bearing, their manners, their dress, they are European young ladies, and there is no-thing exotic in their surroundings but a beautiful royal Brazilian parrot, a fiery red " loro," which they are teaching to talk.

They have profited by their long stay in England : they have adopted the external discipline which regulates life here, the kind of social uniform beneath which the charac-ter can develop at its ease : the respect for a few essential rules and conventions which make so much wild private liberty possible.

Knowing them better every day I have slowly come

to see the riches they contain : what they have chosen and kept for themselves out of their nationality, their education, their experience. What? Were these the two children crushed by fear and poverty whom I picked up one night when with Tassoula I was going through the lower depths of London, just at the moment when they were on the point of being caught and ruined for ever : just at the moment when they were going to throw themselves into the gutter? Picked up on a whim of Tassoula's and because they were compatriots of mine.

I understood, in their society, what it is dwells in a human creature : the principle which preserves it, the continuity of a long inheritance in it, the treasure of reason, sentiments, faculties which it bears within itself. "That is what civilization is built on," I thought, and behind the nice European manners of my two friends I could clearly feel the presence of great social and historical facts : the formation of the American democracies, the conquest, the discovery and farther back still, Spain, and in its origin, Rome. Everything leads up to this.

Nothing important had been lost through the ages. The long line of Emperors and Popes had not lived in vain. . . . I soon ceased to feel that : the details of daily life quickly covered it up again. Now Concha and Socorro appear to me as distinct persons, complete in themselves, and no longer as representatives of a nation or a race.

There was a time of hesitation. I knew their loyalty, and they showed themselves eager to help me, grateful and kindly. And we should have stayed at that if I had not spoken to the elder, Conception, of the particular interest I have in her. I saw her heart come out to meet mine, her intelligence and tenderness welcome and adopt me. I received a freely offered submission of a woman who accepted my love. From that time on our relations were established on a more solid and more definite basis. Socorro resigned herself to her part as the younger sister. I was now the acknowledged master of the house, the respected head of the family. And their old house-keeper, a half-breed whom they had brought over from yonder, replied when I asked her her name :

" Maria, in the service of God and you, my lord."

And gently, little by little, the mother-country reclaimed me, her arms the arms of my beloved.

But I had also hours of uneasiness. Thinking that I was always despised elsewhere I used to wonder if I were not also mocked here in my last refuge. I used to look for ulterior thoughts behind the marks of tenderness Concha gave me. I have sometimes longed to find in her, or Socorro, some trace of boredom, contempt or constraint in my presence : then I should know where I was. Sometimes, again, I would try to judge the situation as if I were a stranger to it: after all, the girls owed everything to me ! Of course it was to their interest to attract me to their house, to keep me, to submit to me, to oppose me in nothing. It was the least they could do. No doubt, when I was not with them, they would take their revenge, and criticize me freely and mercilessly and give their real inclinations full rein. I tried to see only a base servility in their submission, and deep designs in the respect the elder girl mingled with her show of affection. But there was nothing servile in their conduct towards me. Concha's respect was that of a loyal vassal rather than that of a kept mistress : a respect which waved me aside and went straight to the man in me, to the big strong comrade, and not to the master, not to the employer. Sometimes she would tease me and gently take me to task, and be familiar : and then she would set a limit to her dependence.

So I found a new kind of friendship, not based on common tastes, and a kind of passion of which desire is only one of the elements. A feeling not to be expressed in human words, which I tried in vain to translate into a poem. I began :

"Be silent: Explain nothing: Be silent. . . ."

I followed that advice. . . . I have known the irresistible power of gentleness. And I have learned to eat oranges in a certain fashion. . . .

Tuesday.

This morning about eleven, in Bond Street, as I was looking, at the shops, wondering what I could take back to my girls' and hesitating between Lacloche's enamels and Finnigan's travelling-bags, whom should I meet but Gaëton de Putouarey.

" Hello, old chap ! I was very nearly passing you without seeing you. Pity I have to go back to Paris to-night. But you must come and lunch with me and I won't leave you until it's time to catch my train. I have so much to tell you ! "

He took my arm and walked on with me, gesticulating, with his head up and his beard bristling out.

" Don't you love Bond Street ? It is narrow and smells of Oriental tobacco, Russian leather and fresh dung : impossible to walk fast in it : a slight turn in it, just enough

304

to take you by the waist, and the shops draw you to them. And the little horse omnibus going from one end to the other as slowly as possible : and the charming big fair women in blue serge ! . . ."

"Ah ! That is like yourself, Marquis ! "

"My dear fellow ! England is the country for kisses. They are what sweetmeats are in Spain. The little maids in the hotels, the little shop-girls : oh dear ! You kiss their cheeks and they get cross : ' How dare you ? ' and hold out their lips. And the Welsh girls ? Have you been to Snowdon ? "

"No. Probably I shall never go. I am going to America in a fortnight."

"Oh, indeed ! Going away like that without even coming to say good-bye to the Continent or taking leave of Paris ? . . . I suppose you have your reasons. I won't insist. I thought it would end like that, and you would have enough of this aimless life and would be called somewhere. You have your vocation too. I see you are following it with a good face. Not like some of your compatriots : the Marchena, for instance. Just imagine. Those two young rascals kept up a four-days' siege on the roof of their school in Paris when they were wanted to go back to America. They had to wait until they were nearly dead with hunger before they could catch them. They were found fainting with their revolvers by their side. It is different with you, you know all the pleasures of Europe, you have seen what you wanted to see, and after all your chief establishment and everything depending on you are out there. You have found your way. An end of the dilettantism. I too have found my way. I will tell you about it presently on the terrace of my hotel while we smoke. Do you remember our cigars on the Pianello at San Marino?

" . . . Well, this is what happened. I could not stay more than a week at Cettinje. I went without stopping to the house of one of my professors in Germany. I told him what had been at the back of my mind for a whole year : my chief craze : a series of experiments I had made in my laboratory. He was delighted. Impossible to explain without technical terms. . . . So he pointed out a general line of research, and I went for it so energetically that I have really discovered something which partially confirms one of his hypotheses. In his next book the account of my experiments will take up a third of a chapter. You can guess that after that I gave up everything for my laboratory. What I anticipated has happened : one of my crazes has dominated all the rest. When I was fifteen I got my grandmother to fit me up a laboratory in a summer-house in the park at Putouarey, and it was a great comfort to me. It was bound to absorb me some day or other. I had not even realized the importance the craze had for me : I put it on the same level as my collections. Gradually I saw the possibilities of certain experiments : I shall not stop at that : I see far ahead of me. I have begun by publishing one or two studies of minor importance in a non-academic review. I feel I shall have a strong opposition to overcome. To the men who make their living by this science, whose profession is to cultivate it or to teach it, I shall go on being a mere amateur for a long time, a fashionable chemist : and my researches will not receive the attention which I believe they deserve. Already one or two tart little notes have sent me back to the ball-rooms in the

Faubourg St. Germain. But the great man at Munich and one of the great men in Paris have told me to go on with my work, and I know what I am doing. They can call me amateur as much as they like : the advantage I have over them is that I love my work : I love it enough to give up for it the easy life that had been arranged for me. Could they say as much ? Two or three perhaps. For the rest it is a career, almost a business. For them it was a reasonable marriage : to me it is a love match."

" Gaëtan, you amaze me ! One day you will be a member of the Institute, and the people at Putouarey and the Chabots will be flabbergasted."

" Rabot, you mean. And don't you make fun of me. Science is not an affair of vanity like literature. Oh ! I beg your pardon : I was forgetting that you have just published a book of verse. I mean . . . You understand. My work is very modest, subordinate to others : it is a kind of collaboration. It is a question of finding something. Not of making a name for oneself by juggling with ideas and words. Putouarey ? That's finished. You are all the same, provincials and foreigners : for you Paris is only a holiday city : no doubt that is why we Parisians come and amuse ourselves here."

" By the way, what about your latest adventure ? Does your laboratory leave you any time ? "

" I was going to tell you about that. My dear fellow, I am in love. But you won't guess with whom ? My wife, be damned—my wife, my dear fellow ! It was bound to happen. On my return from Germany as I was arranging for my instruments and books to be removed to Paris, I spent part of the night in verifying certain calculations for my experiments. I was pleased with myself. I was just going to sleep when I suddenly felt that things could not go on like that. I wanted my reward. I shall shock you, I know, but I wanted my rations of love. And in Putouarey that was impossible. By Jove, I gathered up all my courage and tremblingly I opened a certain door. . . . My dear fellow, I made her forgive everything. And it is my greatest conquest.

"Vulgar intrigues are charming, but I am tired of them. I must have a certain degree of education as I must have a certain degree of cleanliness. At first they are guarded : but as soon as they become used to you, their natures assert themselves. In every country they have a sort of strangled 'a' which is as vulgar as possible. As soon as you give them enough to live on without doing anything they let go and leave everything in a litter round them : they need three servants at least. And finally they laugh loud and long at meals with their lips shining greasily. Formerly my human sympathy was sufficiently developed to put up with it, even to overlook their laughter. But it's all over : I have turned away from it all : oh ! no doubt at all : it is a stepping back, a reaction. I have my love and it demands the whole of that side of me. As I was on my way here for Christmas, at Southampton I fell in with a band of Italian emigrants who were waiting to be transferred on board a steamer for America. There was a charming little Aretine woman, a widow with two little girls, who was going to join her mother-in-law in Illinois. Such a face ! The little virgin of Bugiardini, don't you know ? She told me her misfortunes in a sweet voice and many ' Ma chè ?—Ma chè ? ' "

"Like you in your Italian days."

"No, resignedly. Formerly I should have taken charge of the whole lot, woman, two children, dolls! Never did the Italian language seem to me so sweet and touching. Then I thought of the woman I love. My dear fellow, it is astonishing, the thing we are all looking for with so much pain and anguish and delight. When we have found it, we hardly notice our happiness at the end of a month. Because it so thoroughly fills the room we had kept for it in our lives. It completes us and we are soothed and calmed. When I am full, do I talk of eating?"

"You have your work, your home. In fine you have settled down."

"Don't be unjust, Archibaldo. I too thought that I had settled down, that is to say, that I had limited myself and my vanity suffered. No. I have not settled down: formerly I was only on the edge of life watching it flow past, sometimes dipping the tip of my fingers into it, sometimes my hand. But I took the plunge, and here I am in mid-stream. I have chosen: I am in possession of the true things. Before I had only hired truths. Before I was all over the place and without any ties. Now I belong to myself and I am no longer alone."

"Putouarey, you have fortified a certain resolution in me. You shall know about it—later on. But in all this what has become of . . . the Myth?"

"The devil! So you remember that? You know I hardly ever think of it. I am a specialist. It is a matter of education: let my grandmother and the Abbé Vernet bear the blame and receive the reward. I don't discuss these things, I am only a layman. It was also a question of conscience. And my conscience is now almost quiet : I obey my vocation and live with my wife."

" And you are happier than before ? "

" Oh, yes. And do you know what I attribute it to ? To my daring now to confess how unhappy my childhood and youth were. I was robbed of six years of my life. I was almost crippled. People pity the men who suffered from hunger or illness in their youth. But think sometimes of those who groaned in these prisons, the châteaux in the provinces, in comfortable bourgeois surroundings lovingly tortured by their preceptors, counting the years, months, days which lie between them and their legal majority. . . . But no doubt it was necessary for me to go through all that. I don't complain. Poor old grandmamma, I wish she was still here ! And my brother Jean must be more or less ashamed of me now in Heaven. . . . Oh, yes, the present time is good enough for me. . . . By the way, what time is it ? By Jove, I must be at Charing Cross in fourteen minutes : my wife will be waiting for me at the Gare du Nord. You will write to me from America ? I'm not likely to come and see you. Good gracious ! I must go up to my room : I was going without kissing Nancy.

LONDON,
8 January·

I see that I am wrong to condemn my past life as a whole. Even in the most misspent years I find some actions which I am still glad to have done. For instance, when I picked up the Yarza girls and saw that they were

310

taught and carefully brought up. Even then I thought that some day one of the two might be an agreeable companion to me.

I had even considered the possibility of my marriage with Concha. But sometimes I regarded it as a mistake, sometimes as an extreme step. I was like a man resigning himself to marrying his mistress. The world would not trouble to discover whether Conception Yarza was or was not my mistress, and " He has married one of the girls he used to keep." I could hear any one of my acquaintances saying those words with the strained accent one hears in clubs. It was precisely one of the things which ought not to happen to me. My marriage, on the contrary, ought to be a masterstroke, surpassing everything that envy of the people of my world could find to say. It should establish me definitely in the great European aristocracy. I used to think of the coronet of Lady Barnabooth of Briarlea.

At other times my marriage with Conception Yarza used to take on a symbolic value. The old puerile idea, the need of *social reparation* was mixed up with it. And what a challenge flung to the world, and how better could I explain to the girls of the aristocracy of birth and money what I thought of them.

How timid I was, and how taken up with public opinion, even in my revolt against it ! But the sign by which I know that I have plucked out the old folly is, that I am thinking—at last !—first of all of pleasing myself. And I know that I am going to be happy : and need I add that I am a little reluctant to be happy ? . . .

I am married, truly married in the English Church, in the Roman Catholic Church, and in the consulate of * * * . We go to-morrow to Liverpool, where on Thursday we embark for Colon.

I am writing surrounded with luggage : boxes from floor to ceiling in every room : my wife is taking away the Rue de la Paix, and I am taking Bond Street with me.

We have just spent four days in Paris, from where I announced my marriage and departure to two people only : Stéphane and Cartuyvels. And I wrote and told Cartuyvels that I was leaving that same day from Havre. He thinks I am at sea. I wanted to avoid his intervention and the useless annoyance of frustrating it. He must have thought it a freak, and said of my going : " Another whim ! " And he will expect to see me come back divorced and repentant. Let him wait for me !

I have said good-bye to Europe. I know there is nothing to keep me from returning to my going from town to town, shop to shop, hotel to hotel. But indeed that was the best part of it ; all the rest, studies, ambitions, doctrines, were boring, Duty, Greek exercises. But I have had enough. I want to be an idle scholar : I give up wanting to pass examinations. I don't even care for larking in the playground. I want the streets, the out-skirts of the town, the sea ! I have got all the good I can out of my hours in school. I am like a beggar giving thanks. I take your handful of coppers : I put on my hat again and addios.

I am leaving all I had and I don't know what is await-ing me. I have not, even in the eyes of Cartuyvels and other reasonable people, the excuse of having something to do over there. My country has been peaceful for four months now. The rebels have come to terms with the government : a new President seems to realize the intelligent and firm dictatorship which the country needs. Hardly six months ago I was receiving letters and emissaries from the provincial government. In exchange for my pecuniary aid they proposed to make me such a dictator. And sometimes I used to imagine myself returning at the head of a fleet of war, firing port and starboard, and landing as a sovereign to the sound of Te Deums and salvos of artillery. Really, was it possible ?

What does it matter ? I am going to land there as a private individual. I shall give my cabin ticket to a clerk of the Norddeutscher Lloyd on the landing-stage ; for the first few days I shall put up like any ordinary European tourist, at the best hotel in the capital. Confused memories whisper to me : the old Spanish colonial softness. . . .

Then I shall take the road to my estates in the interior. I used to try and imagine that existence also : riding on horseback, the ranch, friendships with rough men, daily contact with great plebeian souls. " O camerado close ! . . ." Well, that was Walt Whitman's poetry : a very beautiful thing : but life does not often fit in with the works of the great classics. No. I know nothing of what is awaiting me there, and I have nothing to hold to in this world except these two children, who have nothing in the world but me. All alone, adorned by the chains of my love. I set my face towards the unknown. This time I have given myself never to take the gift away. That at least is real, and all the better if I lose therein the sad love of myself from which I have suffered so much.. O Stéphane, my prince, Stéphane the Better! I am nearer you than you think. . . .

I shall not keep this diary any longer. . . . It will be in Paris to-morrow to be published there. I don't care how or when, with a new edition of my *Borborygmes*. It is the last whim in which I shall indulge. My Chelsea friends asked me to leave them as a souvenir what they are pleased to call my Complete Works. Well, they shall have them : the volume shall be sent them from France. But what they will think of it . . . that I don't care. In publishing this book I am getting rid of it. The day when it appears will be the day when I shall cease to be an author. And I disavow it entirely : it is finished and I am beginning. Don't look to find me in it : I am elsewhere : I am in Campamento (South America).

I have just lifted the blind and peeped out at the night. I saw the square sleeping under its railings, motionless, colourless, in the mist. There are the respectable houses which never put off their dignity even in sleep. And behind them, the false hierarchy of the old world, its little pleasures without vanity or peril, the miserable traps it laid for me, the brilliant career it opened up to my activity : business, politics, literature. . . . I can see myself going on writing poetry in French *vers libres*, every now and then publishing a collection of sketches in the style of the *Ode to Tournier de Zamble* ; spinning out my impressions of Italy—God be praised ! I am not an invalid and there is nothing to keep me to my room. The Dejections will never appear. O little Vanity Fair, O charm of Europe, you would readily take all of me except what I offered you with so much love : the wisdom I have painfully acquired and my spirit of industry and obedience. How beautifully calm are the fronts of the houses, with the window-blinds drawn. But soon they will awake to their ugly existence : servants and masters, and their respectability will consider with an air of haughty disapprobation the disorder of my departure. Ah ! I understand their reproach ; Old World, we are parting after a breach. And I feel so remote from everything people are doing here that I might even stay were it not that for my own game I need Andes and pampas. Old World, forget me as I am already forgetting you. I am even getting out of the way of thinking in French. By dint of talking my native language every day to my family it is becoming my inward language. One by one the Castilian words which recall so many memories, the most obscure, the dearest, the most remotely concealed memories of my life, are becoming once more acclimatized to my kind. . . . Forget me : drag my name and my memory in the mud. There are your coppers : pick them up : do you want my cast-off clothes ? do you want my honour ? I strip myself as it were for death. I go, content, naked. . . .

Four o'clock. I will wait until dawn. I have lit all the lamps in the house : and the parrot, awakened by the light, stirs in his case on top of a pile of bags, and goes on saying :

" Loro . . . Lorito ? . . . lorito réal ! "

EPILOGUE

WITH the white varnish of the narrow corridors,
The low ceilings, the gilded saloons, and the floor
Moving, like a sigh, secretly,
And the oscillation of the water in the bottles,
Here already begins
Before departure and the tide, the new life.

I will recall the European city :
The smiling past resting elbows on the roofs,
The bells, the common fields, the calm voices,
The mist and the trams, the fair gardens and the
Blue smooth waters of the South.

I will recall the summers and the storm,
The purple sky with wells of sun and the warm wind
With its troops of flies, going, violating
The tender nudity of the leaves, and, flowing
Across all the hedges and all the woods,
Singing and whistling and in the royal parks aghast
Thundering.
While above the groves of the vampire tree.
The cedar, raising its black wings, shrieks.

And I will remember that place where winter
Dwells in the heart of the summer months :

That place of ice, and blue rock, and black skies,
Where, in the pure silence,
Above all Europe meet
Germany and Rome.

And I know that soon
I shall see once more that other place, of new waters,
Where the Mersey, at last washed clean of the towns,
Immense, slowly, rank on rank, tide by tide,
Empties itself into the sky, and where,
Europe's first and last voice, on the threshold of the seas,
On its wooden cradle, in its iron cage,
A bell for forty years has been talking to itself.

And so my life, and so the grave and steadfast love,
The patient prayer, until the day
When Death at last transfers *The Secret* to the greater age,
And, with his fleshless hand, shall write

FINIS.